As th[e] ...
assault ...
As his ...
side of ...
drowning in his uncontrollable desire to make ... ...
traction he was used to, but this was something beyond the physical.
He had loved many, but never knew what it was to be in love. And
while he didn't want to believe that he had fallen so quickly, he knew
he would have to search far and wide to find another word to describe what was happening to him. This was it. This was the real
thing.

It was that thought that snapped him back to reality. If this was
the real thing, he knew he had to honor his promise to himself. He
wanted to savor every moment of getting to know her, and if they
moved too fast, deep inside, he knew it would only lead to heartache.

Pulling on every ounce of strength he could muster in his body,
he slowed his touch and stood up, carrying her with him.

Straightening her clothes and catching her breath, Alexis felt the
blood begin to pound in her temples.

Breathless and confused, Alexis stammered, "Wha . . . wha . . .
why did you stop?"

"We're moving too fast," he said, fighting to return to his normal
breathing level.

"Too fast? What the hell is that suppose to mean?" she yelled, as
raw, primitive anger began to overtake her.

"Alexis, let me . . ."

Screaming, she continued, "You take me through the whole seduction of gazing into my eyes, an intimate dance, and . . . ." Waving
her arms around the scattered files and empty desk, "this." With a
sarcastic laugh, she continued, "And I thought it was the woman who
was supposed to be the tease."

Stretching his hand for her, Malcolm started, "Alexis, listen . . ."

Pointing her finger at him, she interrupted, "No, you listen. This
little deal of ours is not working. You can't seem to make up your
mind what you want. Last week it was 'take it slow' and today your
lips are plastered all over my body. Well, I don't have time for
games." At that precise moment, the carousel song ended.

"How fitting," Alexis spat, as she replaced the files on the desk.
Picking up the box of centerpieces, she walked to the door and
turned to him. "I have work to do. Take me home."

JUST FOR YOU

Doreen Rainey

BET Publications, LLC
http://www.bet.com
http://www.arabesquebooks.com

ARABESQUE BOOKS are published by

BET Publications, LLC
c/o BET BOOKS
One BET Plaza
1900 W Place NE
Washington, D.C. 20018-1211

All Kensington Titles, Imprints, and Distributed Lines are available at special quantity discounts for bulk purchases for sales
promotion, premiums, fund-raising, and educational or institu-
tional use. Special book excerpts or customized printings can
also be created to fit specific needs. For details, write or phone
the office of the Kensington special sales manager: Kensington
Publishing Corp., 850 Third Avenue, New York, NY 10022,
attn: Special Sales Department, Phone: 1-800-221-2647.

First Printing: December 2002
10 9 8 7 6 5 4 3 2 1

Printed in the United States of America

Marlin,
    Thanks so much for
your support!
        Enjoy!
            Doreen
            Rainey
                1/03

One

Alexis Shaw waved to the dealer as she drove off the lot into the late afternoon sun. Her temporary tags secured tightly in place, the top down and her shades on, she made one final adjustment to her rearview mirror before picking up speed. Having about an hour before she was to meet her best friend for dinner, she decided to see just what her brand new Mercedes-Benz CLK silver convertible was made of. Merging onto the interstate, she headed north. It was Sunday afternoon, but Alexis had no intention of being a Sunday driver.

Keeping her turn signal on, she quickly moved across three lanes to the far left. Shifting into fifth gear, she mashed her right foot down and let out a "whoop" as she watched the dial move from sixty, to seventy, to eighty miles per hour. Coming up fast on a black Lexus, she flashed her lights and gave a friendly wave as the driver moved to the right to let her pass.

Having come to the dealership straight from the Ritz Hotel in downtown Atlanta, she couldn't help but pat herself on the back for the success of her latest event. One of the most prestigious law firms in the city had just accepted four new partners and wanted to celebrate the occasion in style. That's why they called her. The brunch, complete with imported champagne and food from every country where they had an office, was a huge success. Everyone was especially impressed with the ice sculptures that mirrored the three founding partners of the firm.

Nothing got her more jazzed than bringing the visions of her clients to life. The best part was that seven attendees had asked for her card, three giving her tentative dates of their upcoming events. With her business growing, Alexis had hired three other planners in the past two years, and she was contemplating hiring another. But even as her staff grew, she rarely let one planner handle an entire event on his own. Her ultimate enjoyment was in planning and watching the events unfold before her eyes, so she found it difficult to let her associates handle a single event in its entirety.

Feeling the adrenaline rush through her veins, she turned on the stereo and bobbed her head from side to side as the R&B tunes blared through her custom sound system. Watching the speedometer inch to ninety, Alexis couldn't hide her smile. Life was good!

Celeste Daniels ordered another iced tea and glanced toward the entrance of the restaurant. Pulling out her Palm Pilot, she checked the time and location. She was definitely in the right place. But where was Alexis? She knew her event ended at three o'clock and that she was going to pick up her new car, but that should have been complete at least an hour ago. Calling her cell phone, Celeste pushed end in surprise. Rarely did Alexis not answer her phone.

Dressed casually in powder blue linen slacks and a matching sleeveless top, Celeste rejoiced in being out of the heat. Summertime in Atlanta could be treacherous, and her short haircut, open-toe sandals, and light-colored clothing were a few tricks she used to beat the heat. Pulling out her compact, she quickly patted on powder to touch up her makeup. Her oily skin usually did not fare well during this time of year, so she was glad to see her almond-colored complexion was smooth and dry. Flipping open her cell phone, she started to dial Alexis again when it rang.

Checking the number on the caller ID, she smiled.

"Hey, baby," she said.

"Sorry to interrupt your dinner."

"You're not interrupting, Alexis is late and I have no idea why."

"That's Alexis for you," Kenneth said with a slight chuckle.

"What is that supposed to mean?" she asked, even though she already knew the answer.

"Come on, honey," Kenneth started. "I love Alexis like a sister, but you know she can be a little self-absorbed at times."

Not wanting to admit that he was right, Celeste asked sarcastically, "Did you want something, Kenneth?"

Laughing at her attempt to ignore his comment about her best friend, he said, "Charles called. He needs some help setting up some furniture he just bought. So if you need me, that's where I'll be."

Her mouth curved into a smile as she listened to her husband. Having heard so many of her friends complain about how hard it was to find a good man, she knew she had one of the best. Almost six feet tall, black as midnight, with a body that would make a gladiator jealous, Kenneth worked hard as a professor at Georgia Tech and played hard at being a great husband to her. Married for three years, they had been practically drama free. Of course, they had had their moments, but their bond of trust and love always allowed them to work their issues out.

"Okay, Kenneth. Tell your brother I said hi."

Even though she would never admit it to Kenneth,

Celeste agreed that Alexis could easily lose track of time or get held up at one of her events. That's why they made a deal years ago. After thirty minutes, the waiting party had the right to order or leave. This time, Celeste chose to eat. Signaling the waiter, she opened her menu to make her selection.

Twenty minutes later, Alexis stepped into the restaurant. Spotting Celeste at a corner table, she walked confidently and briskly through the dining area, turning several heads in the process. Dressed for corporate America in a plum-and-white DKNY power suit, she dropped her Prada shades and designer bag on the table and slid into the chair.

"Where have you been?" Celeste said, concern etched in her voice. "I've been waiting for almost an hour. And when you didn't answer your cell, I was beginning to think I had the wrong place or time. Why didn't you call me?"

Signaling the waiter, Alexis ordered a white wine and dropped a piece of paper on the table. "I would have, but I was unexpectedly detained."

Glancing down, Celeste grabbed the paper and skimmed the contents. Her brown eyes widened as she glared at her friend. That's when she noticed the sparkle in Alexis's eyes. "I know you don't take this as a joke. This is a one-hundred-and-fifty-dollar speeding ticket!"

"I know," she answered gaily. "The officer wanted to charge me with reckless driving, but I convinced him to pretend that I was only going ten miles over the limit."

Hearing the laughter in her voice, Celeste shook her head in amazement, "I can't believe you buy a new car and get a speeding ticket all on the same day."

Pausing to allow the waiter to place their food on the table, Alexis was glad to see that Celeste had ordered for both of them. "I've worked hard these last five years. I'm just trying to enjoy some of the fruits of my hard labor. I guess I did get a little carried away with the car."

"A little?" Celeste questioned with a raised brow.

"Okay," Alexis relented. "A lot. But I'm not going to let anything spoil my day—especially after yesterday."

"Now that you've brought it up, I can't believe you didn't stay for the bouquet toss," Celeste said. "Who knows, it may have been your night."

"Oh please," Alexis answered, not wanting to rehash the event. "It was all I could do to make it through the toast. I love Michelle like a sister, but all that wedding crap was getting on my last nerve. It's been twenty-four hours since they tied the knot and my feet still hurt."

Cutting into her chicken, Celeste frowned at her friend. "I thought the ceremony was beautiful and the reception was a blast."

"Ha!" Alexis replied sarcastically, "Easy for you to say. You weren't subject to mandatory participation in all the pre-wedding and post-wedding festivities. All you did was sit through a twenty-minute ceremony and enjoy a wonderful six-course meal at the reception. While I, on the other hand, had to stand under the hot sun—in a purple taffeta dress no less—trying desperately to ignore the numbness in my toes from the dyed shoes I didn't have a chance to break in."

Laughing at her graphic description, Celeste said, "It couldn't have been that bad."

Alexis gasped at her lack of understanding of what took place the day before. Leaning forward, she stared directly into Celeste's eyes and asked, "Who gets married, outside, at one o'clock in the afternoon in the middle of summer, in Atlanta? And in a garden, no less."

Celeste opened her mouth to defend Michelle's actions, but quickly shut it when she realized that she didn't have a plausible answer. She had no idea why anyone would choose to have their ceremony at that location or that time.

"Do you know the number of times I wanted to swat at little buzzing things that were flying around my head? Not to mention it must have been ninety degrees in the shade. I swear there were puddles of sweat forming at my feet."

This was Alexis's second time as a bridesmaid this year and her sixth since graduating from college nine years ago. As a result her patience for these exercises in futility was wearing thin. Her closet was full of one-time wear dresses in an array of colors. There was the black straight velvet dress with the split up the side, the fucshia taffeta dress with the puff sleeves, the emerald-green-and-white tea length, the sweet orange form-fitting sheath, and the yellow spaghetti strap number covered with flowers in every color of the rainbow. Now, she had added the deep purple, off-the-shoulder minidress to her collection.

"I plastered a smile on my face for fifty photos. *Fifty*! Can you imagine how much my jaw hurt by the end of the night?"

"You're the fabulous event planner," Celeste said, reminding her that she could have done something about the wedding location. "Why didn't you help Michelle plan it and steer her clear of a midday, outdoor ceremony in the middle of June?"

"Because I don't do weddings," Alexis replied emphatically.

"Then why did you agree to be a bridesmaid?" Celeste asked, her voice dripping with sarcasm. "You bad-mouth the idea of marriage, but you keep saying 'yes' when you're asked to participate."

"You can't blame me," Alexis replied innocently. "I tried to tell Michelle I wasn't interested, but we were freshmen roommates, pledged our sorority together, and graduated together. She wouldn't let me out of it. That's the problem with college. You join a sorority, get involved in different organizations, and the next thing you know, you're on everybody's bridesmaid list. I may have said yes to six, but I've said no to just as many."

Seeing how worked up her friend was getting, Celeste said, "I have a feeling it's something more than you're telling. I've known you to complain about your wedding party duties before, but this one seems to really be bothering you. What's going on?"

Sighing deeply, Alexis said, "Nothing more than my normal bad attitude about weddings. Of the six weddings I've been in, only one couple is still together, and I'm looking at half of that couple right now. Why bother getting married? The only two things I've witnessed coming out of marriage are heartache and pain. Two things I can definitely live without."

This was not the first time Celeste discussed this issue with Alexis. When she and Kenneth announced their engagement, Alexis threw a royal fit. Claiming that no good would come of the two of them tying the knot, it took months before Alexis relented and began to show support. While it was true that many of their friends had married and divorced, Celeste never lost faith in marriage. Her only challenge was trying to convince Alexis.

"You know my philosophy," Alexis started. "A relationship should just be enjoyed for what it is— temporary. When it's over, it's over. No vows, no rings, no heartache, no pain."

"Is that why your relationships never last for more than a few months?" Celeste asked pointedly.

"That, and the fact that men usually can't handle a successful woman putting her business first," Alexis said.

"I don't know, Alexis," Celeste said skeptically. "I

think you're still single because you don't give relationships a chance to develop."

"Develop into what?" Alexis asked. "Disappointment? Regrets? Bitterness?"

"Those aren't the only things that come from relationships," Celeste answered, hoping that her words could seep through Alexis's hard heart. "There's devotion, passion, companionship and love."

"I've personally witnessed six divorces, including my parents. When my friends were crying and hurt, trying to piece together their broken lives, where was the devotion, passion, companionship and love?"

"Are you saying that you will never commit to a man?" Celeste asked.

"What I'm saying is that I'm not interested in giving any man a chance to cause me pain. There's no such thing as happily ever after. Only the here and now. That's why I can enjoy dating. I'm not looking to hook a man into marriage. I can have fun, hang out, enjoy his company, but when the time comes to go our separate ways—a time that always comes—you can make a clean break."

Shaking her head in disbelief, Celeste offered some encouraging words. "One day you're going to meet your match, Miss Shaw."

"That's what you said when I met Gary," she said, reminding her friend of her last relationship fiasco.

"Yeah, well," Celeste started, trying to justify nudging Alexis to pursue that relationship. "That was my fault. How was I to know he would turn out to be such a jerk."

"Well, jerk or no jerk, he's out of the picture, and as of this moment, there's no replacement in sight."

"Like you're interested in finding a replacement," Celeste said knowingly. "You said yourself that you're not interested in settling down. Besides, you got it going on, Miss Businesswoman of the Year."

Alexis smiled at the reference. She still couldn't believe it. Starting a career in human resources after graduating from college, her job description included planning the company's holiday parties, summer picnics, and recognition dinners. Realizing she had a gift for creativity that was complemented by strong negotiating skills, she began planning personal events for coworkers and friends in her spare time. Soon after, her part-time job began to take over her full-time job. As a result, she left her position five years ago and started Just For You.

Specializing in planning unique events, her place in the Atlanta social scene became solidified when Celeste, working in public relations at the mayor's office, convinced the mayor to use her services to plan his wife's fiftieth birthday party. Choosing to host it at their exclusive country club with an African theme to coincide with the mayor's gift to his wife of a three-week safari, the attendees were so impressed with the life-size stuffed animals and authentic jungle decor, that her client list extended rapidly to include top business leaders and elite members of Atlanta's social scene.

Her services included everything from intimate dinners for two to sweet sixteen parties to corporate events with more than one thousand people. Alexis has created everything from a winter wonderland to the sunny beaches of the Caribbean to an Egyptian night complete with the pyramids and King Tut's tomb. But she drew the line at weddings. Those events she would not do.

To Alexis, it was the epitome of hypocrisy. She saw no reason to expend her creative energy for an event destined only lead to heartache and pain. She had a ringside seat when her parents divorced, and had witnessed her girlfriends' anguish when their marriages ended. She wanted no part of that. Not even for a twenty percent commission.

And lucky for her, she didn't need the wedding market. This year had been filled with phenomenal growth and she loved the challenge that each event gave her. Her goal was to give the client something beyond anything they could ever expect or imagine. And her hard work paid off when she was notified last month that she was voted Businesswoman of the Year by *Image Magazine*, one of the top African American business magazines in the country. She could barely contain her excitement when she opened the certified letter. *Congratulations, Ms. Shaw.* Image Magazine *is proud to award you with this year's Businesswoman of the Year in the category of small business.*

Image Magazine had been one of her favorites for many years. Its recognition of top minority leaders in various fields was held in high esteem by the business world and she was amazed and honored when she was notified that she had been selected. Not only would she be on the cover of its anniversary issue, along with the winners from the midsize and large business categories, but her accomplishments would be recognized at an awards banquet next weekend. A writer from the magazine was scheduled to interview her the next day. Yes, indeed, life was definitely good!

Breaking into her thoughts, Celeste said, "I'm still not giving up on your love life. I know there is a Mr. Right for you somewhere."

Alexis chuckled, "The closest I could probably hope for is Mr. Somewhat Right."

Malcolm Singleton glanced at his watch for the third time in as many minutes. He decided to wait five more minutes and then he was leaving. He should have said no, but when Rick called about meeting for a drink and dinner, he figured he needed a break. Having just finished an article on the rise of African American clothing lines in the twenty-first century, he was contemplating what to do about a meal when Rick called. However, if he had known Rick was going to be a half hour late, he would have passed on the offer. There was another looming deadline on the horizon, a stressed-out editor breathing down his neck, and an early morning appointment on his plate. An appointment that he hadn't fully prepared for. Checking the time again, he planned to finish his drink and head out. He'd have to catch Rick another time.

"You look too serious, bro. What's up?"

"You're late," Malcolm answered, not hiding his agitation.

"Sorry, but Candice called as I was leaving," Rick answered, curving his lips into a sly smile. "You know I had to have *that* conversation. I'm meeting her later tonight."

"I thought you were seeing Tawana?" Malcolm asked, raising his brow.

"That was last week," he replied, taking a seat. "You need to keep up, Malcolm."

"You need to slow up, Rick," he answered sarcastically. "One of these days you're gonna play the wrong woman."

"Who said anything about playin'?" Rick asked with an air of innocence. "Everybody knows the deal . . . I know the deal . . . Candace knows . . . Tawana knows . . . Renee knows . . . Lisa knows . . . Crystal . . ."

"I get the picture, Rick. It's a wonder none of those women get upset that you're seeing so many other women."

"*If*, and that's a big if," Rick stated with confidence, "they get wind that they aren't my one and only, it just takes two dozen pink and red roses from Peachtree Florist and I'm back in their good graces."

"You're a sick brother," Malcolm answered, releasing a grin and allowing some of the tension to leave the air. He had been dealing with Rick's antics since college and should have been used to them by now. Malcolm just wished that he would outgrow some of his immature ways.

Rick was what Malcolm's mother would call a slickster. He walked around in fine clothes, with a sly grin on his face, thinking he was God's gift to the female population. It always surprised Malcolm that more women didn't see through his game.

Rick only gave out his cell number, never his home. Rarely bringing a woman back to his apartment, he also didn't stay the entire night at theirs. If you add it all up, it would seem that Rick was married. But that wasn't the case. Rick just didn't want the women in his life to get too much information on him. That way, when he moved on, his girlfriends would have limited information on him. He was on his third cell phone number this year. Malcolm had no idea how a thirty-five year old man could still be playing such juvenile games.

"Well . . . ," Rick answered, surveying the restaurant, "if I'm a sick brother, then I'll need someone to nurse me back to health." His eyes stopped and focused on a table in the far corner.

Following his gaze, Malcolm saw his resting spot. Two women sat laughing and talking. With the dim lights, he could only make out a few features, but he could tell both were quite attractive.

"Watch a master at work," Rick said confidently, as he motioned to the waiter.

A few minutes later, Malcolm and Rick watched as the waiter arrived at the ladies' table with a bottle of champagne. Rick raised his glass to them as the women glanced over at them. His smile quickly faded when the waiter left the table, carrying with him that same bottle of champagne. The women looked the men straight in the face and began to laugh, shaking their heads.

"Ouch!" Malcolm said, amused. "I think we just got the brush-off."

"I can't believe it," Rick answered, his voiced laced with agitation. Standing, he began making his way over to their table.

"Let it go, man," Malcolm said, as he followed Rick. But Rick ignored him and kept walking. Malcolm sighed. The last thing he wanted to do was cause a scene, but knowing his friend, that was just what he was about to do. The one thing Rick didn't like, and refused to accept, was rejection.

"Looks like we have company," Celeste whispered to Alexis, nodding her head in the direction of the two approaching men.

"Oh, brother," Alexis murmured.

"Ladies, ladies," Rick started, in his friendliest voice. "I see you refused our kind offering."

"If you're referring to the champagne you sent over," Alexis said, without glancing their way, "thanks, but no thanks."

"Excuse me?" Rick said, annoyed by their disinterest.

"Look Rick," Malcolm said, grabbing his arm, "the women aren't interested. Let's just go back to our table and have dinner."

Alexis glanced up when she heard his voice. The tone, nothing like she had heard before, kissed her ears with melodic notes. It was deep. It was smooth. It was extremely sexy. The rich timbre and smooth sounds lingered in her ears and it took her a moment

to recover. When her eyes focused on him, she realized
his voice was a perfect match for him. Deep bronze
skin, a smooth, clean-shaven face, and sexy light brown
eyes.

She smiled. Malcolm noticed.

"What are you ladies . . . gay?" Rick asked incredulously.

Her smile vanished. Malcolm noticed.

"Look you Casanova wanna-be," Alexis started, jumping up, almost knocking her chair over in the process.
"I know this may be hard for you to believe, but guess
what? You guys are not irresistible. For your information, this is ladies night, and we don't need Frick and
Frack," she paused, glancing from one to the other, "to
make it enjoyable."

Totally ignoring the shocked expression on both
their faces, as well as the stares her outburst garnered
from the people nearby, she maintained her challenging stance as she watched their retreat, Rick giving her
a final sneer.

"P.S." she said to their backs, "We are not gay . . .
we're just not interested in either of you!"

Malcolm turned toward her at her final words, his
jaw clenched and his eyes slightly narrowed. This was
the first time he could honestly say he had been rejected with such finality. The woman stood motionless,
as if daring him to another round. His eyes, locked with
hers, seemed to analyze her extreme, emotional response. And instead of being angry, he found himself
curious—about her. For a moment, all sights and
sounds became background as they stared openly at
one another. Malcolm had to admit that Rick could
definitely pick them. With her warrior stance, smart
mouth, and "I dare you to say something attitude," Malcolm was forced to admit that, without a doubt, she was
gorgeous. But he never forced himself on a woman,

and he wasn't about to start now. Giving her a brief
nod, he turned and followed Rick back to their table.

Alexis remained standing, even though the two men
were gone. She found herself feeling a little put out by
the cool, aloof demeanor of the second man's departure.

Celeste stared in amazement. "Was all that necessary,
Alexis?"

"I can't believe the audacity of some men," she answered, taking her seat.

Having witnessed the silent exchange between her
friend and the second gentleman, Celeste said, "I can't
believe you let that one walk away."

Alexis stared at her with a questioning gaze.

"I saw the way you looked at him. His friend may
have been a jerk, but maybe . . ."

Alexis interrupted by raising her hand, "You know
what they say . . . birds of a feather . . ."

Malcolm stepped out the shower onto the cold ce-
ramic tile. As he dried off, he remembered the long
dinner he had to endure with Rick. The entire conversation revolved around Rick's belief that women didn't
know a good man when one stood directly in their face.
He openly wondered how women could constantly
complain about the lack of eligible men and then turn
a man down after he made such a classy gesture. In
Rick's mind, something was wrong with the women of
today. Reminding him that he was the biggest player in
the city didn't seem to faze him. Rick expected to get
whatever and whomever he wanted, whenever he
wanted it. Knowing that made Malcolm highly uncomfortable.

Malcolm thought about their college days. Both
young and dumb, they split their time between chasing

girls and studying. They even made bets on who could get dates first with certain girls. The loser actually had to pay for the date the winner went on. Smiling, Malcolm recalled only paying for one date while Rick shelled out money for many.

But thirteen years later, Malcolm could look back and see how stupid they had acted. If any of those girls had found out what they were doing, they probably would have slapped them both, passing the word along so that neither Malcolm nor Rick would ever get a date again. Thank goodness Malcolm had outgrown those childish behaviors. But watching Rick tonight, Malcolm wondered if he was the only one who had left those collegiate ways in the past.

Putting Rick out of his mind, he slipped on a pair of sweats, retrieved the FedEx package left at the security desk of his condo, and went into his home office. Booting up his laptop, thoughts of the two women in the restaurant crept into his mind . . . again. Especially the spunky one who told them off. Her image was as clear to him now as it was when she was standing right in front of him.

Holding a stance that indicated she was ready to take on any challenge, the slender curves of her body were defined by the fitted material of her suit. Her chestnut brown skin, her stylish shoulder-length cinnamon hair, piercing eyes, and plum-covered lips were branded in his memory. Actually, it was the image of her lips that he lingered on the longest.

Closing his eyes, he could see the solitaire diamond earrings and the matching pendant necklace that dipped into the "V" of her silk blouse. He wanted to go back to their table and apologize for his friend's behavior, but he put it off too long, and the two women left before he had the chance. Shaking her image out of his head, he acknowledged his missed opportunity.

The ring of the phone snapped his mind back to the present. *Get it together, Malcolm.*

"Hello," Malcolm said, trying to erase that picture from his mind.

"Hey, big brother."

Not fully recovered from his daydreaming, he asked, "What's up, Jackson?"

"You sound a little preoccupied." Wondering if he had caught his brother with someone, he teased, "I'm not interrupting anything, am I?"

Annoyed with himself for letting a stranger affect him this way, Malcolm snapped, "I'm in the middle of working. Did you want something?"

Not quite believing his brother, Jackson said, "Must be some story."

Hearing silence on the other end, Jackson continued, "Just wanted to confirm our game tomorrow night. I reserved the court for seven."

"I'll be there."

"The way you sound, I hope your mind will be there as well. Matt and his guys have beaten us the last two games. I don't want to lose again."

"Don't worry about my game," Malcolm answered. "You're the one who missed four three-point shots last week."

After several minutes of discussing who had better skills on the basketball court, Malcolm hung up with his brother and within seconds, the woman from the restaurant popped right back in his mind.

Thinking about her complete rejection of him, he clenched his jaw in slight irritation. Was her reaction necessary? He reasoned that she must have major life issues if she responded with such a vengeance. It was probably a good thing that nothing came of their meeting. Imagine trying to get to know a woman with that much attitude. A woman needing an attitude adjustment was the last thing Malcolm needed. What man in his right mind would want to deal with a woman like that? Definitely not him. He didn't have the time or the energy. Based on their brief encounter, he understood that any relationship with her would be a constant battle for power and control, and she struck him as the type of person that didn't relinquish either easily.

Determined to put that woman out of his mind, Malcolm turned his attention to his work. There was no purpose in spending any more time thinking of her. In a city this size, the chances of seeing her again were about one in a million.

Needing to prepare for his next interview, he settled at his desk to review the information his assistant sent over. Opening the package, he pulled out the bio and picture. Taking a closer look, Malcolm blinked twice. Were his eyes playing a cruel trick on him? After several moments, his mouth curved into an unconscious smile. He was going to get a second chance at making that apology after all.

TWO

The receptionist sat poised and professional as she answered the multilined switchboard.

"Just For You. Sherry speaking, how may I help you?"

Standing near the receptionist desk, Malcolm looked around at the small, but well-decorated lobby. Enlarged, framed photos of various types of events graced the walls. The cushioned chairs, positioned around a table adorned with magazines, looked warm and inviting. Glancing at some of the titles, he was glad to see his magazine among them.

"Sorry to keep you waiting, sir. How may I help you?"

"I have an appointment with Ms. Shaw. I'm Malcolm Singleton, from *Image Magazine*," he answered, handing her his business card.

Sherry took his card with an appraising look. Without a hint of shyness, she rose just a little in her chair to get a better view of him. His frame, over six feet, was accentuated by his commanding air of self-confidence. Without hurry, her gaze traveled over every inch of him. From his short cropped hair with slight waves on top, to his smooth golden bronze skin, down to his tantalizing lips. Moving from his face to his body, she stifled a moan as his muscular build did amazing things to the casual pleated brown linen slacks and the multicolored, button-down shirt he wore.

Finally, her eyes fell to the floor. His black Gucci loafers had style and money written all over them.

Standing completely, she offered her sexiest smile, and said, "Just one moment, I'll let her know you're here."

Alexis sat at her desk selecting items for the twenty-five gift baskets for an upcoming dinner party. This event was being handled mostly by Samantha Downs, the latest planner added to her staff, but Alexis wanted to make sure the selection for the baskets were perfect. As she looked through the catalog of imported chocolates, she realized she had been on the same page for the past fifteen minutes and hadn't made one selection.

Closing the catalog, she closed her eyes and tried to clear her mind of the distraction. But it wouldn't go away. All through the night and that morning, she thought of him. It was the way he looked at her before he turned and walked away. His eyes were compelling—almost magnetic—as if he were drawing her to him, probing the very depths of her soul. It made her feel . . . Alexis struggled as she tried to capture a word that would describe how she felt.

In an instant, she opened her eyes and sat forward. The word flashed in her head and it set off warning bells: *vulnerable.* Alexis immediately rejected that word, him, and all it represented. She could not recall a time she felt this way with any man and there was no way she was going to start now. Especially a man who could be so juvenile in his approach to a woman. How unoriginal and lame. Sending over a bottle of champagne. What did he expect her to do? Fall right into his arms? What a joke!

Reopening the catalog with fierce determination, she flipped through the pages. It was not her nature to let her mind get so easily disgraced by a man, no matter how attractive he was, and she wasn't about to begin now. Besides, in a city this size, she knew the chances of seeing him again were one in a million.

"Come in," Alexis said a few moments later when she heard the knock on her office door.

Stepping into the tastefully decorated office, Sherry danced over to Alexis's desk.

"Girlfriend, today is my lucky day!" she exclaimed.

"What are you talking about . . . and what are you doing away from the receptionist desk?"

"The reporter is here from *Image Magazine*."

Alexis closed the catalog she was reviewing and stood. This award would finally put her company on the map, garnering her national and possibly international attention. "And how does that fit into it being your lucky day?"

"The fact that this man is the finest example of the male species I have ever seen—and the fact he will not leave here without having my phone number—makes it my lucky day."

Alexis couldn't hold back a burst of laughter as she watched her receptionist's animated gestures. Sherry Pearson had worked for the company less than three months and was best known for her carefree lifestyle. Enjoying life to the fullest, she kept everyone abreast of all the best spots to hang out, the latest fashion trends, and the best ways to attract and get rid of men. Alexis had counted four boyfriends since her first day. That was life on the fast track.

"Before you sweep him off his feet," Alexis said, "do you think you could show him to my office, offer him something to drink, and hold all my calls until the interview is concluded?"

"As you wish, madame," Sherry answered lighthearted-ly as she playfully bowed and headed for the door, "but I can't imagine having a coherent conversation for any length of time with somebody that *fine!*"

"Sherry?" Alexis said seriously.

Hearing the tone in her voice, Sherry straightened up, "Yes?"

"I'm a little nervous about this. This is my first interview by a national magazine. Do I look okay?"

Sherry stepped back into the office and gave her boss an assessing look. Dressed stylishly in a Chanel dark green pantsuit, her emerald accessories and matching pumps added flair. At five feet five inches, Alexis loved the height and power her high heels provided her. Her hair hung loosely on her shoulders in large curls and her flawless skin was smooth and clear, highlighted by a light dusting of powder and her favorite shade of lipstick. Watching her smooth out her blazer with her hands, her nervousness was evident.

"You'll be just fine," Sherry reassured her.

"Yes," Alexis answered more confidently, "I'll be okay."

"Besides," Sherry added, with a mischievous grin, "that reporter will be so taken with me, that he'll hardly even notice you."

Malcolm thought about the receptionist's brazen assessment of him as he waited patiently for her to return. He should have been used to it by now. Dubbed the "pretty boy" in college, his smooth skin and light eyes always got him second glances from women in all shapes, sizes, professions, and marital status. He had to admit that he enjoyed the attention, and years ago he played the dating game like a master. Taking pause, he wondered if he had ever been as bad as Rick. But he quickly realized that Rick treated women as objects, disregarding their feelings. Malcolm always treated women with respect. And on top of that, he left the game playing alone a long time ago.

At thirty-four, Malcolm was tiring of the string of six-month relationships that usually ended when his girlfriends got tired of taking a backseat to his work. Writing had always meant everything to him and he found it hard to pursue personal relationships when he was so committed to his work.

Carving out a successful writing career, Malcolm has interviewed everyone from entertainment stars to heads of state. Traveling the world on assignments, he'd spent time on just about every continent for a variety of publications. But three years ago, he returned to his hometown and accepted a position with *Image Magazine*. Since coming on board, Malcolm had produced more cover stories for the monthly publication than any other writer, and had been given credit for pushing the magazine's circulation numbers and advertising income past those of *Ebony* and *Black Enterprise*.

Having a large readership of African American women, it was Malcolm's idea to develop the annual Businesswoman of the Year award. The award would highlight three women who had accomplished extraordinary goals in starting and running a successful small, midsize, or large business. His editor jumped on the idea and the selection committee had chosen this year's recipients last month. Malcolm's role included writing the feature articles on the three winners. He had already completed two of the interviews and was completing his final one today. He'd had no idea that one of the women selected would tell him off the night before their meeting.

"Ms. Shaw will see you now," Sherry said, returning to the reception area. "Please follow me."

Walking behind her, Malcolm acknowledged her sexy walk and the slight switch of the hips. It was apparent that this little show was especially for him. Looking young and fresh, he guessed she was in her very early twenties. Her jet black hair, hanging straight

down to the center of her back, swung loosely against
the sway of her hips. The short skirt and fitted top was
borderline professional, but showed off her best assets.
If Malcolm was in the market, he might have made a
move. But he decided after moving to Atlanta that the
next relationship he pursued would be for keeps, and
the woman moving seductively in front of him didn't
strike him as someone looking to settle down.

Alexis paced in front of her desk. Always confident
and poised, she was slightly irritated with herself for
feeling so jittery. While this was her first interview for a
magazine, she was no stranger to talking with people
on a one-on-one basis. She had made it her profession.
Working closely with clients to understand their pref-
erences for their event was her niche. Now, her hard
work was beginning to pay off. When this issue of *Image*
hit the newsstand, she was preparing to have more business than she could handle.

Hearing the approach of Sherry and the reporter,
Alexis discarded the last of a mint and patted her hair
one last time.

"Thank you, Sherry. It was a pleasure meeting you. I
think I can handle it from here."

Alexis froze at those words. That voice. There was
something very familiar about it. It was deep. It was
smooth. It was extremely sexy. Ignoring the chill bumps
forming on her arms, she strained her neck to get a
glimpse of the man standing in the hall. She hoped her
ears were playing an awful trick on her. But as she
thought about who that voice belonged to, an un-
pleasant taste began to form in her mouth. No matter
how smooth he may sound, it could never excuse his
immature behavior last night.

If it was him, Alexis questioned whether she could
spend the next few hours with a man who was obnoxious, self-centered, and arrogant. Granted, those were

words that described the actions of his friend, but she couldn't imagine someone putting up with that type of behavior if they didn't possess those same characteristics. Putting on her best professional demeanor, she said a quick prayer that she would be able to hold her tongue on her personal opinion of him and focus on the professional.

Having been notified a week ago of the name of the person conducting the interview, she was initially pleased. She had read *Image Magazine* consistently for the past few years, and was familiar with his articles and cover stories. Malcolm Singleton was good. Very good. His writing had style and flair. With his talent and skill, he had a way of taking any topic and presenting it with power and excitement. What he wrote about had influence over the business community, and she had to, regardless of her personal feelings, make a great impression. Inhaling deeply, she stood tall and confident with her resolve to take the high road. She moved toward the door and mentally prepared herself for introductions.

But no amount of mental toughness could override her physical response. When Malcolm Singleton stepped into her office, every cell in her body came alive. Her heart jolted and her pulse pounded as a ripple of complete awareness traveled from her head to her feet, warming her every place in between. Last night, the restaurant was dimly lit, and she couldn't quite make out his features, but today with rays of sunlight reflecting off him, there was only one thought that came to her mind. Sherry was absolutely right. This man was gorgeous. Dressed casually, his presence filled the room and she found herself short of breath. Forcing her gaze away from him, she immediately chastised herself. How could she have such an intense attraction to someone who was obviously a jerk?

With extreme effort, she controlled her expression and stretched out her hand. "Mr. Singleton, it's so nice to meet you."

Leaving her hand hanging, he said, "Oh, this morning it's Mr. Singleton. Last night it was Frick . . . or was it Frack?" Stroking his chin, he appeared to be in deep thought over that question.

Appalled and enraged, Alexis withdrew her hand and snapped, "It was well deserved, and as a matter of fact, I can think of a few more names I could call you instead of either one of those."

Malcolm, stunned at her curt response, thought this woman must not have one humorous bone in her body. Wanting to quickly diffuse the situation, he raised his hands in defeat and said, "Don't shoot me, it was just a joke."

His astonishment was obviously genuine and Alexis inwardly admitted that she noticed humor in his eyes. Immediately, she regretted her outburst, but something inside her refused to let her outwardly acknowledge it. So she said, "I thought you were here to do a job. Or am I to assume that I could add unprofessional to the growing list of adjectives that describe you?"

Dropping his hands, Malcolm furrowed his brow at her attitude and adjusted his shoulder bag. *She won't affect my professionalism.* With deliberately casual movements, he looked around the office for the first time and saw a conference table on the opposite wall. "My apologies, Ms. Shaw. Why don't we take a seat and get started with the interview."

She watched him walk over to the conference table and remove items from his leather bag. Notebook, pencil, and a minicassette recorder. Pulling back one of the six chairs around the table, he took a seat. Never looking up at her, he opened his pad and began writing.

For the first time since Alexis had been conducting business in this office, she felt uncomfortable. Throughout her career, Alexis thrived on being the one in control. And now she felt just the opposite. Shifting her weight from one foot to the other, the silence in the air was deafening. Refusing to let him get the best of her, Alexis lifted her chin defiantly and strode over to the table and took a seat.

Watching Malcolm unwrap a new cassette tape and load it in the machine, Alexis debated on breaking the tension that now permeated the room. She contemplated if perhaps she had overreacted to his joke. He could have been just trying to break the ice in what could have been an extremely awkward situation. Realizing that it was not good business practice to alienate the very person who had the ability to give her company more media coverage than she had had in all the five years she had been in business, she decided to take action.

Clearing her throat, she hoped to gain his attention to at least offer a smile, letting him know that she could set aside her personal feelings for the sake of the interview. He never looked up. Failing to get a reaction, she felt slighted. Taking a deep breath, she decided to offer an olive branch.

"Mr. Singleton, would you like something to drink? Coffee, maybe some juice?"

Answering in the negative, he continued to write. Having spent most of the night staring at her picture and reviewing her bio, Malcolm created an image of her in his mind. During the selection process for the award winners, he was duly impressed with the portfolio he'd received about her company. But that positive impression grew when he placed a face with the statistics. Alexis Shaw was breathtaking and he was mesmerized. Starting a business was never an easy task, and for Alexis to have accomplished all that she had in the short amount of time spoke volumes about her. She was smart, beautiful, and had occupied his thoughts throughout the night.

But that image was immediately shattered by her funky attitude and snooty demeanor. He had seen it many times before, successful women with a chip on their shoulder. Well, her chip was the size of a boulder, and he had no intention of trying to knock it off. He would get his story, attend the awards banquet, and never have to see Alexis Shaw again.

"Why don't we just get started with the interview," he answered. Pushing the record button, he slid the device to the center of the table. "Why don't we begin with how you got started in the event planning business?"

Never one to let loose ends dangle, Alexis refused to begin the interview without clearing the air. Grabbing the small recording device, she pushed the "stop" button, much to Malcolm's surprise.

"What do you think you're doing?" he asked incredulously.

"Before we get started, I want to take a moment to clear the air. What I said a moment ago was uncalled for."

Malcolm started to nod in agreement. *Now we're getting somewhere.*

"I didn't give you the opportunity to apologize."

Malcolm stopped nodding and, once again, became appalled at her audacity. Apologize? Wasn't she the one who had just insulted him? She must be out of her mind. Having no intention of honoring her request for an apology, he reached for the recorder, pushed the red button again, and repeated, "Why don't we begin with how you got started in the event planning business?"

This time, Alexis grabbed the recorder, pushed "stop" and placed the device behind her back. With a courteous, yet patronizing tone, she said, "Mr. Singleton, I don't want your interview to be skewed by our chance meeting last night. Now, I'm willing to overlook your childish, egotistical behavior, but at the very least, you can apologize."

Glancing at the spot where his recorder had disappeared, Malcolm struggled to ignore her condescending remark and called on every piece of restraint he had in him. Opening his notepad, he repeatedly tapped his pen on the table and said, "Why don't we begin with how you got started in the event planning business?"

Irritated at his outright ignoring of her attempt to get them started on the right foot, Alexis said, "I hope this rudeness will not be around during the awards ceremony."

Staring at her with contemptful eyes, he felt his last bit of professionalism fading. "If you are going to be there, then yes, rudeness, I'm sure, will be there as well."

Alexis gasped and slammed the recorder back on the table, neither acknowledging the batteries that came flying out of the back. "I should have known better than to attempt to develop some sort of professional relationship with you. You are obnoxious, rude, arrogant, and . . ."

"That's it!" Malcolm yelled. Standing, he returned all the items he had taken out of his bag less than ten minutes ago. "I can't believe you received the most votes. We should have gone with the pet groomer." Never looking back, he slammed the door on his way out.

Alexis stared at the closed door for several minutes, seething with anger. *How dare he walk out on me? Who does he think he is? The man who holds my company image in the palm of his hand!*

"Damn," she yelled at the empty room. Stomping over to her desk, she grabbed the receiver, and continued her tirade under her breath. Punching in the three-digit extension, she was betting on the fact that he had a deadline and was probably pacing the floor in the lobby, waiting for her to come out.

"Sherry, please ask Mr. Singleton to come back to my office."

Hearing the slight hesitation on the other end, Alexis began rubbing the bridge of her nose. "Sherry?"

"Um . . . sorry, Ms. Shaw . . . Mr. Singleton left."

Celeste had constantly warned Alexis that her temper would someday get the best of her. It would seem as if that day had arrived. Her short fuse had successfully alienated the one person who had the capability to publicly damage the good reputation of her company that she worked so hard to build.

Malcolm Singleton's magazine was read by millions of people every month. What would the business world think of her when they read of her actions today? Why had she let herself get carried away? She had come across rude men before, and ignored them. Business associates whistled, made snide remarks, and even propositioned her, some using extremely colorful language describing what they wanted to do to her. She had politely, and sometimes not so politely, told them where to go. But she found this man difficult to set aside.

She hated to admit it, but when she realized that sexy voice from the night before was standing in her office, she had a flash of fantasy that would set the world on fire—two bodies, hot and naked in her bed. And after their chance meeting, it was the last reaction she wanted to have. He was obviously a man who didn' know how a woman should be treated, and that's the reason she had lashed out. She only wanted to prove that he was the jerk she labeled him. That way, she could justify ignoring the fact that she was being drawn by those piercing eyes, his muscular build, and that devastating smile.

But her plan backfired. The only thing she accomplished was the possibility of ruining her chances for the cover of *Image Magazine*. What was she going to do now?

In the parking garage, Malcolm gripped the steering wheel of his Cadillac Escalade while inhaling deep breaths. Never in his life had he felt such complete, unhindered annoyance at anyone. The nerve of that woman accusing him of being egotistical. How dare she! She didn't know him. Where did she get off making assumptions like that about him? *From Rick's behavior last night.*

He cursed under his breath as he realized he was guilty by association. Rick was everything she said he was and he couldn't blame her for being upset about last night. That could explain her behavior, but it didn't excuse his. Malcolm realized that there was no excuse for the lack of professionalism he displayed in her office. Never had he walked out on an interview, not even when he interviewed a top leader from the Ku Klux Klan. So what was it about Alexis Shaw that set him off? He had hardly known the woman twenty-four hours, and yet she had managed to put him completely off balance. If this got back to his editor, he'd never hear the end of it.

Removing the key from the ignition, he got out of the truck and took one final deep breath. His experience told him that he could spend about two hours with her and get all the information he needed for a strong, in-depth article. With renewed determination, he made his way back into the office building.

Alexis stood in the reception area grilling Sherry about anything Malcolm may have said on his way out. Did she have any idea where he was going? Did he leave a number?

"I told you," Sherry said, "he stormed passed me, mumbling something about the impossibility of dealing with women with a chip on their shoulders."

Exhaling, Alexis contained her anger at that remark and turned toward the sound of the elevator opening. Out stepped Malcolm. They glared at each other like two bulls preparing to charge.

Alexis broke the silence first, "Why don't we go back to my office?" Not waiting for a response, she turned on her heels and strode confidently down the hall.

Upon entering the office, Alexis shut the door behind them and moved to the conference table. Malcolm followed. Neither took a seat, but stared openly at one another.

"Well," Malcolm started, "here we are . . . again."

"Yes," Alexis replied, "you, me, and the chip on my shoulder."

Exasperated at the amount of energy he was expending on what was to be a very simple interview, Malcolm decided to ignore that comment. Again, taking out his pen, pad, and the small recorder, he replaced the batteries, sat down, and pushed record. "So, Ms. Shaw, why don't we begin with how you got started in the event planning business?"

Professional. I can be as professional as he can. All I have to do is answer his questions and everything will be just fine. I can do this.

Taking a seat opposite him, Alexis adjusted her jacket, put on a smile, and began telling of her beginnings in Human Resources.

After several more questions, Alexis visibly relaxed and Malcolm got into the groove of his interview.

Much to his disappointment, Malcolm found himself drawn to this woman. Her confidence and passion came through when she spoke of her work. How could someone with such passion and business savvy be the same person who had him seeing smoke an hour ago?

"Just a couple of more questions and we'll be done." Glancing down at his notes, Malcolm asked, "When you think of event planners, the first thought that usually comes to people's mind is weddings. But Just For You doesn't plan weddings. Why not?"

Alexis was personally very clear about why she didn't plan weddings. Marriage was a farce, and while she stood with her friends and watched them say their "I do's," she could never take someone's money for a wedding. She would consider herself an accessory to a relationship crime. But Alexis didn't believe that she wanted this information passed on to millions of readers. So she opted for the other answer that also reflected the truth.

"Wedding planning is a niche in the industry that I have chosen not to pursue. Our focus is more on the unique events that our clients are looking for."

"But since most of the population gets married, aren't you leaving a fair amount of business on the table?"

Pointedly, Alexis said, "Mr. Singleton, I'm looking to add several other planners to my staff over the next year. I don't need, nor do I want, weddings."

Her emphatic statement caused Malcolm to take pause. Was there something about weddings—or marriage—that didn't sit right with Alexis? Realizing that this question was more for his personal benefit, he decided to move on to his final question.

"Tell me about Alexis the person. Where did you

grow up and what impact has your family had on you and your career choice?"

Alexis stiffened, but quickly recovered. Forcing a smile, she answered, "I'm sure your readers aren't interested in my family."

Malcolm had been a reporter for a long time, and what made him so good at it was his natural instinct. Very rarely was he wrong. Alexis purposely avoided his question and the first word that came to his mind was "why."

Rising, Alexis took off her blazer and laid it across the chair, exposing a sleeveless blouse that showed off her toned arms and slim waist.

For a moment, Malcolm was caught up in the scent of perfume that floated through the air, but then the reporter in him kicked in and he figured that removing the jacket was probably a nervous gesture. Why would talking about her family make her nervous? Deciding not to push it, he figured that if he needed it for the article, the information shouldn't be too hard to get.

"Well, Ms. Shaw," Malcolm said, closing his notebook and pushing stop on the recorder, "I think we're done. This will be a great story."

Alexis visibly relaxed as she realized he was not going to pursue her personal life. Malcolm noticed. He had become an expert at reading body language and hers indicated that whatever was going on in her family life, she was glad that he hadn't pushed her to reveal it.

Rising, he placed his work tools back in his bag as silence engulfed the room. Neither spoke as he picked up his bag and headed for the door. Stopping with his hand on the knob, he turned to her and opened his mouth to ask her to lunch. While their initial meeting was quite intense, he couldn't deny the flare of curiosity that burned inside him, drawing out a desire to get to know her better.

But as fast as the thought came, he quickly dismissed it. Their truce was temporary as he needed his story and she needed him to tell her story. Experience had taught him that you can't let the fantasy created by a subject during an interview spill over into real life. There were many times when the interviewee became a different person when the questions ended or the cameras were off.

He recalled the time he spent with an Oscar-winning actor who volunteered at inner city schools and donated money to various charities. After the interview, he invited Malcolm to a party to celebrate the end of filming on his latest movie. It was at the party where Malcolm watched him snort cocaine. The actor reminded Malcolm that whatever he thinks or believes he saw at this party was "off the record."

There was also the time he interviewed a woman recognized for her achievements in the research on breast cancer. After his tour of the state-of-the-art research lab, he witnessed her cursing and demeaning other researchers and assistants.

This time, he would not be fooled. Alexis Shaw, a sharp, professional woman on the rise in the business world, may not be a drug user or rude to her staff, but she had a short temper and a hot head. With a combination like that, the only thing he could get out of any relationship with her was a third-degree burn. It would serve him well to remember that.

Instead of lunch, he opted for the safe route. "A limo will be picking you up for the award ceremony. All the arrangements have been made. I'm sure I'll see you there."

Alexis didn't know what was on his mind, but that statement was not it. He seemed to have changed his mind about what he was going to say at the last minute, and Alexis felt an odd twinge of sadness. With a forced smile, she covered up her disappointment and replaced it with a professional facade. If aloofness and reserve was what he wanted, then that was exactly what he was going to get.

"Yes, I'm sure you will." Turning to her desk, she picked up the phone. "If we're done, I have calls to return."

Three

Alexis opened the door to her condo and was immediately greeted with the aroma of herbs and spices. Setting her packages down, she kicked her pumps into the corner of the foyer. The three other pairs of shoes that were in the corner that morning were now gone. Making the short trip into the living room, she saw the overnight bag and the Dior purse she had given as a birthday gift on the sofa. The Sunday paper she left scattered about was neatly stacked on the coffee table. Glad for the unexpected company after such a stressful day, she shed her blazer and made her way to the kitchen.

"I hope it tastes as good as it smells. I haven't had a home-cooked meal since the last time you were here," she said, stepping into the entryway. "And that was six months ago."

"Well, hello to you too little sister," Melanie said.

Walking over to the stove, Alexis playfully bumped her sister out of the way and dipped a nearby spoon in the simmering sauce. Letting the flavor penetrate her taste buds, she closed her eyes and moaned in pleasure. "Oh, Melanie, this is fabulous."

Grabbing the spoon from her sister's hand, Melanie quickly covered the pot. "You ain't seen nothing yet, girlfriend. What we're eating tonight is guaranteed to set your mouth on fire."

"Did you just say 'ain't'? I know that type of language is not tolerated at Winston Marks Financial Services," Alexis teased. "And speaking of your job, what are you doing here? I don't think I've ever known you to come visit and not call. Not that I mind, but it isn't a holiday and I don't recall you ever taking a day off from work you didn't absolutely have to."

"I'm off the clock, so I can do or say whatever I want—including ain't," Melanie answered defensively, pushing loose strands of jet black hair behind her ears.

Alexis raised a brow at her tone, and held her tongue as she watched her fool with her hair. The last time Melanie came to Atlanta, she claimed she was fed up with long hair and wanted to try something different. Yet, when Alexis made an appointment at her favorite salon, Melanie backed out at the last minute because she wondered what her fiancé, boss, and their mother would think if she went through with the cut. Unfortunately, the hair thing was just one issue of many.

Last year, Melanie wanted to get a tattoo right above her butt, but feared repercussions from her job. Mentioning that the CEO, COO, and Senior Management team probably wouldn't find out unless she dropped her pants in a board meeting didn't seem to make a difference. She still didn't do it. Two summers ago, Melanie wanted to spend two weeks at a cooking seminar in Paris, but her mother convinced her that a Greek Isle cruise with the Women's Business League would be a much better way to spend her vacation. True to form, Melanie relented and canceled her flight to Paris. A few weeks after her return, she admitted to Alexis that she'd hated every minute of it. It was the one thing about her sister that got on Alexis's last nerve. Melanie didn't have a mind of her own.

A few inches taller than Alexis, Melanie could easily pass for a model instead of an uptight corporate executive. Her coffee brown skin, pronounced cheekbones, and perfect smile would be breathtaking if she didn't hide behind glasses, used a little more makeup, and bought one piece of clothing that didn't make her look like she was on her way to a meeting of the Censervative Club of America. Even now, in the kitchen cooking, she had on dress slacks, a silk blouse, and pearl earrings. Alexis always wondered if she owned any casual clothes.

"I stocked your refrigerator. I've never been in a house with no eggs or bread. What do you eat?"

Opening the dishwasher to get a glass, Alexis shrugged. "If I don't have an event, I usually grab take-out." Slamming the door shut, she looked around the kitchen before asking, "Where are the glasses?"

"In the cabinet where they belong," Melanie answered, reaching up to hand her one. "There were clean dishes in the dishwasher, dirty dishes in the sink, and a weird smell coming from your refrigerator. No doubt compliments of some of your take-out. I hope you don't mind, but I did a little spring cleaning before I started cooking."

Remembering her sister was a neat freak, Alexis said, "Now you know why I can never find anything after you leave. I still haven't found my taupe slingbacks."

"I told you I put those shoes in the repair shop on the corner to fix your heel." Pausing, Melanie began to laugh. "Please don't tell me your shoes have been in the shop for six months?"

"Fine," Alexis said, sticking her tongue out in a childish gesture. "I won't. I'll leave you to your sauces and spices while I go and change. But when I get back, I want to know why you are in Atlanta instead of New York, and no fancy meal is going to get you off the hook from answering that question."

Twenty minutes later, Alexis returned to the kitchen casually dressed in cotton shorts and a tank top. She had pulled her hair back in a ponytail and had cleansed her face of makeup. She was home, and at home, she relaxed to the fullest.

Melanie had already set the table in the formal dining room off the kitchen and poured each of them a glass of wine. With the cherry wood table, matching chairs, curio cabinet and a glass centerpiece, it was a room worthy of a home designer's magazine. Taking a look around, Alexis furrowed her brow and frowned. She had spent a significant amount of money on this room, yet couldn't remember the last time she had eaten in it. Alexis watched silently as Melanie carefully placed the scrumptious dishes on the table. Her mouth started to water at the aromas drifting to her nose. This was one of the best things about having her sister come visit—the great food.

Vice president of US Loan Acquisitions with Winston Marks, one of the largest financial institutions in the world, Melanie spent her days running to meetings, crunching numbers, and dressing in stuffy suits. Her entire closet was filled with blacks, browns, and grays. Alexis could honestly never recall seeing her sister in any other colors. The only African American VP and only one of three women in the company to reach that position, she worked hard and played little. But Alexis often wondered if she was living out her passion or just following the rules that were laid out for them before they were born.

Every time Alexis asked how her career was going, Melanie would say that things were fine, but there was always a hint of longing, of dissatisfaction that told Alexis that while things may be fine, that didn't mean she was happy.

Alexis knew several woman who had taken the corporate world by storm and were loving every minute of it. But that didn't seem to be the case with her sister.

Watching Melanie in the kitchen earlier almost prompted Alexis to ask why she was wasting her artistic culinary skills by working at a company that epitomized corporate America. But she quickly decided against it. That conversation was old and tired, and after the last twenty-four hours she'd had with Malcolm Singleton, she was not in the mood for another argument. And Alexis knew that if she broached the subject of her sister's career choice, there would definitely be a disagreement.

When they were young, Melanie spent a lot of time in the kitchen with the family cook, creating dishes and baking pastries. Some were good, some were bad, but most were downright awful, though Alexis never minded being the guinea pig. Alexis always felt honored when her big sister let her be the first to try her food.

As Melanie got older, her cooking skills dramatically improved, and in her junior year in high school, she announced she was wanted to go to culinary school. From the immediate reaction from their mother, one would have thought Melanie revealed she had robbed a bank. It was quite apparent that their mother had no intentions of letting that career choice be an option for Melanie. No daughter of hers was going to waste her life cooking for other people. Where was the status in that profession? Mother's expectations were clear and there was never room for negotiation. Melanie and Alexis would attend the best colleges, followed by obtaining professional or graduate degrees, and become what their mother deemed acceptable. It wasn't that they couldn't choose a career, they just had to choose one from their mother's short list. Doctor. Lawyer. Director. President. Chief Executive Officer. Anything that would make her so-called friends stand up and take notice.

The moment Melanie made her grand announcement in high school, their mother sat Melanie down and reminded her that this family was about status, not slaving over a hot stove in a restaurant—or worse, in someone's house.

Melanie was gravely disappointed, and for a brief moment, considered defying their mother. But the thought of going against her wishes was unfathomable. So she stopped helping in the kitchen, buried her dream, and focused on her studies. She never brought up the topic of culinary school again. It was more important to Melanie to make her mother happy and proud than to follow her own dreams. And she continued to do just that for her entire adult life.

At her high school graduation, Melanie appeared to be excited about college, but Alexis believed it was all an act. She gave up her first love because she didn't know how to stand up to a domineering mother.

Graduating with a degree in finance, she went on to receive her MBA and CPA. Now, ten years into her career, she had an apartment on the Upper West Side, a vacation home in the Caribbean, and a social calendar that reeked of who's who in the New York business world. But deep down, Alexis knew that the little girl who made her eat pineapple chicken with cornflakes and oatmeal when she was seven years old was still there. She had just been smothered by the pressures of people-pleasing.

Whenever she came to visit, Alexis, who had trouble boiling eggs, knew this was Melanie's time to pretend that she had followed her dream. Her official title wasn't Chef, but when she came to Atlanta, that's exactly what she was.

Watching Melanie set the table, Alexis didn't offer to help and she knew Melanie didn't mind. Watching her work, Alexis realized that being a chef was similar to being an event planner. The preparer pours her heart and soul into the creation. From beginning to end it was her baby. Alexis cringed when her clients offered to help set up decorations or meet a vendor. And Melanie was the same way about her food. It wasn't just about cooking. It was about a total experience—from hand picking the ingredients at the market, to arranging the finished product on the table. So Alexis sat back and watched as she placed jambalaya, a salad, and fresh baked bread on the table.

After enjoying several bites, Alexis took a sip of wine and glared at her sister. "Okay, sis, spill the beans. You come to Atlanta unannounced and fix me the best meal I've eaten since . . . well . . . since the last time you were here. This unexpected visit is completely out of character for you. What's going on?"

Watching Melanie wipe the corners of her mouth, followed by taking a sip of wine, Alexis wasn't fooled by the delay tactic.

"Actually," Melanie started, "it's not what's going on with me, it's what's going on with you."

Pausing with her fork in midair, Alexis stared curiously at her older sibling. "What on earth are you talking about?"

"Marissa Johnson called me yesterday."

Making no connection to her sister's high school friend and her being in town, Alexis shrugged. "So?"

"She told me she had just spoken to Jessica Montclair, who had just played tennis with Carmen Milestone."

Not in the mood to play along, especially after her day with Malcolm Singleton, Alexis sighed and asked, "What's your point, Melanie?"

Not put off by her sister's obvious irritation, Melanie took another bite of salad and chewed slowly.

"Melanie, I'm not in the mood for this tonight. If you

want a free place to lay your head, you will stop with the riddles and spit it out."

Staring pointedly at her sister, Melanie answered, "Carmen Milestone had just left her mother's house."

Watching her taking pause to add more salad to her plate, Alexis's last nerve snapped. "Look, Melanie, either you spit it out or . . ."

"Alice Milestone sits on the board of McKnight Publishing, who owns . . ."

". . . *Image Magazine*," Alexis answered, as the light-bulb clicked on.

There was a moment of silence as Alexis rested her head in her hands.

Watching her closely, Melanie shook her head in disbelief. "What is your problem, Alexis? Why didn't you tell us you were chosen as one of *Image Magazine*'s Businesswomen of the Year?"

Raising her head, her expression grew hard and resentful. "You know why."

Ignoring the evidence of anger swelling on the inside of Alexis, Melanie said, "You've separated yourself from the family since you left for college. Don't you think it's time to let us back in?"

"I let you back in. It's just Mother that's out," she answered pointedly.

"Alexis . . . ," Melanie started.

"You know how she is, Melanie," Alexis interrupted. "I have never had one moment that was truly mine. She finds a way to weasel herself, her money, her name—something—into everything I do, and I refuse to let that happen anymore. Not in my business and not in my life. This award is special to me and I plan to enjoy it without the interference of mommy dearest."

"But I'm not your mother, I'm your sister. Why didn't you tell me?" she asked, confusion etched in her voice.

Alexis exhaled slowly and reached across the table

and squeezed Melanie's hand. "Because you would have told her."

Seeing the hurt flash across her face, Alexis tried to justify her response. "You didn't have to endure her after the divorce."

Melanie pulled her hand away and placed it in her lap. This was not the first time they had had this conversation, and it always ended with them angry at each other. Eventually they would make up, but Melanie was tired of the fight and wanted to mend her family once and for all. With five years separating her and Alexis, Melanie had already left for college when their parents divorced. With no one to keep their mother occupied, she made her life's purpose her younger daughter. And with time and money on her hands, it was not hard to do.

Alexis often complained about her mother's interference in her life, but Melanie always believed that Alexis exaggerated. Melanie hoped that as Alexis grew up and stepped out on her own, she would realized that her mother was just acting out of love, and she would look back and see how ridiculous her complaints were.

"Mom has always had your best interest at heart," Melanie answered quietly.

"Is that so?" Alexis asked, obviously not convinced. "My freshman year in high school, I made the cheerleading squad, even though there were several girls better than me who didn't make it. I just thought I underestimated my talents—until the squad got new uniforms compliments of our mother. When I tried out for the school play my junior year, I begged my teacher not to tell Mother and I got the lead. Only to find out later that the principal ran into mother a week before auditions at a community meeting. The drama department suddenly had the money for new props. By my senior year, I was known as 'the kid most likely to succeed because of my mother.'"

"But that was high school, surely you can't still hold that against her."

"High school? How about the fact that I was wait listed for admission to college, only to find out that there was a 'clerical error,' and my acceptance was secured?"

Melanie shook her head in denial, "Surely you don't think Mother had anything to do with that?"

Putting her fork down, Alexis fought to control the knot forming in the pit of her stomach. "Don't you get it, Melanie? She always has something to do with it. She had something to do with the clothes I wore, the friends I had, and the places I went were all crafted by her. And we can't forget about her role in the clubs I joined, the positions I held, and the boys I dated. It was never about what I wanted, it became about impressing her friends. By the time I went to college, I had enough."

Melanie shook her head in denial. "You make it sound as if she was a puppeteer and you were helpless to do anything on our own. That's ridiculous."

Leaning forward, Alexis stared directly in her eyes and asked, "Forget about me for a moment. How do you think you got into that management program at Winston Marks after you graduated?"

A flash of panic widened her sister's eyes, but it quickly disappeared. "There is no way she could have had anything to do with that. She didn't even know I was asked to apply."

Alexis threw her hands up in frustration. "Whatever you say, Melanie."

"My goodness, Alexis, don't you know that you would have accomplished all of those things without her help?"

Their food going untouched, Alexis released a slow,

deep breath and felt some of the tightness in her stomach dissipate. "That's just it, Melanie, there is no way I will ever know. But with this award, I do know. I started this business without her help and I built it into something I could be proud of—all on my own ability. When I pick up that award this weekend, there will be no doubt in my mind that this accomplishment completely belongs to me."

"That's exactly my point, Alexis. Telling her about the award would prove to her that you are capable of taking care of yourself, of making your own way."

"That's the difference between me and you, Melanie. I don't have to prove anything to her. I only have to prove it to myself."

Choosing to ignore the fact that her last remark touched a nerve, Melanie said, "It's obvious you accomplished this on your own, so why don't you invite her to the ceremony? Let us celebrate with you."

"You're welcome to come, Melanie. But Mom? I don't think so. We usually end up arguing and I don't want that to happen on my one special night."

Melanie knew the chances of changing her sister's bullheaded mind was slim, but she tried anyway. "Will you at least think about it?"

Pausing a moment and looking toward the ceiling, the lines of concentration deepened along her brow and underneath her eyes, as Alexis appeared to be in deep thought. For a brief moment, it seemed as if she was considering inviting her mother. But as she turned her attention back to Melanie, she replied sarcastically, "Thought about it, and the answer is still no."

"You're tough, Alexis," Melanie said.

"No, Melanie" Alexis said, sitting forward to resume her meal "just at peace."

* * *

Malcolm bounced the ball at the free throw line, took his stance, and released the ball. What should have been an easy basket, ended up missing its target by a mile. Ignoring his teammates' questioning gaze, he ran down court, attempting to focus on defending his man. But it was no use. Stepping to the left, and then quickly to the right, his opponent went right by him and scored an open three-point shot.

Just as he prepared to take his offensive position at the opposite end of the court, his brother called time-out. Hesitantly, Malcolm jogged to the side of the court, knowing that he was in for it. He played basketball with Jackson and his cousin, Brent, as often as their schedules allowed it, and even though he was no Kobe Bryant, he could hold his own. But tonight, he was way off his game, and he was sure it did not go unnoticed by his teammates.

"Man, what is going on with you?" Jackson said, standing on the sideline catching his breath. "We've beaten these guys many times, and tonight, you can't even score a basket."

"Yea, Malc. I passed you the ball twice, and it went right through your hands," Brent said.

Grabbing a towel and wiping his face, Malcolm was not in the mood to recap his game. He was there when it happened. "Why don't we just call it a night. It's just a pick up game."

After the fellas called the game, Malcolm headed for the showers. As the hot water pounded against his body, it failed to help his tightened muscles relax. Stressed since this morning, he had hoped this game would release the tension. No such luck. And horrible play only served to annoy him more. Wondering what the problem was, his mind worked at lightning speed to determine the cause. Unfortunately, he kept coming back to the same conclusion: Alexis Shaw.

As her name occupied his mind, her face flashed before his eyes and his body reacted like that of a seventeen year old. Stretching his memory, he couldn't recall the last time he reacted this way to any woman. Betrayed by his body, he turned the water ice cold, hoping to quench the fire that began to burn inside him. But when he headed back into the locker room, he cursed under his breath as he realized that as long as her face was in his head, there wasn't enough cold water in the city to cure his ailment.

Putting the last of his stuff into his gym bag, Malcolm slammed the locker shut and turned to his two teammates. "I'm going home."

Grabbing his car keys, Jackson answered, "Oh no, you're not. You owe us a beer and an explanation after that horrendous showing."

"Just a beer?" Brent asked, glancing from one to the other. "Make that dinner and dessert."

Twenty minutes later they were seated in a booth at a popular downtown restaurant. The waitress took her time taking their orders, giving each of them an inviting smile. Whenever the three of them went out, attention from the opposite sex was never a problem. Jackson, with his short twists and goatee, and Brent, with his rugged five o'clock shadow, always made it a point to collect several numbers.

"Do you want to tell me what's going on with you?" Jackson asked, concern etched in his voice. Getting no response, he tried again. "Is it a story you're working on?"

Taking a swig of his beer, Malcolm continued to ignore his questions.

Not dissuaded, Jackson continued, "Do I need to repeat the question, or should I move on to the next one?"

Malcolm glared at his brother and continued to respond with silence. His brother was an attorney and, at times, could take his interrogation techniques too far. Malcolm had no intention of being a witness on the stand.

"If it's not work, it must be a woman," Brent said.

The slight twitch in Malcolm's jaw was a dead give-away. Brent knew he hit the nail right on the head. "Who is she?"

"She's nobody," Malcolm answered.

"For a nobody, she sure has *somebody* worked up," Jackson said with a sly grin.

Malcolm finished his beer, threw a few bills on the table, and stood, "Good night, fellas."

"What is it with you, Malcolm?" Jackson started. "You're late to our game, you play like an amateur, and now you refuse to tell us what's going on with you."

Brent chuckled, "She must really have you whipped."

Narrowing his eyes, Malcolm answered, "The last thing I am is whipped. What I am is irritated, aggra-vated, angry, agitated, and . . . and . . . annoyed beyond words. And that's saying a lot for a journalist. This woman is hard-headed, brash, temperamental, and"—pausing a moment, Malcolm plopped back down and sighed—"the sexiest woman I have ever met."

"And that's a problem?" Brent asked, thinking of the last part of his statement. "Sexiness always outweighs everything else—hands down. Not to mention that being sexy is usually the only thing that has mattered to you. Why would this one would be any different? Just do what you always do, ignore the negative part and focus on the only thing that matters. The sex appeal."

"Yea," Jackson continued, "What difference does it make if she's irritating? Your relationships never last more than six months anyway. By the time you get re-ally agitated at her bad qualities, you'll be ready to move on. So what's the big deal?"

Malcolm took in the advice and immediately dismissed it. What they just described was the story of his life. His relationships, never built on anything solid, consisted of sporadic dates around his work, so-so sex, and shallow conversations. And frankly he was tiring of the same old routine. He now longed for something more. Something different. Someone different.

"The big deal is that I'm tired of relationships that aren't going anywhere," Malcolm answered. "I'm not looking for another six-month affair. I want something more real, something permanent."

Shocked was a mild adjective to describe the look on their faces. Jackson's mouth literally hung open. Four years younger than Malcolm, Jackson got his drive to succeed from his older brother. Getting an education and establishing a solid career was the path that Malcolm preached. Every thing else came second, including love. Professional achievement was the name of the game, and while it was acceptable to enjoy the company of the opposite sex while you built your career, it was always understood that if there was ever a choice, the woman always came in second . . . a distant second.

And Malcolm was the best at sticking to that rule. Never dating any women more than a few months, there was a time when Jackson couldn't keep up with Malcolm's girlfriends. But ever since Malcolm moved back to Atlanta, he'd noticed that his big brother had changed. He recalled hanging out and double dating with his brother when he first came back to town. But he had to go back over a year to think of the last time they double dated.

"If you're looking to settle down—and that's a strong, debatable if—" Brent said skeptically, knowing of the short-lived relationships for which Malcolm was famous, "then this woman doesn't sound like the one to do it with," Brent said. "Perhaps you should let this one pass you by." Signaling the waitress for another round, he continued, "If you want the minivan and the two point five kids, then this woman, whoever she is, doesn't seem to fit that mold."

"I agree," Jackson said. "Let her go, man. No woman could be worth this much trouble—and she definitely can't be worth playing really bad basketball."

Malcolm listened to their advice and realized that it made perfect sense. Why set himself up for a relationship that was doomed to fail? Alexis Shaw grated heavily on his last nerve, and to consider anything beyond a professional relationship was absurd. There was no way he could see himself with someone he would probably spend most his time arguing with. But even as he tried to convince himself that no good thing could come out of pursuing a personal relationship with her, he couldn't get her beautiful way out of his mind.

Could it be that they just got off to a bad start? Perhaps when he saw her at the awards ceremony, things would be different. With the pressure of the interview behind them, maybe he could get to know the real Alexis Shaw. But that rationalization sounded weak to Malcolm. Deep inside, he knew the bold, outspoken woman with the feisty attitude was the real Alexis Shaw. And that type of woman had never appealed to him. Yet, he couldn't deny that he was looking forward to round three. It was just too bad he had to wait until the weekend to see her.

Four

After dinner, Alexis relaxed on the oversized living room sofa with fluffy down cushions, while her sister sat Indian style on the floor, enjoying a slice of homemade cherry cheesecake. Alexis, who never made anything from scratch, enjoyed the rich flavor and fresh cherries. Putting her fork down after eating the last bite, Alexis watched as Melanie cut herself a third piece.

Grabbing the remote off the coffee table, Melanie clicked the power button and asked, "Is this a new TV?"

"It sure is," Alexis said proudly. "A high definition, flat screen, with surround sound, satellite, and TiVo."

Channel surfing, Melanie said, "I can't believe the money you spend on toys and trinkets. I saw those bags in the foyer. Saks, Neiman's, and some name I won't even try to pronounce. I know there can't be anything in those bags that you actually need."

"You don't know what I need," Alexis said defensively. Seeing her sister fold her arms across her chest, Alexis tried again. "They were having a sale?"

"Alexis, your kitchen has more appliances than the best restaurants, your jewelry box should be locked in a bank vault, and you have a computer system to rival any corporation."

Feeling a lecture about to take place, Alexis said smartly, "Then you definitely don't want to see what's in my parking space."

Clicking off the television, Melanie eyes widened in disapproval as she stared at her sister, "Tell me you didn't"

Alexis shrugged.

"You just bought a new car two years ago." Being ignored, she continued, "You know Alexis, contrary to your belief, toys can't grow old with you and keep you warm at night. You should have learned that from our mother."

Alexis tried to turn the tables, "This, coming from someone who owns a summer house and original artwork?"

"Investments, Alexis. My purchases are investments." Looking around the living room, she inventoried the top of the line stereo system with several loose wires dangling in the back, a large collection of CDs stacked carelessly in the cabinet beside it, and several magazines and newspapers that were neatly stacked because Melanie did so earlier in the day.

Hoping to get her point across, Melanie continued, "You buy stuff just to buy. I bet you don't wear most of the clothes in your closet and you probably have shoes that have never touched the outside ground."

Realizing Melanie was making some valid points, Alexis still refused to give in. "I think you're exaggerating."

"Is that so?" she asked. "I used your food processor this afternoon and I had to take it out of the plastic. I think you buy material things to replace something that may be missing in your life."

Knowing what was coming next from her sister, Alexis responded, "Please Melanie, not that 'you need a man' lecture again. I don't want to hear any talk about love and happily ever after. I've already had my dose from Michelle's wedding this past weekend."

"You just don't get it, do you?" Melanie asked, moving

to sit beside her on the sofa. "You did it, Alexis. You accomplished the American dream. You built a successful business, you have the fifteen-hundred-square-foot condo, complete with three bedrooms, an office, gym, and a few rooms you don't even use. You're driving a new car and your bank account is growing. But so what? What you buy is not what's important in life. What's important is love and family."

A picture of Malcolm flashed in her mind, and Alexis felt an unwelcome surge of excitement flutter in her stomach—and that pricked her nerves more than this conversation. "Either change the subject or check into a hotel."

"Fine, Alexis," she said, knowing her words were falling on deaf ears. Taking another bite of her cheesecake, Melanie cynically asked, "What would you like to talk about?"

"Why don't you tell me the real reason you're here?" Alexis challenged.

"What do you mean?" Melanie asked, sliding back on the floor.

"I know you were shocked that I didn't share the news of winning the award, but I doubt very seriously that would cause you to jump on a plane and fly down here." Leaning forward, she said, "I've never known you to do one impulsive, unplanned thing in your life. Usually when you come to visit, you tell me weeks in advance, e-mail me your itinerary, and call me from the plane a half hour before you land to make sure I have the right flight information. Mind you, you are confirming the same flight information that you had already e-mailed me."

Shifting uncomfortably, Melanie said, "I can be spontaneous."

"Yea, right!" Alexis said. "You don't have one spontaneous bone in your body. Not only that, you usually have to be forced to take time off. The only reason you visited six months ago was because it was the holidays. And here you are, on a Monday, sitting in my house one thousand miles from home and not looking concerned about getting back. That just isn't you."

"Maybe I've changed," Melanie said, as she finished off the last of her cheesecake.

"That's your third piece of cake and the only time I've seen you eat like that is when there's a man involved. And this must be a doozy because not only are you overeating, but you flew a thousand miles to do it. So what's up. Problems with your man?"

"I have no man problem, because I have no man," Melanie replied emphatically.

"I thought you were so in love with Darius," Alexis said, placing her hands dramatically over her heart.

"No, Darius is in love with Darius, I've just been there to give him someone to talk to."

"Oh, no," Alexis cried sarcastically. "Don't tell me there's trouble in paradise. Last I heard, you loved Darius completely. You wanted to spend the rest of your life with him. He was the perfect man for mom—I mean you," Alexis said, making the slip on purpose.

"I'm not interested in spending one night with him, and definitely not the rest of my life," she answered unconvincingly. "And what does Mother have to do with this?"

"How can you ask that? When she introduced you two at the annual Sweetheart's Ball at her country club, I know she had everything mapped out. The three-carat platinum setting Tiffany engagement ring, the Vera Wang strapless, hand-beaded gown, a June wedding with several hundred of her closest friends. Not to mention what comes next. The two perfect grandkids, one purebred dog and a white picket fence."

"That's not true. So she may have introduced us, but

I choose who I date or don't date. It doesn't matter what our mother thinks."

Not believing her, Alexis decided to let the topic go. Emotions ran too high between them when that woman was the center of their discussion. Melanie was blinded when it came to their mother. "So what happened?"

"We had a fight last night and I needed to get away from him."

"It must have been one hell of a fight if it drove you to drop work and come here. But I'm not surprised. I told you a long time ago, sis. Relationships aren't meant to last. No matter how good you think it is."

"I didn't say it was over," she countered defensively.

"Then why are you here?" she asked smugly.

"I was offered a promotion last week. President, International Loan Acquisitions," Melanie said quietly.

"That's great!" Alexis squealed, moving to give her sister a huge hug. She didn't know what she expected to hear, but this was not it. It took her several seconds to realize that Melanie didn't share in her enthusiasm.

"What is it, Melanie?"

"I don't know if I want to accept the offer and that's what caused the fight. Darius finds it absolutely absurd that I told the Board I wanted to think about it."

Taken aback that her sister needed time to think about accepting such a coveted position, she asked, "What are you thinking about?"

Melanie shook her head and spat, "It shouldn't matter what or why I'm thinking about it. The man I'm suppose to marry should support whatever decision I make." Melanie's growing anger was apparent as she stood and began to pace the floor. "Do you know he demanded that I stop this charade and accept the offer. He actually ordered me to make the call. I told him to take that job and shove it up his . . ."

"Melanie!" Alexis exclaimed. "First you say 'ain't' and now this?"

Alexis was known for placing a well chosen word here and there, but Melanie? Alexis couldn't recall one bad word ever coming from her lips.

"Nose," Melanie said sarcastically. "I told him to shove it up his nose. I just couldn't bring myself to actually say the 'A' word."

They both stared at one another in complete silence, then Melanie cracked a smile and a few seconds later they were in uncontrollable hysteria. Melanie doubled over in laughter and Alexis held her side to keep the cramps from coming. Neither had enjoyed a laughed this hard in a long time.

As their laughter subsided to giggles, Alexis said, "I don't know why you're surprised that you've come to this place in your relationship. I hate to sound cold, but the truth must be told. Relationships are not meant to last. People are just too selfish."

"I don't think he's selfish," she said slowly, as if trying to convince herself.

"Darius is from one of the wealthiest families in the state. I'm sure he knows exactly what type of wife would be acceptable to him and his family. As long as you were on the rise at Winston Marks, you fit that mold. Beautiful, successful and an accepted member of his social class. But now, it looks as if you may step outside that mold. And if you do, he will drop you like a hot potato."

"He loves me, Alexis."

"All I have to say is that you had a good run with Darius, but his actions just serve to prove my theory true. There is no such thing as 'until death do us part.' When it comes down to it, people are too selfish to totally commit to another person. This situation proves that he's only concerned about himself."

Melanie refused to believe those words and replied, "You say that, but there are men out there looking for that special someone to spend the rest of their lives with."

Rising, Alexis collected the dishes and headed for the kitchen. "The only place you'll find a man like that is in the pages of a romance novel," Pausing, Alexis said, "Take this guy I met last night."

"You met a guy?" Melanie asked, her mood quickly changing to enthusiasm. Following her, she said, "That sounds promising. Was he cute?"

"I meet lots of guys, Melanie. Meeting them is never the problem."

"Yea, yea, yea," she answered impatiently. "But was he cute?"

"What he was, was a certified, Grade A jerk," Alexis said, refilling their coffee cups and taking a seat at the kitchen table. "And that's exactly what I told him when he came to interview me this morning . . ."

"Interview you?" Melanie asked, completely confused. "Wait a minute, back up, I thought you said you met him last night?"

Alexis recapped the sparring rounds she had over the past twenty-four hours with Malcolm Singleton. Standing, she began to pace the floor as she concluded her story. Even now, she still couldn't believe he said she had a chip on her shoulder.

"Just because you are tall, handsome, and possess a devastating smile, does not mean that you can treat people any kind of way. Can you imagine asking a woman if she's not interested because she's gay? What an ego!"

"I thought you said his friend asked if you were gay?"

Glaring at her sister, she answered, "Same thing."

"Alexis, I don't think . . ."

"And how about storming out of my office? How unprofessional! It's a wonder he's made it as far as he has in his profession. I can't believe that type of behavior is tolerated by his boss."

"But didn't you call him egotistical, arrogant, and rude first?"

Stopping her pacing, Alexis turned and shot daggers at her sister with her eyes. "Whose side are you on?"

Ignoring her look, she answered with amusement, "If he's cute, I'm on his side."

Relaxing her stance, Alexis conceded that one point and sat back down. "Okay, I will admit that the man is two parts ooohhhh, three part aaahhh, and four parts ump ump ump, mixed with some Lord have mercy." Remembering the way he made her feel, Alexis stopped smiling and said with conviction, "But I could never go out with him."

With a knowing look, Melanie said, "I don't recall you saying that he asked you out."

"He didn't." Alexis replied defensively. "I'm just saying that if he ever did, the answer would definitely be no."

"Um hum," Melanie said slowly.

Ignoring the smirk on her sister's face, she quickly changed the subject. "So what are you going to do about Darius? It's not like you can avoid him forever. You have to make a decision about the job and go back to New York at some point."

Acknowledging her dilemma, Melanie sighed. "You're right. But I'm taking a break. I haven't taken a real vacation in over four years. I'm going to hang out with you for the next month—maybe longer. I've given that company thirteen years of my life, they can give me thirty days to make a decision."

"And what about Darius?"

"I don't know. I'll just have to see when I get back to the Big Apple."

Glancing at the clock on the microwave, Alexis said, "You know you're welcome to stay as long as you want. The spare bedroom is all yours and there are fresh towels in the guest bathroom, but it's getting late and I have an appointment at an antebellum mansion tomorrow morning as a possible location for a fund-raiser."

"Nonprofits pay your outrageous fees?" Melanie blurted out in amazement.

"First of all," Alexis said, "I work very hard for my clients and my fees are not outrageous. Secondly, I periodically waive my fee to help a good cause raise money. I solicit vendors that I use on a continuous basis to offer steep discounts for their services. One of my clients told me about this youth organization several weeks ago that helps prepare young men for college. When I looked into it, I was impressed with their mission. That was when I found out they were planning a fund-raising dinner. I contacted the coordinator last week and offered my services. Not only am I committed to running a profitable business, I want to give back and help those less fortunate."

"I have to admit, Alexis, I'm impressed," Melanie said proudly. "With your fancy car, expensive clothes, and the 'I don't need anybody' attitude, I never would have pegged you as community service oriented."

Shrugging, she said "Yea, well, just don't let it get out. I have my reputation to think of."

Pleased that her sister was not totally callous, Melanie smiled. "Good night."

"Night."

Malcolm slammed his laptop shut after he read the same sentence four times. He had thought of working from home, but hoped the hustle and bustle of *Image*

Magazine's office would take his mind off Alexis Shaw. As demonstrated by his lack of concentration, his plan was not working.

When he got home from the game the night before, he gave himself a pep talk, reminding him of all the reasons he shouldn't get involved with a person like Alexis Shaw. His time with her would be filled with the battle for control. He would probably only be able to stand her for a week, and then he would want out. There was no use starting something he knew would come to an end—quickly.

With that decision firmly planted in his mind, he slid under the covers, welcoming a good night's sleep. He would put the events of the past two days and Alexis Shaw out of his mind. Unfortunately, his mind had another agenda, and as he lay in bed, the only thing that he could do was think of the woman who'd managed to be a constant in his thoughts since he first laid eyes on her.

After two hours of staring at the ceiling, he decided to stop fighting, and instead entertain the thought of spending time with her. Already a proven fact that something about her settled in him and would not go away, he hoped to understand his strong reaction to her if he could figure out what that something was.

She was beautiful, but he'd met beautiful women before, and none had stuck to his thoughts like this one. She was successful, but Malcolm was constantly surrounded by successful people, so he eliminated that. She was passionate about her work, but most successful people were. He searched for other words to describe her that might clue him in on why she had taken up permanent resident in his thoughts. Bossy, brash, demanding, and hotheaded immediately came to mind. And for some unknown reason, instead of being put off by those adjectives, he found that on her, it was quite appealing. In the few hours he had spent in her presence, she managed to pique his interest like no other woman had ever done before.

Shaking her out of his head and returning to the present, he raised the screen on his laptop and tried, once again, to focus on work. But his mind kept thinking of her and it actually bought a smile to his face.

"My seventeen-year-old son had that same goofy look on his face last night when his new study partner, Sheila, left our house."

Clearing his throat, Malcolm erased his grin and began typing on his keyboard, hoping to look hard at work. "I didn't hear you knock, Susan."

"Why don't you tell me her name, just in case she calls," she said, eyeing her boss with a hint of humor in her voice. "That way, I can put her right through."

"What are talking about?" he said, attempting to sound impatient. Susan was known as information central, and the last thing he needed was to have her thinking he was interested in a woman. The news would spread throughout the entire organization before lunchtime.

"That grin. The only thing that can put a smile like that on a man's face is a woman."

Malcolm started to argue against her analysis, but quickly changed his mind. That would only add fuel to the fire she was fanning. Susan, married at age twenty, had celebrated her twenty-fifth wedding anniversary three weeks ago and found it hard to fathom the thought that someone could be in their midthirties and still be single. Raising three kids, with only her youngest son remaining at home, Susan took on a motherly role with everyone in the office. Embracing that role with passion, Susan made a special point of offering advice—whether requested or not. Over the three years that Susan had been his assistant, she subtly, and sometimes not so subtly, worked on getting Malcolm to the altar.

He ignored her comment and changed the subject. "Is there a reason why you are in my office, or did you stop by just to aggravate me?"

"Me? Aggravate you? I wouldn't dream of it," she answered, her voice dripping sarcasm.

"I just wanted to let you know that the voicemail system has been down all morning, so I've been taking messages for you."

Placing the small, pink slips on his desk, she turned to leave, but paused just outside the door. "Are you sure you don't want to tell me her name?"

Malcolm could still hear her laughter long after she shut the door.

Leaning back in his leather chair, he flipped through his messages, not wanting to admit that he hoped that there would be one from Alexis. Technically speaking, their professional relationship would end on Saturday night, after the award's dinner, but there was a small part of him that wanted to continue that relationship on a personal level.

Reading the last message he contemplated the request. Picking up the phone, he dialed the cell number to confirm that he would give it his best shot. Checking his watch, he headed for the door. It would be close, but he could make it. Walking out, he stopped at Susan's desk.

"I have to run an errand, but I'll be back in the office this afternoon."

Five

Alexis turned down the long driveway and admired the trees lining the road. The branches from each side met overhead to create a naturally beautiful arch. The entrance, almost a mile long, helped calm her down after the horrendous traffic that had delayed her. The accident on I-85 put her almost thirty minutes behind schedule, but she called the owner of the mansion, Sylvia Harris, and was glad to learn that the fund-raising coordinator from Men of Standard had already arrived.

The organization worked with young men between the ages of eight and eighteen to assist them with schoolwork, computer skills, job placement, and getting into and paying for college. Men of standard set itself apart from other organizations because the program was run entirely by men, a rarity in the charity world. Speaking with Brent Harrison last week about assisting with the fund-raiser, he was noticeably apprehensive about bringing in an outsider. But he quickly warmed to the idea when Alexis mentioned the possibility of a free venue. Now that she thought about it, she should call Malcolm and let him know about this part of her business. He may want to mention her community service in the article. Alexis frowned. Was she searching for a reason to contact him?

That's ridiculous! That man is nothing but trouble. I just want him to write the best article possible.

Pulling into a parking space, she cut the engine. Riding with the top down, she checked her hair and makeup. She was heading directly to the home of Samuel Dobbs, the owner of several malls in the state, after this meeting. Hosting a dinner party for fifty of his closest friends, he and his wife wanted to share what they had experienced from their recent trip to India. Wanting to make the evening as authentic as possible, Alexis worked with each guest to provide traditional Indian dress for them to wear, as well as contracted several well-known chefs to prepare authentic Indian dishes.

The guests were scheduled to arrive at six o'clock, but she planned to meet with the decorators at two this afternoon to oversee the layout of the tables and the pillows that the guest would be sitting on. By the time everyone arrived, they would have a hard time believing they were dining in a friend's home in Georgia, as opposed to the Taj Mahal. Pulling out her cell phone, she made one quick call to confirm with the musicians and dancers.

Not wanting to delay the start of the meeting, Alexis instructed Sylvia to start the tour without her, as she was already familiar with the facility.

As Alexis approached the entrance, she admired the large wraparound porch, the stately pillars, and the oversize double doors made of solid wood. It was a breathtaking structure that was perfect for any occasion. The mansion had been in Sylvia's family for the five generations. Receiving ownership after her mother died, Sylvia and her husband raised five children in this house, who had now all moved to other states. When her husband passed four years ago, instead of selling the estate, she remodeled and began renting it out to the public for functions. Alexis had held six events there since she started Just For You, and she was pleased when Sylvia agreed to waive the rental fee for the charity event they were planning for September, especially since they were asking for a Saturday night. Alexis knew that most Saturdays during that time of year were reserved for weddings.

Entering the grand foyer, she was not surprised that no one was there to meet her. There were only two people on staff when no event was scheduled, and they rarely worked on the same day. Assuming that Mr. Harrison and Sylvia were still touring, she set off in the direction of the main ballroom. Having torn down several walls on the first floor, the room could easily accommodate up to three hundred people. She knew she made a good choice as she heard Sylvia's voice explaining the different options for seating arrangements.

"As you can see, we offer a variety of setups and decor. However, I've worked with your planner on several other events and I'm sure she'll have several other ideas for your fund-raiser."

"That's good to know, because I'm substituting for the event coordinator. He was called into an emergency meeting and couldn't get in contact with the other committee members. I'm the pinch hitter." Laughing, he continued, "It's a good thing we have a planner, because I have no experience in fund-raising events. I have only been a part of the organization for less than a year, and only in the capacity of a tutor."

Alexis felt a flurry of butterflies in her stomach as she stood in the entrance. That deep, smooth, sexy voice that had haunted her dreams the past few days had found its way back into her life. Hoping beyond hope that her mind was playing a sadistic trick on her, she shut her eyes and walked in the room. She prayed silently that when she opened them, she would not see Malcolm Singleton.

Slowly, she opened her eyes.

So much for prayer!

Turning at the sound of heels on the hardwood floor, Sylvia smiled, "We were just speaking of you."

Alexis genuinely smiled and offered the woman a friendly hug. "It's good to see you again, Sylvia. I'm excited to be working with you again."

Malcolm watched as Alexis greeted the elderly woman and forced himself to focus his attention on the conversation. *What was she doing here?* Brent and Jackson were heavily involved with Men of Standard, and Malcolm pitched in to help out with tutoring young boys in English, but rarely got involved with the administrative side of the organization. The message he got from Brent was to meet with the owner of the facility where the event was to be held. He made no mention of a planner, and Malcolm didn't expect one, until Sylvia told him otherwise when he arrived. It seemed that he couldn't get away from Ms. Shaw if he wanted to. And much to his dismay, that thought pleased him immensely.

As Alexis continued her conversation with Sylvia, Malcolm took advantage of that time to study her, his eyes seductively perusing her body like an eagle.

Alexis felt his gaze sear into her. *What in the world was he doing here?* Knowing she couldn't ignore him any longer, she turned to Malcolm and said, "Hello, Mr. Singleton."

"Ms. Shaw," he answered with a slight nod.

Sylvia glanced from one to the other as an uncomfortable silence ensued. They stared openly at each other as if they were daring the other to make the first conciliatory gesture to a private dispute. She was glad she wasn't made of wool, as the electricity in the air would definitely cause permanent damage.

"I see you two know each other."

Not moving his gaze from Alexis, he smiled and replied, "Yes, Alexis just won a very prestigious award for her business accomplishments, and I was honored to interview her for *Image Magazine*."

"Oh, how simply wonderful, Alexis," Sylvia beamed. "You are the best."

"Thank you, Sylvia," she said, continuing to stare at him. Alexis felt her heart rate increase and swallowed deliberately. What was it about this man that caused her insides to quiver with excitement? Trying to act nonchalant, she soaked in his sultry eyes and sexy grin. Dressed casually, she had to admire his taste in clothes. This man definitely had style. Feeling her thoughts could be read in her face, she forced her attention away from him.

Looking from one to the other, Sylvia loudly cleared her throat. Giving the couple a knowing smile, she said, "Since we have finished with the tour, I'll leave you two to discuss the details of the program. If you need me, I'll be in my office."

Snapping back to reality, Alexis turned to Sylvia, and said sweetly, "Thank you, Sylvia. We'll be in shortly to discuss menu options once I get a feel for what type of affair Mr. Singleton plans on having."

As soon as she left the room, Alexis turned to Malcolm and whispered angrily, "What is your problem?"

"My problem? What are you talking about?" he asked.

"How dare you stand there and ogle me in front of her."

"Excuse me?" he asked, wondering if he heard her correctly. "Ogle? First of all, sweetheart, I don't ogle, I admire. And second of all, I could ask you the same question."

"What do you mean 'you could ask me the same thing'?" *Did he just call me sweetheart?*

Taking a step forward, he leaned to her ear and whispered, "Are you trying to tell me that you weren't checking me out?"

Taking one step back, Alexis said through gritted teeth, "Don't flatter yourself."

"I don't have too," he said confidently. "The way you were looking at me was flattering enough"

"What way?" she spat.

"You know the look. The one that says you could sop me up with a country biscuit."

Stepping to his face, she pointed her finger at his chest and emphatically declared, "Not if you were the last man on earth."

"Is everything all right?"

Alexis and Malcolm both turned to the voice and both immediately responded with a sugary smile.

"Of course, Sylvia," Alexis drawled, "I was just sharing with Malcolm some ideas on how to make his event a success."

Looking from one to the other, she paused and released a grin. "I see. Well, I'm going out to the garden to meet with the landscapers. If you need me, I'll be back in my office in about fifteen minutes."

After she made her exit, Alexis turned to Malcolm and asked accusingly, "What are you doing here? What happened to Brent Harrison? Are you following me?"

"Now, don't you flatter yourself," he replied sarcastically. "Brent couldn't make it, so as a volunteer at Men of Standard, I told him I'd stand in for him. He had an unexpected meeting at work and he didn't want to cancel this appointment."

"Why didn't he call me?" she asked suspiciously.

"You'll have to ask him," he answered, crossing his arms over his chest.

Irritated at this turn of events, Alexis said, "I can't believe someone like you actually volunteers his time. I would think with an ego as big as yours, you would have little time to help other people."

"You should be one to talk. I find it hard to imagine that you have one nice bone in your body."

Putting one hand on her hip, Alexis sneered, "My body is none of your business."

Malcolm braced himself for the onslaught of anger and annoyance to overtake him, as no woman had ever talked to him this way. Most didn't give him a hard time because they were too busy trying to impress him. But Alexis Shaw didn't have that problem. The last thing on her agenda was impressing him. The amazing thing about this entire situation was that he found himself duly impressed. So instead of coming back at her with a snide remark, he paused to take a look at the body that was so aptly being discussed.

As the corners of his mouth formed a seductive grin, he leaned back. His eyes lazily traveled the length of her body, taking in every supple curve. It was in this moment that he realized why this woman got under his skin and made it crawl.

Alexis Shaw, with her hands resting firmly on fine hips, was tantalizingly attractive. There was no doubt that her body would cause any man to take a second look. Her eyes, filled with fire and determination, glared back at him with the grit of a lion, and her lips, pouty with agitation, screamed silently to be kissed. Moving down her slim neck, he focused on the exaggerated rise and fall of her chest, indicating she was bucking for a fight. Moving to her slim waist and shapely thighs, Malcolm realized he liked everything he saw. Gazing lower, he admired the ankle-length black flare pants and his smile grew complete at the bright-red nail polish on her ten perfect toes. Pulling his eyes all the way up, he said nothing. He wondered if she was fighting her attraction to him as much as he was fighting his attraction for her.

"Excuse me!" she said, shocked at his brazen appraisal.

He took a few steps forward and watched her mouth start to protest but quickly snap shut. His smile left and his expression became filled with hunger and desire. Pulling her close by the waist, she slammed into his rock hard chest and gasped as she realized what he was going to do. Forming her lips to say no, she paused when she looked into his eyes and saw them grow dark.

Malcolm paused inches from her lips and tauntingly said, "Is your body still none of my business?"

Immediately becoming flushed with humiliation and embarrassment, anger at herself began to rise from the pit of her stomach when she realized she actually wanted his kiss. Taking a step back, she straightened her shoulders and her temper began to swell like a tidal wave. "Malcolm Singleton, go to . . ."

The ringing of her cell phone interrupted her and snatching it off the holder on her hip, she hastily answered, "Hello!"

"Alexis? Is that you?"

"Yes, Celeste," she answered, as she watched Malcolm tip his head in a gentlemanly gesture and head toward the exit.

Egotistical jerk!

"If this isn't a good time . . ."

Watching him disappear through the double doors, Alexis turned her attention back to her friend. "No, no. This is a good a time as any."

"What's going on? You sound preoccupied. Anything you want to talk about?"

"Not particularly," she answered, wiping the sweat from her brow as she thought about the almost kiss. "What's up?"

"I was wondering what you were up to tonight. There's a great new restaurant that opened in Buckhead and Kenneth is working late. Are you interested?"

"It'll have to be late. I have the Dobbs dinner tonight, but I should be out of there by eight o'clock."

"That's fine. I'll meet you at eighty thirty. I'll make the reservations."

"Make it for three. Melanie's in town."

"No problem. See you tonight."

After hanging up, Alexis took a few moments to get herself under control. She had a string of curse words running through her mind that would make a sailor blush, and she knew that if she went into Sylvia's office now, she was liable to say every last one of them at Malcolm. After counting to ten to calm down, she realized she was still livid. So she counted to ten again. By the fifth count, she felt calm enough to see him again without wanting to punch him.

Entering the office off the entrance, she was surprised to see Sylvia working alone.

Putting on her most professional demeanor, she asked, "Where is Mr. Singleton?"

Removing her glasses, Sylvia smiled. "He already left. Did you still need him? He said he left everything in your hands."

Hearing the double meaning in that statement, Alexis assured Sylvia that everything was fine, and after they reviewed menu options, said good-bye and headed out.

As she headed toward her next appointment, her agitation grew with every minute. Never one to let any man walk away getting the best of her, she dialed information. It only took a few seconds to make the connection.

"*Image Magazine*, how may I direct your call?"

"Mr. Singleton, please."

"I'm sorry. He's not in the office. Would you like to speak with his assistant? Our voicemail system is down at this time."

"His assistant will be fine, thank you."

Waiting to be transferred, she thought of all the ways she could torture him.

"Malcolm Singleton's office, Susan speaking."

"Hi Susan, my name is Alexis Shaw."

"Ms. Shaw! Congratulations on the award."

"Thank you," she said. "I understand that Mr. Singleton is out of the office."

"Yes, but he should be back this afternoon. Is there a message?"

"Even though we've completed the interview, there are a few more things I'd like to add. Could you have him call me?" Pausing to listen, Alexis smiled. "Thanks, Susan. Have a great day."

An hour later, Malcolm returned to his office and retrieved his messages. Flipping through them, he paused when he saw her name. He reread the message several times, wondering if this was a good or bad sign.

"She must have called," Susan said.

Glancing up at his door, he erased his smile and said, "You have got to stop sneaking up on people, and what are you talking about?"

"That grin. It's the same goofy one you were wearing this morning. Now, let me think about all the women that called today. There were about six."

"Susan," Malcolm warned.

Ignoring the tone in his voice, she continued,

"There was Denise Edwards from Advertising. But that was disaster the first time you guys dated, so I can't imagine you going back to her. Too possessive."

Stepping into his office, she took a seat. "Then there was Peggy Johnson from Morehouse College. You're suppose to be speaking to her journalism class. But I don't think it would be her, she sounded old enough to be your great-grandmother."

"I don't believe I invited you in," he said, hoping she would take the hint.

She didn't. "The next call came from Angela Barnes. She's from your cleaning service. Now she seemed a little too young and fresh for my taste. She came right out and asked if you were single. I think she would be all wrong for you . . . too fast. Next, there was Arlene Lopez. She didn't leave any information, so she's a possibility. Next there was . . . ."

Rising out of his chair, Malcolm pointed to the door and said, "Out!"

"But Malcolm . . ."

Trying to sound firm, he warned her, "You are an employee-at-will. I can fire you anytime."

Standing, she headed for the door, "Just to let you know, I'm not the least bit bothered by your idle threats. But I do have to get back to work. I'll just continue to go down the list when I get back to my desk."

Relaxing his stance, Malcolm knew his threats were empty, and confirmed it by stating, "You're lucky you're the best assistant in this whole company. Now get out of my office and mind your own business."

Alone, he picked up the phone and toyed with the idea of calling her. Quickly changing his mind, he replaced the receiver. He had something else in mind for Ms. Shaw.

* * *

Later that evening, Celeste and Melanie enjoyed a wonderful dinner while listening to Alexis tell of her latest encounter with the seemingly ever-present Malcolm Singleton. Barely eating half her food, Alexis talked nonstop about her escapades with the handsome magazine writer. After she finished, the two women exchanged knowing glances.

"Excuse me," Alexis said, darting her eyes from one to the other. "What do you two find so amusing? Did I not just sit here and tell you what a terrible few days I've had dealing with a complete idiot? Not to mention that I called him"—pausing, she glanced at her gold watch—"almost eight hours ago, leaving my cell, home and business number, and he has yet to return my call."

Cutting her eyes at Melanie, Celeste said, "You're her sister, you tell her."

"Well you're her best friend, you tell her."

Not amused, Alexis said, "Have you both completely lost your mind? Tell me what?"

"I think thou dost protest too much," Celeste said.

Melanie shook her head in agreement, "Way too much."

Realizing what they were indicating, Alexis sighed. "Besides being a successful writer and a gorgeous specimen of a man, what else does he have going for him?"

Melanie laughed. "Girlfriend, what else does he need?"

Alexis glanced at her sister strangely, "This comment coming from a woman who sleeps in flannel pajamas and hasn't gone out with anyone but Darius for the past five years?"

"But she's right," Celeste said. "If what you say is true, Malcolm may have more on his mind than magazine articles and fund-raisers."

"Now that statement I will agree with," Alexis said confidently. "He does have more on his mind. To con stantly think of ways to get under my skin and agitate me to the point where we can't be in the same room with each other."

"Almost kissing doesn't sound like two people who can't stand to be in the same room with each other," Melanie said.

Pondering the events of the past few days, Alexis relented and admitted, "Okay, there may be a slight physical attraction to the man."

"Just a slight attraction?" Melanie said, convinced it was a major attraction.

"What are you going to do about it?" Celeste asked.

"I'm not sure," Alexis said slowly, "I'm not seeing anyone now, so maybe I'll indulge in a summer fling."

Melanie stared at her sister, confused, "Did you just say what I think you said?"

"If you think I said 'short term, hot and heavy, get my groove on, summer fling,' then yes, you heard right."

"You can't be serious? No wonder your relationships never last. Look at the attitude you have when you start one." Turning to Celeste, she asked, "Is she always like this?"

Nodding, Celeste said, "If it lasts the entire summer, I'd be surprised."

As the waiter cleared the dishes away, Alexis smiled. "A man usually lasts three months, four at the most, before he realizes that I'm an independent woman who doesn't need him. That's when he decides to move on to find someone who has time to cater to his every little whim. I don't see Malcolm being any different."

"Why?" Melanie asked.

"Because he's a man," Alexis answered, looking at her sister as if she had just asked the dumbest question ever spoken.

Leaning closer to the two women, Melanie lowered her eyes and her voice, "I can't believe you, Alexis. You sit here, planning the end of a relationship before you begin it. How can you do that?"

Celeste put her fork down and leaned in as well. "Yes, Alexis. I've always wondered how you could stay so emotionally detached. Don't you want something more from your relationships?"

Alexis mockingly moved forward, as they did, and whispered back sarcastically, "Well, little Miss Prissy, just because you and Kenneth have been together since birth, doesn't mean that all relationships last forever." And turning to her sister, she continued, "You have only been with one man your entire life. A man who—by the way—will let you go the minute you decide to turn down that job. So I don't think my way of handling my relationships is so bad."

Leaning back, she continued, "Whatever attraction Malcolm and I have for each other, it will be for a season, and then it will be over. That's just the way my relationships works."

Six

Alexis glanced at the blinking red light on the answering machine when they returned home and pushed play. She hated to admit that she felt a slight tremor of excitement in the center core of her being as she anticipated hearing his voice.

Beep.

"Melanie, this is Darius. I got this number from your mother. Stop playing these childish games and come back to New York. It doesn't look good to keep the Board waiting, and it definitely isn't good to keep me waiting. I'll be out tonight, but call me tomorrow and let me know when you'll return. I'll have a car pick you up from the airport."

Alexis glanced at her sister with questioning eyes. "You can **hit** delete," Melanie said, not quite ready to deal with her fiancé.

Alexis obeyed, and waited for the next message.

Beep.

"Melanie?"

Alexis cringed at the voice and forced herself to listen to the rest of the message.

"I've been trying to reach you the last few days, but I can't get through on your cell phone. I don't understand why you have that phone and then never answer it. Anyway, I spoke with Darius. Melanie Shaw, you need to end this nonsense this instant. Have you completely

gone mad? Do you know what you have? A job that gar-
ners respect and status, and a man from one of the
wealthiest families in the state. I just don't understand
what the problem is. Anyway, I hope you'll be home by
the Fourth of July. The Clarkstons are planning a fabulous barbecue and it will make Mary Clarkston spit
nails when she sees you with Darius. She swore he
would choose her daughter over you. In any case, I've
talked long enough. Call me."

Alexis stared incredulously at her sister and asked,
"Why did you tell her you were coming here if you
wanted time to sort things out in your life?"

"I didn't want her to worry," she answered, knowing
Alexis didn't approve.

This time, it was Alexis who said, "I can hit delete on
this one too."

"She's just concerned about us," Melanie said.

Throwing up her hands, Alexis was dumbfounded.
"Is that what you think? Do you realize she called my
house and never said one word to me? Can't you see
she only cares about herself? What would she tell her
friends if you declined that job and broke it off with
Darius? She's all about status."

"You're not being reasonable, Alexis."

"Not reasonable? Can you believe she's telling people I'm still considering law school? How ridiculous is
that? This just proves that she's selfish and self-centered
and I, for one, don't want to have anything to do with
her."

Watching Alexis erase the message, Melanie said,
"She's our mother."

"That title does not give her carte blanche to run our
lives."

"She's just wants the best for us."

"Why do you keep defending her? What she wants
is for us to make her look her best in front of her sid-

dity friends. You didn't have it so bad before the divorce because daddy served as a buffer, but after he left, she was determined to maintain her status in the community.

"Everyone knew that she came from nothing, and if it wasn't for David Shaw and his medical practice, she would still have nothing. When he left, she may have gotten millions in the settlement, but she always felt her social circle saw her as less deserving, making her work twice as hard to prove her spot in the New York elite was deserved. And that included forcing her children to live up to some crazy expectations. She made me join clubs, attend country club parties, and hang out with people I couldn't stand. All in the name of her image. I couldn't wait to get out of New York."

Melanie said, "Let's just drop it."

"Fine," Alexis answered.

Alexis listened to two more messages, neither of which were from Malcolm. Not wanting to show her disappointment to her sister, she deleted the last message. *I don't care if he ever calls!*

Putting their earlier disagreement aside, Melanie tried to cheer her up. "You said your call was in reference to your interview, so I'm sure he'll call you tomorrow, during business hours."

"Whatever," Alexis answered, heading for her bedroom.

Following her sister, Melanie plopped on her bed. "Tell me about the awards ceremony."

Pushing Malcolm out of her mind, Alexis thought about Saturday. "It should be very exciting. Top business leaders from around the country will be attending, and it'll be covered by other media outlets, including the *Atlanta Journal and Constitution*. I have tickets for my staff, along with Kenneth and Celeste. And since I don't have a man, get ready to dress up and step out on the town."

"It sounds like it will be a great event," Melanie said hesitantly.

"You sound like there's a 'but' coming."

"I was just thinking that if you want to invite Mom, I'm sure she'll be glad to catch a plane and be here for you."

Cutting her eyes at her sister, she said, "Did you not hear that message? There is no way I want her here. If you don't want to go, that's fine, but that ticket will not go to Mom."

Rising, Melanie headed for her room "Fine, I'll go. But I didn't bring any formal wear, so I hope you have something in that overstuffed closet of yours that can fit me."

Alexis skipped her morning workout and arrived in the office early the next day. Her only appointment was that afternoon, followed by a status meeting with her staff. Hoping to take full advantage of her free morning to complete some paperwork, she made a mental list of tasks she needed to accomplish.

Stepping off the elevator, she stopped short when she saw Sherry and Malcolm laughing and talking over coffee and croissants. Leaning over the receptionist's desk, Alexis's breath caught as she admired the view from behind. His body filled out those blue jeans and the cotton shirt highlighted his broad shoulders. Sherry's flirty laugh snapped Alexis out of her trance.

Hearing the phone ring, Alexis said sharply, "Sherry I believe I pay you to answer phones."

Flashing a quick smile at Malcolm, Sherry picked up the call.

"Good morning, Ms. Shaw," Malcolm said.

"Mr. Singleton," she answered eyeing him suspiciously. "What are you doing here?"

Standing confidently, he casually leaned against the desk.

"It was you who called me, not other way around."

Having transferred the call, Sherry glanced from one to the other, extremely interested in the exchange.

Noticing her nosy receptionist, Alexis looked at Malcolm and said, "Follow me."

Placing his empty coffee cup in the trash can beside the receptionist's desk, Malcolm smiled at Sherry and winked, "Thanks for the great conversation, Sherry. It's been fun."

"Anytime, my brother," Sherry said, stretching her neck to admire him from behind. "Anytime."

Agitated at their friendly demeanor, Alexis cleared her throat and said, "I don't have all day, Mr. Singleton."

Shutting the door, Alexis moved quickly behind her desk and took a seat. Hoping her pounding heart could not be heard, she felt her palms grow sweaty. Seeing him again reminded her of their almost kiss the day before and sent her senses into a tailspin. Giving no indication of her inner turmoil, she said, "A return phone call would have sufficed. You didn't have to come to my office."

Moving around her desk, Malcolm took a seat on the edge. Leaning forward, he curled the corners of his mouth and said, "I figured you were calling because you wanted to finish what you started yesterday."

Knowing he was trying to get a rise out of her, Alexis refused to let him see how much his sultry voice and smoldering eyes affected her. Clearing her throat she said, "If anything, Mr. Singleton, you are here because *you* want to finish what *you* started yesterday."

Malcolm relaxed and reached for the paperweight

on her desk. Fingering the crystal object, he took a moment to gather his thoughts. After several moments of comfortable silence, Malcolm said, "You intrigue me, Ms. Shaw."

"Should I be flattered?" she asked flatly.

Replacing the paperweight, Malcolm stood, not the least bit deterred by her smart remark. "Your message said you had something to add to the interview. Was that true, or was that just a ploy to see me again?"

Standing, Alexis picked up a file off her desk and walked to the file cabinet on the opposite wall. When she called him yesterday, she was prepared to give him a piece of her mind, telling him that in no uncertain terms would she consider giving her lips, and definitely not her body, to someone as ornery as himself. But now that he was here, she had to admit that she wasn't sure if that objective was still true. Malcolm Singleton. He was successful, intelligent, and handsome. And the more she thought about it, the more she realized he intrigued her as well.

Turning to face him, she answered smugly, "If it was a ploy, it worked. You're here."

Walking toward her, he stopped within a few feet of her. "And now that I'm here, what are you going to do with me."

Wanting to set him off balance, she said with a sly grin, "What I always do with my men. Enjoy them while the thrill is there, and when it's gone, it's over."

"And how can you be so sure that the thrill will end?" he challenged.

"It always does, Mr. Singleton," she answered, stepping around him. "It always does."

Turning, he asked, "Are you proposing that any relationship between us will be temporary?"

"Have you ever had a relationship that wasn't temporary?"

In the midst of the absurdity of this conversation, Malcolm saw the truth in her statement. As evidenced by the fact that he was not married, all of his relationships were, in fact, temporary. But he had a different inkling about Alexis Shaw. He was used to dating women whose sole purpose was to grab the diamond ring, and all that came with it. When that didn't come into fruition, they moved on to find the next brother who could lead them to their pot of relationship gold. And that was perfectly fine with Malcolm. His career had always come first, and he had no problem letting any woman go that could not understand that.

But now that he wanted more, he found it quite ironic that he had to meet a woman who had no interest in developing a long-term relationship. Still, he couldn't resist her fiery personality, her challenging nature, and the proposition she just laid before him. Maybe he could turn the tables on her. Prove her wrong. Show her that, when the right two people got together, there was nothing temporary about it.

"Maybe there's a man out there just waiting to change your mind about that."

"I doubt it," she said confidently. "I have divorced parents and five divorced friends to assure me that no one, not even you, can change my mind about that. People are too selfish to hang in there when the times get tough. And if more people recognized that going into a relationship, then they would be better prepared when it ended."

Thinking back to their interview, he said, "Is that why you don't plan weddings, because you believe the relationship won't last?"

Not forgetting who he was, she raised a brow and said, "Off the record."

"Off the record." And he meant it. This conversation was one hundred percent personal.

"One of the main reasons why my events are so successful and unique is because I wholeheartedly believe in the goal, in what's trying to be portrayed or accomplished. There is nothing about weddings or marriages that I believe in."

"That's a strong statement to make, Ms. Shaw. If that's how you feel, then I'll have to go along with it." Malcolm said, "You're on."

Confused, Alexis said, "For what?"

"A temporary relationship."

"What are you suggesting?"

"That the two of us become involved."

"In what?" she asked incredulously.

"In a temporary relationship."

"Why would I want to do that?"

Moving one step closer, Malcolm lifted her chin with his forefinger and stared directly into her eyes. Lowering his voice, he whispered, "Because you find me just as enticing as I find you."

Alexis struggled to control her breathing, as she found herself captivated by his words. Never one to get sucked in by a smooth line, she fought for control. Retreating one step, she asked, "And what happens when it ends?"

Malcolm had no intention of having it end. He wanted this relationship to be different. In the past, he never took the time to really get to know a woman. This time, he vowed to make this relationship different. He wanted to take the time and make the effort to get to know Alexis. To build a relationship where the conversation could move beyond world events and business. He wanted to know a woman's heart before he came to know her body. Understanding that he couldn't share these thoughts with Alexis, he answered, "We'll be going into this with our eyes wide open. When it ends, it ends. No hard feelings."

Growing up with a domineering mother, life was never about what Alexis wanted, it was all about what her mother wanted, and when Alexis became an adult, she vowed never to hesitate to go after what she wanted. And she wanted Malcolm Singleton. "You've got yourself a deal. Shall we shake on it?"

"I've got a better idea," Malcolm said, lowering his eyes to her lips.

"Alexis, Elaine Barr is on line one. She says it's urgent," Sherry's voice interrupted on the intercom.

"Thanks, Sherry." Feeling disappointed at what didn't happen, she took little comfort in seeing the same reflected in his eyes. "She's spending twenty-five thousand dollars on her son's graduation party. I have to take it."

"Then I'll let you get back to work."

Alexis was unsure of what to say or do now. Isn't this the point where he asks her out, invites her over for dinner, or wants to know the next time they could get together?

Raising her hand to his mouth, he gently kissed the back, grazing his tongue along her soft skin and giving it a slight pull with his teeth. "See you at the awards ceremony on Saturday."

The caress of his lips on her hand set her insides aflame and she felt the heat move from the palm of her hand, through her arms, and down to her feet.

"Alexis," Sherry's voice interrupted again, "Line one."

Opening the door, he said, "I'll see you Saturday night."

Alexis stood still for several seconds. If his lips on her hand could cause that type of reaction, imagine what she would feel when his lips touched her . . .

"Alexis," Sherry buzzed. "Line one."

Snapping back from her fantasy, she fanned herself as she moved toward her desk.

Picking up the phone, she took a deep breath. "Elaine, what can I do for you?"

Laying her dress on the bed, Alexis called out to Melanie, "What did you decide to wear tonight?"

Melanie stepped from the walk-in closet into the master bedroom with several outfits thrown across her arms, "I can't believe your closet. How can you find anything in it?"

"It's not out of order, it's just slightly unorganized."

Melanie laughed. "Did you say slightly? It's more like a major disaster. You have beautiful designer clothes, but they are all over the place."

Not wanting to admit that she could be a little messy, Alexis tried to sound convincing when she said, "At least I know where everything is."

"Sure you do," Melanie said mockingly.

Pulling the selections out of Melanie's arms and holding them up one by one, Alexis said, "If you think this closet is bad, you should see the one in the other bedroom. Being an event planner, I have to fit in with the theme. I keep all of those clothes in there. I probably wouldn't be caught dead in any of those outfits outside of a theme party."

"I can't imagine you dressing in anything that would make you look less than impeccable," Melanie said, vetoing the first two dresses that Alexis picked. Too short and too colorful.

"Then it's a good thing you didn't see me in the red-and-white polka dot dress that flares out when you twirl around. I wore that to the reunion of the 1975 Square Dance Championship Team."

Melanie laughed as the picture flashed through her

mind. "Is it really necessary that you fit in with the theme? I would think that as the planner you would be excused from dressing as a participant."

Discarding the last of the dresses that Melanie brought out, Alexis walked to her closet to search for more clothes. "I guess it's not necessary, but it's my way of letting my clients know that I'm one hundred percent committed to making their event a success."

Shaking her head in the negative to the next three dresses Alexis held up, Melanie asked, "But how many different kinds of parties can you have? Don't you get tired of doing the same thing over and over again?"

"That's just it. Every event is unique. Last year, I wore doctor's scrubs when my client threw a birthday party for her *ER* loving husband. The entire ballroom was turned into an emergency room, complete with an Eric LaSalle impersonator. Oh, and I definitely don't want to forget the cowboy boots, stirrups, and holster ensemble. That's what I wore when the owner of a chain of outdoor stores wanted to teach his son about the black rodeo."

Melanie, laughing hysterically by this point, said, "Please tell me you didn't have live animals."

"Would I do anything less?" she responded. Holding up the last dress in her arms, "This is perfect."

Melanie took a look at the strapless red satin dress with the gold trim. Sifting through the discarded clothes on the bed, she held up her choice. "I'll think I'll wear this."

Alexis scrunched up her nose and said, "That's a simple black dress."

"Exactly."

"Boring!" Alexis answered.

"Not boring, classic," she answered, holding it up against her body.

"Aren't you tired of being 'classic'?" Alexis asked, snatching the dress out of her hands.

"What are you talking about?"

"I saw your expression when I held up that red satin dress. You would look fabulous in it."

Fingering the smooth garment on the bed, Melanie contemplated, but then quickly came to her senses, "I can't wear that, what would people think?"

"What people?"

"You know . . . people?"

"You're being ridiculous. Stop being a people pleaser. It's not about what anyone thinks, it's about feeling good about yourself."

"Call it what you want," Melanie replied. "That dress is not me."

Taking a peek at the dress Alexis selected, she said, "You want me to believe the only reason you chose that dress is to feel good about yourself? I don't think so. I think you made your selection with a certain magazine writer in mind."

"Well, maybe I considered him just a little when I chose that dress," she said, picking up the outfit that took her four days and eleven boutiques to find.

"Speaking of Malcolm, can you explain to me again how you can make a deal to have a temporary relationship?" Melanie asked, still confused about their arrangement.

"It's quite simple, Melanie," she answered, pulling an overnight bag off the shelf. "We are both adults, capable of enjoying each other's company for however long we want to,"

Watching her throw in a teddy and silk robe, Melanie raised a questioning brow and asked, "Not coming home tonight?"

"I always come home . . . but you never know." Alexis hadn't heard from Malcolm since he left her office, but she was sure that being together tonight was a top priority for him.

"How can you be so sure that he's ready for a physical relationship? You two just met."

"How can I be sure?" Alexis said. "It's quite simple. First of all, he's a man. Second of all, he's a man."

"And that's okay with you?"

"Look, Melanie," Alexis said, stepping in the bathroom to start the shower. "If you must know, I am very attracted to him. He's smart, gorgeous, and there's something that draws me near him. I don't know quite what it is, but I'm looking forward to getting to know him."

Following her sister into the bathroom, Melanie asked, "But how can you be so sure it will be temporary? What happens if you fall in love with each other?"

Alexis turned her sister and laughed. "Love? Don't be ridiculous. Our parents were in love, and they stopped speaking to each other five years before our father died. Not to mention that I stood at the altars of several churches with five of my good friends after they fell in love, only to have them end up in divorce court—some left to raise a child on their own. And let's not even talk about your situation with Darius. So as you can see, Melanie, I have absolutely no interest in falling in love."

"But what about Celeste and Kenneth? They're in love and have been together since high school. They're extremely happy together."

"That's only one couple. Hardly enough to build a case on."

"So let's assume you beat the odds and fall in love with Malcolm. Would you be able to walk away?"

"That is a moot question"—she answered, pushing her sister out of the bathroom—"because there is no way that Malcolm Singleton and I will do anything more than have some fun and enjoy each other's company. And when we decide to move on, it will be a clean break."

Alexis shut the door, slid off her silk robe, and stepped into the shower. As she lathered up, using her favorite scented body gel, she thought about her sister and her fantasy world of falling in love. There should be a diagnosable psychological condition for people who claim to fall in love. That way, they can be treated before they get trapped, only to end up with a broken heart.

When her parents divorced, her father said that her mother was asking too much of him and her mother said her father was asking to much of her. If love were so great, why were people so easily willing to give it up?

To avoid the heartache that usually came with giving away your heart, Alexis never allowed a man to get too close. Most people said she was too hard on men, but she didn't agree. Her theory that selfishness was the name of the game and people would rather get what they want, regardless of what it costs the relationship, had been proven out by the men she had known.

She thought about Gary Thompson. Celeste had introduced them because he seemed to be someone that would be a good fit for Alexis. Gary worked for a public relations firm for several years before branching out on his own. Celeste reasoned that he would understand the time constraints and the pressures that come with running your own enterprise. But Alexis soon realized that Gary was full of ulterior motives for dating Alexis.

A short time after they began dating, their conversations began to revolve around Alexis's work and what events she had coming up and for whom. Soon after, he began showing up at her events uninvited, asking to be introduced to her clients. Explaining that her events were not the place for an uninvited guest to network did not register initially. Eventually, he finally stopped showing up unannounced, but then began to constantly ask her for referrals. She told him she would be happy to present his marketing packages to clients who expressed an interest in his line of work. But that wasn't good enough for him. He constantly asked Alexis for the names and numbers of people she worked with.

One morning, she got a frantic call from Sherry. Only on the job for a month, she had gotten to know Gary through his phone calls and visits to the office. That's why when he showed up unexpectedly at the office with a story that Alexis had asked him to get some information from her office, Sherry relented. However, only a few minutes passed before she began to feel antsy about allowing someone into her boss's office. She called Alexis, who promptly told her that she asked Gary to do no such thing and held on the phone while Sherry went to ask him to leave. She caught him going through Alexis's Rolodex, copying down names and numbers. Alexis, outraged at his boldness, proceeded to tell him by phone, in words that left no room for interpretation, not only to get out of her office, but out of her life. That was the last she heard from Gary Thompson. And it was good riddance to him.

As she rinsed off, she moved her thoughts from Gary to Malcolm. There was no comparison. She dated Gary for several months, but there was never anything about Gary that set her soul on fire. But that wasn't the case with Malcolm. Everything about him excited her. From the moment she heard his voice at that restaurant, to the current of passion that passed between them when he gently kissed her hand, Malcolm had never been far from her thoughts. If she was the falling in love type,

Malcolm would be the type of man she would choose.
But, as she cut off the water, she realized that would
never happen. Love was for those who were gluttons
for punishment. She'd seen it too many times to believe it could be anything different—no matter who the
man.

Seven

Malcolm adjusted his tie and reached for his dinner jacket. Security had just called from the gated entrance to his condo community to let him know that Brent had arrived. Deciding to go dateless, he invited Brent and Jackson to the awards ceremony. Having to file a brief on Monday, Jackson passed, but Brent, who loved these events to scout out single women, accepted on the spot.

Walking down the hallway to his bedroom, he paused to straighten a painting he bought last month. A fan of jazz music, the watercolor of a cotton club scene caught his eye the moment he walked into the gallery.

When Malcolm moved to Atlanta, he knew in his heart that he had returned to the city that he wanted to call home. Having lived in three other major cities throughout his career, Malcolm's living quarters had always reflected his lifestyle—the ultimate bachelor.

Scarcely furnished to accommodate his hectic travel schedule, Malcolm had no problem with living off the bare minimums. Take out food was a staple in his life, there were no plants to water and no pets to care for. There was nothing in his life that gave the impression of permanency. But when he accepted the position at *Image*, he knew it was time to make a change in his life.

Susan had offered to scope out rental units, but Malcolm decided to take some time and find a home.

The three bedroom condo he chose had become just that. He spent a significant amount of time his first year back furnishing his place to reflect his style, and he loved the atmosphere he created. His living room, comfortable and inviting, was perfect for entertaining and his office, complete with a custom built desk, created the perfect place for his creative juices to flow.

Managing to create such a haven caused Malcolm to dread leaving for assignments. There was something comforting about being home, and that was a new feeling for Malcolm. The only thing missing was someone to share it with.

Entering his bedroom, he searched his dresser for his gold cufflinks. Grabbing one, he struggled to hook the link through his sleeves and grimaced in frustration. He had dressed himself a hundred times for formal affairs, but tonight, it had taken him twice as long. The tie didn't want to cooperate and it took him four tries to get the knot perfect. Now, his cufflinks had slipped through his hands twice. What in the world was going on with him? He felt like a seventeen-year-old getting ready for the prom. This couldn't possibly be nervousness?

Normally, when he attended functions like this, his main focus was to work the room, speaking with editors, other writers and advertisers. But tonight was different. For the first time in his career, his number one objective had nothing to do with a hot news story or idea. It had to do with a certain business owner who had wormed her way into his every thought.

Hearing the doorbell and the phone ring at the same time, Malcolm reached for his cordless as he made his way down the hall. "Hello," he answered. Opening the door, he signaled for his cousin to enter.

"Hi there, Malcolm."

"Denise?" he asked, surprise evident in his voice.

"I see you still recognize my voice. I'll take that as a good sign."

Inwardly groaning, Malcolm led Brent to the living room and motioned for him to have a seat.

"I'm getting ready to go out, Denise. Is there something that you wanted?"

"Now isn't that a loaded question," she said, followed by a breathy laugh.

Not getting a response, Denise cleared her throat and continued, "I heard through the grapevine that you were coming to the event tonight dateless."

"My personal life is none of your business," he said, trying to hold his agitation in check. It had been quite a while since Malcolm had spoken to her, but that didn't diminish his sour reaction.

Trying to ignore the cold response she was getting, she said, "Did Susan give you my message?"

"Yes."

Realizing he wasn't going to elaborate on why he didn't return the call, she said, "I was just hoping that you would save a dance for me."

"I don't think that would be a good idea, Denise."

Brent eyed Malcolm with a questioning gaze when he heard the name.

"Malcolm, I know things were screwed up with us in the past. But I'm coming alone tonight and I just thought that we could have one dance. That's all."

"We'll see, Denise. But I really have to go."

After hanging up, Brent said, "Wasn't that the Denise that you dated several years ago? The one that works in the advertising department at *Image*?"

"The one and only."

Remembering all Malcolm went through after their breakup, Brent asked, "Wasn't she the one who called

you relentlessly every time you were out of her sight?"
Watching Malcolm nod in the affirmative, Brent said,
"That is one possessive woman."

Malcolm thought of his earlier conversation with
Susan and realized she used that same adjective to describe Denise. Walking into his office three days after
he started with *Image*, Denise, having always admired
his work, welcomed him to the publication by offering
to buy him dinner. Over the next few months, they
spent quite a bit of time together, but Malcolm soon
realized that she wouldn't be the one to find a permanent home in his heart. Denise, though successful in
her professional life, was extremely needy and inse-
cure. So instead of dragging on a relationship he knew
was going nowhere, he broke it off.

For the next several weeks, she contacted him just
about every day, hoping to get an opportunity to work
things out. Initially, Malcolm was cordial and respect-
ful. He knew that her feelings for him ran deeper than
his for her, so he put up with the impromptu visits to
his office and the late night phone calls. But after a
month, he told her emphatically that they could always
be friends, but nothing more.

Not taking the news too well, Denise stepped up her
attempts to convince Malcolm that if he just took the
time to get to know her, he would see that they could
be good together. She began to show up at the
strangest times. He would be at the gas station, and she
would appear. He would be hanging out with his
friends, and there she would be. He was glad that he
lived in a gated community as her attempts to get by security failed.

But the phone calls and the unexpected visits didn't
prepare him for the grand finale. She showed up at a
restaurant where he was dining with another woman.
Introducing herself as Malcolm's ex-girlfriend, she

proceeded to share with the young lady that once he got her in the bed, he would leave her—just like she had been left.

Furious at her boldness and the outright lie, he went to her home the next day and threatened to file stalking charges if she didn't leave him alone. The thought of getting arrested must have scared her, because he hadn't had to deal with her antics since then. On the occasions when they had to work together, she had been professional and aloof. That's why this call had been such a surprise. Why would she call him now?

"What did she want?" Brent asked.

Grabbing his keys, he turned out the lights and headed toward the door. "Nothing. Let's go."

"Come on, Alexis," Melanie yelled from the living room, "everyone's waiting and the limo is here."

Melanie stood with Celeste and Kenneth waiting for the guest of honor to make her grand entrance. Looking elegant in their evening best. Kenneth was in a classic Hugo Boss tuxedo, Celeste in a purple chiffon cocktail dress, and Melanie, deciding to throw caution to the wind, was in the red satin dress.

"All right, all right," Alexis said entering the room, "I'm ready." Twirling to give a complete view, she asked, "How do I look."

All three pairs of eyes smiled in approval. Her hair, pinned up tightly in a French roll, had not one strand out of place. The floor length, silver-lace halter dress with flesh-tone straps looked amazing on her model-size body. Diamond-strapped high-heeled sandals completed an ensemble that screamed sophisticated and successful.

Stepping to her sister and giving her a hug, Melanie answered, "Oh, Alexis, you look absolutely stunning."

Sniffling slightly, she continued, "I'm so proud of you.' Stepping back she frantically fanned her face, saying with a laugh, "No tears tonight! I spent too much time on my makeup to ruin it before we get there."

Celeste pulled a tissue out of her evening bag and quickly agreed, "That's right ladies, no tears."

"Oh, brother," Kenneth whined. "If I knew you ladies needed a 'women's moment,' I'd have waited in the limo."

Nudging him playfully, Celeste said, "Now, Kenneth, you have to admit that this is a very exciting night."

Heading for the door, Kenneth answered, "Exciting? Yes. Emotional? No."

All three ladies followed Kenneth out of the condo, each with a tissue in hand.

The Hyatt Regency on Peachtree was alive with activity when Alexis and her guests arrived. Entering the grand hotel, Alexis was immediately escorted to a private hospitality suite while her friends were directed to the ballroom.

The moment Alexis entered the suite, every fiber in her body came to alert. Malcolm stood across the room speaking to a couple that she did not recognize. His broad shoulders filled out the custom tuxedo, and he stood confident, comfortable, and in total control. Momentarily paralyzed, Alexis had a revelation that caused a flutter in her stomach and literally took her breath. For the first time in her life, Alexis Shaw was in awe of a man.

"Ms. Shaw, how nice to meet you."

Turning to the voice, she focused her attention on the approaching woman, "Good evening, Ms. . . ."

"Just call me Susan."

Alexis gave a genuine smile to the elderly woman standing in front of her. Dressed elegantly in a floor-length black sequin gown, her accessories seemed out of place, as she had reading glasses hanging on a chain around her neck, a clipboard in her hand, and a walkie talkie on her hip. "I recognize you from the picture you sent to us. I'm Malcolm's assistant and I spoke with you last week when you left the phone message." At the mention of Malcolm's name, Alexis unconsciously smiled. Without intending to, she glanced his way and marveled at her complete attraction.

Watching Alexis's expression, Susan followed her gaze and saw the object of her attention. Instantly, Susan recalled Malcolm's strange behavior earlier in the week and turned her eyes back to Alexis. Thinking back on the women who called that day, she realized Alexis was one of them. Was it possible?

"It's nice to meet you, Susan," Alexis said, offering her hand.

Deciding to watch them closely tonight, Susan said, "I'm the coordinator of this event, and knowing what you do for a living, I hope everything meets your expectations."

"Don't worry about me. I know that everything will be perfect." Leaning forward, she whispered in her ear, "If the truth be told, it's nice to be a guest for once and enjoy all the hard work that someone else has done to put an affair together."

"Well, just relax, have something to drink. In about thirty minutes, I'll escort all of the award recipients into the ballroom for their introductions. After dinner, a short bio of each recipient will be given and then the awards will be handed out. Each recipient will have about fifteen minutes to make their acceptance speech. After that, there will be a band and dancing."

"It sounds like a fabulous evening, Susan."

Catching a signal from the hotel catering manager, Susan excused herself.

"The bar is in the corner, and there are light snacks on the table against the wall. Enjoy the evening."

Alexis said polite hellos to the people she passed as she made her way to the bar to order a glass of sparkling water. While this event could be viewed as social, she considered it business, and Alexis never drank alcohol during business.

As she thought about receiving her award tonight and her private after party with Malcolm, a shiver of anticipation filtered through her body. Hoping to have a few words with him before the evening began, she retrieved her drink and turned to the area where he stood when she entered. But her mood slightly deflated when she realized Malcolm Singleton was nowhere to be found.

Spending the next several minutes being introduced to staff members and other honorees, she was finishing up a conversation with Jeremy Michaels, Editor-in-Chief, when Susan made the announcement that it was time to move to the ballroom. As Alexis followed the others into the hallway, she made one final sweep of the room for Malcolm. Where did he go?

The three honorees were taken through a small staging area that lead to the back of the ballroom. Alexis, having planned several events at this hotel, knew exactly why they were doing this. It would be awkward to have them walk from the entrance at the back of the ballroom, as they would have to weave through tables to get to the head table. The area off the front of the ballroom, where the servers entered and exited with food, was the perfect place from which to enter. It was a straight path to the front.

Jeremy entered first and took his place at the podium. His salt-and-pepper hair and beard gave him an extremely distinguished appearance. As the editor at *Image* for the past ten years, he had shared with

Alexis earlier that this was one of his favorite events. As the master of ceremony, he welcomed everyone, gave a few opening remarks, along with a joke that loosened up the crowd before he moved to introductions. When he called her name, Alexis was escorted to the head table amid the applause and cheers. As she took her seat, she quickly scanned the room for Malcolm. There was still no sign of him.

As the final recipient took her seat, Alexis saw Malcolm make his way to the head table from the back of the room. When he looked her way, she gave him a questioning gaze, to which he responded with a brief nod before he turned and took his seat. Curious, Alexis could only wait until later to find out where he had disappeared to.

The dinner hour passed quickly and Alexis barely touched her stuffed chicken breast as the excitement and anticipation totally dissolved her appetite. As the program was about to begin, she excused herself to freshen up. Seeing her leave the ballroom, Celeste and Melanie excused themselves as well. They found her in the lounge touching up her lipstick and practicing her acceptance speech one more time.

Pulling out her own lip gloss, Melanie said, "Celeste thought that Malcolm Singleton was the gentleman sitting beside the editor of the magazine."

"He is. Why?" Alexis answered, pulling powder out of her small evening bag.

Melanie turned to her sister and let out a slow whistle, "Your description of him was on point. I thought Darius was handsome, but this man would put him to shame. If he wasn't already taken by you, he would be a nice diversion from what's going on in my life right now."

"Are you looking for a diversion?" Alexis asked, her curiosity piqued.

"I'm looking for anything that doesn't remind me of New York, Darius, corporate mergers, power lunches, and acquisitions. Preferably something that's in a neat little package like Mr. Singleton."

"Let me get this straight," Alexis said. "In the week that you've been here, you've gone from Miss Straight and Narrow, Do Everything By The Book, Don't Ruffle Any Feathers to Miss Footloose and Fancy Free?"

"It must be the dress," Melanie answered lightly, trying to explain the new feelings of freedom she was experiencing since coming to Atlanta.

"Or the fact that the ballroom is filled with young, eligible men just waiting to meet some fine, successful sisters like us," Celeste interjected. "If I wasn't married, I would give both of you a run for your money."

"Both of you are too crazy," Alexis laughed, dropping the powder into her evening bag and snapping it shut. "I need to get back out there. They're going to present me the award in a few minutes. Do I have lipstick on my teeth?"

"You look perfect." Following Alexis out of the restroom, none of them heard the stall door open or saw the woman stare at their retreating bodies. If they did, they would have seen eyes black with envy and cold as ice. "So Malcolm has a new woman. Well we'll just see about that."

Returning to her seat, Alexis nodded and smiled at the other two women receiving awards tonight. Amanda Bradshaw, who owned a string of boutiques on the West Coast, was being honored in the midsize business category, and Catrena Powell, owner of an IT consulting firm, won in the large business category, with government and private contracts in the tens of millions of dollars and hundreds of employees in her organization. All the women were thrilled at receiving such a prestigious honor, but hadn't had much time to get to know each other. Hopefully that would happen tomorrow, when they were meeting to shoot the cover for the anniversary issue.

The soft jazz sounds playing in the background died out as Jeremy, once again, took his position at the podium.

"Ladies and gentlemen, it brings me great pleasure to stand before you tonight to honor three outstanding women in the world of business. *Image Magazine* prides itself of being a source and a resource for all issues concerning our business community. Over the years, we have cultivated an environment that promotes excellence, and these women who will stand before you tonight exemplify that level of excellence.

"I would like to take credit for this award coming to fruition, but unfortunately, that would make me a liar. Three years ago, in one of the best business decisions I've ever made, we welcomed Malcolm Singleton to our family. His fresh approach and trendsetting stories have done incredible things for this publication. When he came to me with this business award, it was just another example of his commitment to improve the quality of our magazine while recognizing the achievements of women. It's only fitting that he will be the person to present the awards to our recipients this evening."

Alexis could barely contain her nervous energy as she watched Malcolm step forward to the microphone. There was a brief biography of each woman and their accomplishments in the program book, but she knew that when Malcolm presented the accolades, it would only serve to magnify how important this award was. Since the small business category was the first to be recognized, Alexis mentally rehearsed her speech one last time.

"*Image Magazine* is proud to honor Alexis Shaw," he started.

As Malcolm waited for the applause to die down, Alexis found herself momentarily mesmerized by his assuming presence. She ventured a quick look around the room, and noticed several other women coming to that same conclusion. There were some who were speaking with their eyes, batting fake lashes and seductively raising a brow, while a few others tried the fake cough approach, only to smile when his attention was diverted their way. But the room finally settled down, and Alexis's complete attention went to the man standing before her.

"Many people may think, 'How hard could it be to plan a party?' You order some food, send out invitations and let the fun begin. However, if you want to make your party a memorable event, that requires special attention. And Alexis Shaw, owner of Just For You, is the person to call. Starting her business five years ago, Ms. Shaw has developed a company that encompasses class, elegance, style, and creativity."

As Malcolm spoke, Alexis closed her eyes and let the sound of his enchanting voice overtake her. Smooth, melodic, and tranquil, it was the sound that first attracted her to him. As his words caressed her and she felt the goosebumps rise on her arms as she fantasized about them together she couldn't wait to have him speak only to her. Opening her eyes, she was glad of the semidarkness to hide the flush in her cheeks, as she realized she had daydreamed right through the remainder of her introduction.

"Ladies and gentlemen, I introduce to you, Alexis Shaw."

The applause was thunderous as she took her place at the podium. Shaking hands with Malcolm as he handed her the plaque, both were taken aback by the

ripple of electricity that passed between them. Her
heart hammered in her chest as she realized that there
was something very tangible happening between them.
Momentarily, time stood still as they both stared at each
other with a new awareness. Malcolm snapped out of it
first as his lips curved into a congratulatory smile and
he stepped aside to give her the opportunity to make
her speech.

"Thank you. Thank you," she started, glad that her
voice didn't reflect the nervous quiver as her body did.
The spotlight was bright in her eyes and she could not
see past the first few tables, but she could visualize
Melanie, Celeste, and Kenneth, clapping and cheering
the loudest.

"To the staff at *Image Magazine*, honored guests,
friends and family. Thank you for this award. I am honored to receive this symbol of excellence in the
business community."

As Alexis continued her speech, Malcolm stood behind her in unspeakable awe. When she walked into
the hospitality suite earlier, his train of thought was lost
in midsentence. She was absolutely breathtaking. Formal affairs were commonplace to him, and women
always look stunning in evening attire. But never had
he bore witness to a vision as perfect as Alexis Shaw.
That dress had to be specially made for the contour of
her body. Her hair and makeup were meticulous and
her eyes sparkled with excitement and confidence. The
entire package was a lethal combination and the only
thing Malcolm could think about was how he wanted
to begin their temporary relationship immediately—in
his bed. And that thought went against everything he
was trying to change about his relationship with
women. Especially this woman. Needing to clear his
head, he excused himself from the conversation and
stepped out on the balcony.

As he stood looking out on the glittering skyline of Atlanta, he wrestled with himself and the feelings this woman envoked. Having had his share of temporary relationships, he remembered his promise to himself. No more six-month flings. No more physical relationships without love. No more getting to know a woman's body before capturing her heart, mind, and soul.

Inhaling deeply, he pondered breaking his promise one last time. Reasoning that there were no guarantees in life, even if he took it slow with Alexis, that wouldn't necessarily lead to a relationship that would be more than just temporary. But deep down, Malcolm knew that wasn't what he wanted. He had experienced the world, accumulated wealth, and had all the trappings of material success. But the bottom line was that while he had many women who had shared these things with him, he was still alone. And Malcolm was tired of being alone. Taking one last look at the glittering city, he turned to head back inside. With renewed faith, he silently solidified his desire to take things slow. He wanted the real thing, and when Alexis Shaw stepped into the room this evening, he got the feeling that she may be it.

An hour after the presentations ended, Alexis finally greeted her friends at their table. It had taken her that long to work her way through the crowd, as guests wanted to offer their congratulations. Several asked for her business card, and Alexis was glad she remembered to put a small stack in her evening bag before she left home.

Almost talked out by the time she made it to the table with her sister and friends, she was glad to see Samantha Downs, Eric Wilson, and Olivia Banks, her three planners, had come to support her. As they offered her congratulations, Alexis was struck with the most incredible thought: She had always taken pride in the fact that she had built this company on her own, not using her mother's name or money. But looking at her staff, she realized that she wasn't building this business alone anymore. She had help from a committed staff. Samantha, Eric and Olivia were creative, competent, committed and contributed significantly to the expansion of her client base.

Her staff often complained that Alexis's management style could be classified as overbearing, as she always followed up on the details of her planner's events. It wasn't that Alexis didn't trust their abilities, it was just that she had put her blood, sweat and tears into building her business, and it was a little tough to let it go. Realizing it may be time to change her ways, she resolved to show them how much she appreciated them.

"Oh, Alexis," Melanie said. "I am so proud of you. You have got to find a special place to hang that plaque."

"Yes, Alexis," Celeste said, "when you started your speech, I couldn't hold back the tears."

"We know, Celeste," Kenneth said sarcastically. "As a matter of fact, our whole table knew. You needed just about everyone's napkin."

Punching him playfully in the arm, Celeste laughed. "Don't believe him for one minute, Alexis. See"—she said, opening her purse—"I bought my own supply."

They all laughed at her stack of tissues.

"Come on, honey," Kenneth said, leading Celeste out to the dance floor. "I think they're playing our song."

Melanie and Alexis watched as Kenneth swung Celeste into to his arms and whispered something in her hear. Celeste giggled and kissed him lightly on the lips.

"How wonderful to be in love," Melanie said, staring longingly at the couple.

"For some it is wonderful; for most, it's a living hell," Alexis answered.

Facing her sister, Melanie said, "You know, I saw that little exchange between you and Malcolm when he introduced you."

Knowing exactly what her sister was talking about, Alexis answered, "What you saw was lust. Pure and simple." But as she said the words, she realized that wasn't totally true. She had dealt with lust before, and there was something different about this.

"All I'm saying is, tonight might be the start of something real for you, Alexis."

"Or it won't. Look Melanie, I know you are in love with the idea of falling in love. But that doesn't appeal to me in the least. We'll enjoy that attraction for however long it lasts and . . ."

"I know, I know," Melanie said, mocking her sister's favorite phrase, "When it's over, it's over."

Not put off by her sarcastic tone, Alexis smiled, "Exactly." Scanning the room, Alexis continued, "Have you seen Sherry? She told me she would be here."

"She's here. When the music started, she said she was going to mingle."

Alexis curved the corners of her lips upward, "Why am I not surprised? That girl has probably got some poor guy's tongue hanging out of his mouth." Scanning the dance floor, her eyes squinted to make sure she was seeing correctly and she inhaled deeply. Melanie followed her sister's gaze and saw Malcolm swaying to the music with a very attractive woman.

While there was nothing inappropriate in their movements, Alexis decided she didn't want to watch. "If you'll excuse me, I'm going to the bar to get a much needed glass of wine."

Denise inhaled deeply as she enjoyed the music and the man in her arms. "You look good, Malcolm."

"Thanks," Malcolm said as he glanced around the ballroom looking for Alexis. The last place he wanted to be was on the dance floor with Denise. Trying to make his way to Alexis, he was stopped by colleagues just as the band began to play when Denise approached the group and extended an invitation to dance. He felt compelled to accept to prevent an awkward moment in front of her coworkers.

"How about me?"—she asked, tilting her head and seductively curving the corners of her mouth—"do I look good?"

Turning his attention back to her, he said, "I don't think this conversation will get us anywhere."

Thinking of the women in the restroom, her smile faltered and she asked, "Are you seeing someone, Malcolm? Someone in this room?"

The song ended. "Now I know this conversation won't get us anywhere." Stepping out of her arms, he said, "Enjoy your evening."

Denise watched him walk off the dance floor, leaving her standing alone. But she wasn't discouraged. She had him before, she could get him again.

It took Alexis several minutes to work her way to the front of the line, and as she ordered, she felt his presence behind her before he said a word.

"That dress looks as if it as made for your body."

Chill bumps tingled own her arms as that now familiar voice caressed her ear. Turning toward the speaker, Alexis feigned agitation and said, "I thought we had an understanding that my body was none of your business."

"That was before our deal."

"Ah, yes, Mr. Singleton, our deal," she said, retrieving her glass of wine and stepping away from the bar. "So how do you propose we start off this temporary arrangement?" Not giving him a chance to answer, Alexis continued, "Perhaps a midnight dinner, in a suite, right here in this hotel. Followed by a late break-fast in the morning."

Not getting an immediate response, she asked matter of factly, "Or will you be otherwise occupied with your dancing partner?"

At that comment, Malcolm raised a brow. Was that jealously he heard in her tone?

"It was just a dance, Alexis. Nothing more," he said with a sly grin.

Realizing how she must have sounded, she quickly backtracked, "Doesn't matter. What matters is our deal. So what about it, Mr. Singleton?"

Leaning forward, he whispered "Your offer sounds enticing, Ms. Shaw, but if we come out of the starting gate too fast, we could lose steam and fizzle out."

"We'll fizzle out anyway," she reminded him.

"Then it won't matter what we do, right?"

Shrugging, she didn't answer.

"Unfortunately, I'm leaving tomorrow morning for an industry conference in San Francisco."

"Tomorrow?" Alexis said, disappointment evident in her tone. "When will you be back?"

Staring at her intently, his voice dropped, "Alexis, if I didn't know better, I would think you would miss me."

Masking her emotions, she looked away and said, "How much could I miss someone I've only known a week?" *A lot.*

Knowing that she was lying, he said, "I was hoping we could get together next Saturday, about five o'clock?"

Taking a sip of the dry Chardonnay, Alexis shook her head in the negative. "No can do. I have Arleon Enter-prises's annual picnic next Saturday from one in the afternoon until after dusk."

"Do you have an event every day?"

Laughing, she answered, "No, it just seems that way."

"Luckily, your previous engagement won't be affected. I was talking about five A.M."

Alexis choked on her wine.

Patting her on the back, Malcolm was glad that he had finally caught the controlled Alexis Shaw off guard.

Recovering with a final cough, she asked, "Did you say five in the morning?"

"Are you not a morning person?" he asked with a twinkle in his eyes.

"You can't be serious?"

Before Malcolm could respond, they were interrupted.

"Well, well, well, what do we have here?"

Alexis and Malcolm turned to the approaching voice and Alexis felt a strong uneasiness in her stomach. She didn't know his name, but she recognized him immediately.

"I don't believe we have been formally introduced, even though I tried to arrange that when I sent over a bottle of champagne," he said as his eyes slowly traveled the length of her body.

Alexis felt invaded.

"Malcolm, why don't you introduce me to your lady friend?"

Unconsciously, Alexis took a step closer to Malcolm. Not going unnoticed by Malcolm, he wondered what would cause her to seek him out as protection. Wanting to give her a sense of security, he slipped his arms around her waist.

"Alexis Shaw, I'd like to introduce to Rick Satchel, a staff photographer for *Image Magazine*."

Stepping between Malcolm and Alexis, he forced them to break their connection. Rick turned his complete attention to Alexis and offered his hand. Not wanting to cause a scene, Alexis shook his hand, but the minute she made contact, that queasy feeling in her stomach intensified.

"Mr. Satchel," she said politely, quickly breaking contact.

"Please, call me Rick," he said. "Had I known that you were one of our honorees, I would have sent over a more expensive bottle of champagne."

For an unknown reason, Alexis didn't want to spar with Rick, and while she had several smart remarks on the tip of her mouth, she opted to remain silent.

"But I see you found it in you to give one of us another chance," he said, taking a quick glance at Malcolm. "You know, me and your man here go way back. So let me warn you, he can be a slick one. Did you know that in college we actually used to bet on who could get with a girl first? But you know what? No matter what tactics I used, my buddy here always seemed to snag the best ones."

Looking directly into her eyes, Rick said, "I guess some things never change."

Malcolm stared at Alexis for a moment, surprised at her silent response. Fortunately, by her expression of indifference, he hoped she wasn't buying into all that Rick was saying. Wanting to cut him off before he continued to embarrass himself any further, Malcolm turned his attention to Rick and asked, "When did you get back in town?"

Rick continued to stare at Alexis a few more seconds, before returning his gaze to Malcolm, "My flight got in late last night. I'm assigned to this event," he said.

Alexis noticed the camera equipment around his neck and the large bag on his shoulder.

"And," he said, glancing back at Alexis, "I've been enjoying every minute of it."

Turning to Malcolm, Alexis said, "I think I'll freshen

up." Giving Rick one final look, Alexis said, "Have a good evening, Mr. Satchel."

Malcolm watched Alexis head for the ladies lounge and hoped her special night wasn't ruined by the man standing beside him.

"Now that's something I would love to get in to . . . literally," Rick said, his eyes following Alexis.

"Watch it, Rick," Malcolm said, agitated at Rick's barbaric comment.

Rick's eyebrows arched and one corner of his mouth slid into a wicked smile. "That's exactly what I'm doing, my man. Babygirl is definitely something to watch."

Grabbing his arm, Malcolm stepped within inches of Rick's face, commanding his full attention. "I mean it, Rick. Alexis Shaw is off limits to you."

Rick gently, but definitively, removed Malcolm's hand and stared him directly in the eyes. "It looks like someone beat me to the punch . . . again. I just hope you can handle it. She looks to be a feisty one. If you can't, be sure and pass her on to me. I'll take real good care of her."

Before Malcolm could respond, they were interrupted by the shrill sound of a high-pitched voice.

"There you are, Ricky. I've been looking all over for you."

Both men turned to the young woman who now stood beside them. Dressed in a loud, strapless dress that seemed to be one size too small, she hooked her arm through Rick's and poked out her bottom lip.

"Ricky, you promised me a dance."

Malcolm took this as an opportunity to make his exit, "Enjoy the evening."

Eight

"Five in the morning?" Melanie exclaimed. "You've got to be kidding me."

Sitting at the table, Alexis returned from the restroom feeling refreshed and sat with her sister, enjoying the sounds of the live band, watching couples show off their best moves.

"That's exactly what I said. Who in their right mind would get up at five A.M. to do anything other than work?"

"When have you worked at five o'clock in the morning?" she asked. "I've never known you to be a morning person. I always figured most of your events were in the evening."

"Not always," Alexis said. "Last year, a woman wanted to arrange a fishing expedition for her father. He used to take her as a little girl. He was turning seventy-five and he hadn't been fishing in over twenty years."

Intrigued, Melanie asked, "How is that an event worthy of a planner?"

"It was on a ninety-foot yacht, with about sixty of his closest friends. The fishing was followed by an elaborate brunch with the main dishes being made from the fish they caught."

Confused, Melanie asked, "How could you be sure they would catch something?"

Alexis stared pointedly at her sister with a look of complete confidence.

After several seconds, Melanie caught on. "No way. How could *you* arrange for them to catch fish?"

Smiling, Alexis simply said, "Scuba divers."

Pretending to bow before her like a queen, Melanie said, "I have definitely underestimated what you do. No wonder you're winning awards."

"I'll take that as a compliment."

"You should. Now back to your five o'clock date. I think it's romantic, Alexis," Melanie answered thoughtfully. "A mystery date. Who knows what he has planned for you."

"But five A.M.? What happened to the traditional dinner and a movie?" Alexis said.

"Since you are anything but traditional, I think this invitation was a smart move on his part." Pausing a moment to think, Melanie continued, "Maybe he wants to take the time to get to know you a little better. I think you want the same thing, according to that look on your face when he handed you that award."

"What look?" Alexis said.

"The look of finding something special, something worth your time and effort."

"Don't be so melodramatic, Melanie. I told you earlier what you saw. L-U-S-T. In its purest form."

Reaching across the table, Melanie grabbed her sister's hand and said, "Lust doesn't ask for a five A.M. date a week from now when there's a suite available tonight."

Alexis started to respond, but decided against it. Melanie was in love with the idea of being in love, and arguing with her would be an exercise in futility. While she would allow herself to admit that she had never felt such a strong attraction to a man before, she was not ready to admit that it could mean a more meaningful relationship. Looking out on the dance floor, she watched Kenneth pull Celeste into him arms as the up-tempo song ended and was replaced with the slow sounds of a Luther Vandross classic. *They're the exception.*

"Good evening, ladies." Malcolm stood tall and majestic with another man who was also quite attractive.

Introductions were made and Brent could see why Malcolm's world had been turned upside down since this woman came into his life. But he also had to admit that beauty ran in the family, as he shook hands with her sister. Looking amazing in a red strapless dress, he was fascinated by her big brown eyes surrounded by dark lashes.

"May I have this dance?" Malcolm asked. "I've been patiently waiting the entire evening."

Brent took Alexis's seat as Alexis and Malcolm headed to the dance floor.

Malcolm reached for her hand and gently turned her to him. As she rested in his arms, Alexis let her body completely relax. Swaying from side to side, she now understood the meaning of "floating on a cloud." While she would never admit this to anyone, the feeling that had been invoked by his touch, his smell, his very presence, was something that she didn't want to attach the word temporary to.

"So have you made a decision about my offer?" he asked.

Taking a small step back, her eyes brimmed with seduction. "Have you made a decision about *my* offer?"

Pulling her back to him, Malcolm's laugh was deep and rich. "As tempting as your offer is, I think my offer is better."

Alexis realized she was enjoying the change of pace Malcolm was taking with their relationship. Most men she dated were usually focused on rushing through the standard number of dates as quickly as possible, hoping to move the courtship to a more intimate level. But Malcolm was different. He seemed to be in no hurry to jump from one stage to the next. It was as if he was enjoying each moment to the fullest. And Alexis liked it.

"Five A.M. next Saturday? It's a date."

"May I cut in?"

Malcolm turned to the voice and wondered who this man was. Standing slightly shorter than six feet, his rented tuxedo hung loosely around his shoulders. Not turning his gaze from him, he answered, "If the lady doesn't mind."

"The lady and I go way back. I'm sure she won't mind one dance," he said confidently.

Knowing the intruder would not have any qualms about making a scene, Alexis released her hold from Malcolm. "It's okay, Malcolm."

As the gentleman pulled Alexis to him, Alexis stood firm to keep a respectable distance.

"Why am I not surprised to see you here, Gary?"

Giving her a cocky grin, he answered, "I was so hurt when I found out you were being honored tonight with the business elite and didn't bother to tell me of your great accomplishment. I came to offer my support and congratulations."

"Don't play games with me," she said, unfooled by his faked sincerity. "You are not here to wish me congratulations, you are here doing what you always do. Scouting out people for your next business deal."

"Now that you mention it, I could use a few introductions."

"Sorry, but I think I've done quite enough for you in that category."

"Now, Alexis," Gary responded, pretending to be hurt by her response, "I know you can't still be upset about that mix-up in your office?"

Alexis stopped dancing and took a deliberate step

back. "Mix-up! Are you talking about the day you lied to my receptionist, weaseled your way into my office, and began to steal my clients' information?"

"Is there a problem here?"

Both turned to Malcolm, and Gary's eyes twitched in annoyance. Although Malcolm was taller, Gary was about thirty pounds heavier and felt he could knock this guy out with one punch. But he quickly squashed that idea. He was here to grow his business, not get in a scuffle with some hotshot writer. "No problem, just reminiscing over old times." Leaning forward he whispered in Alexis's ear, "Congratulations, sweetheart. And take it from me, you can do much better than this clown."

Feeling a chill take over her body, she watched Gary step back, give Malcolm a significant look, and head to the other side of the ballroom.

Pulling Alexis back into his arms, they danced so as not to look awkward on the floor.

"Who was that and what did he say to make you so upset?"

"Just someone I use to know."

"A temporary relationship?" Malcolm asked, feeling his own twinge of jealousy at the thought of her with another man.

"We never made it that far. More like a few dates."

Malcolm was relieved. The thought of her in another man's bed didn't sit right with him. It struck him that this was the first time in his life he ever felt that way about a woman. "What is he doing here?"

"Who knows, probably leeching."

Not wanting to discuss the subject on her special night, he decided to change the subject. "When's your next event?"

"I'm helping Olivia with one tomorrow."

"Another company picnic?"

"No. One of the largest investment clubs in the state

is having their annual dinner and I'm creating the New York Stock Exchange."

Duly impressed, Malcolm said, "That's amazing. If I didn't have to catch my flight tomorrow, I would love to come and see how you pull that off."

Alexis secretly smiled. Whenever Gary mentioned wanting to see her creations, she always felt uneasy, never hearing a sincere interest in her work reflected in his tone. With Malcolm, it was different. She realized she wanted him to see what types of fantasies she arranged for her clients. She took pride in her work, and for the first time in her career, she wanted to share that with someone—with him.

Leading her back to table where Melanie and Brent appeared to be in deep conversation, they were soon joined by Celeste and Kenneth.

Kenneth shook hands with Malcolm and said, "I heard about your initial encounter with the wrath of Alexis." Leaning closer, he continued, "You know, her bite is just as bad as her bark."

"Kenneth!" Celeste said. "That's enough." Turning to Malcolm, she said "It's nice to see you again."

"Are we ready to go?" Alexis said.

"Actually," Melanie said, "I think I'll stay a little longer and have a cup of coffee with Brent."

Alexis stared at her sister in astonishment. For as long as she could remember, Melanie was the one that walked the straight and narrow. She rarely did anything that was out of sync of what was deemed acceptable and proper. Growing up in a strict household, there were few occasions when either of them had the opportunity to walk outside of that line.

During Melanie's career and courtship with Darius, she continued with that same trend. Periodically, Melanie expressed discontentment with her job and her man, but she always allowed their mother to talk her into staying the course she was already on.

When Melanie showed up in Atlanta last week, Alexis listened to her express her uncertainty about the promotion and her engagement, but Alexis believed that at the end of her vacation, she would catch a plane back to New York, accept the job, and marry Darius. That was why Alexis was taken aback by her statement.

Wearing the dress was a BIG move for her. But going out on a last minute date with a guy she just met was not something that Melanie would do. She was the type to exchange work numbers first, have a few lunch dates, meet at the restaurant for evening dinners, and finally reveal her home number and address. Now she was telling Alexis that she was headed out into a strange city with a man she hardly knew.

As if reading her mind, Melanie said, "I'm sure Malcolm can vouch for him."

What could she say? Melanie was an adult and she seemed to have made up her mind. "Okay, I'll see you at home later."

Brent and Melanie stayed behind and Alexis, Malcolm, Kenneth and Celeste made their way through the lobby. As they waited for the limo, Alexis reflected on her evening as she held her award close to her chest. It was absolutely perfect. Not even Rick or Gary was able to spoil her good time.

Celeste and Kenneth got in the limo when it arrived, while Alexis said good-bye Malcolm. The area was filled with people mingling in the calm summer air. Hardly the place or time for a romantic moment.

"What time does your flight leave tomorrow?"

"At seven." Malcolm thought about his promise to himself to take things slow, as she stood before him sexy, desirable, and causing that familiar physical reaction that had become commonplace when she was around.

Giving her a chaste kiss on the cheek, he paused and whispered in her ear, "I'm using every bit of restraint to keep my lips off of yours. But I don't think this is the time or the place."

Alexis felt a pool of comfort fill her entire body as she acknowledged his statement with a small smile. She silently agreed that she felt the same way, and reluctantly stepped into the limo.

Stepping back, he said, "I'll call you."

Pleased that she was affecting him the way he was affecting her, she said, "You don't have my phone number."

"I'm a reporter. I have your phone number."

Malcolm entered his condo and dropped his keys on the table in the living room. Loosening his tie, he pulled it from around his neck and headed for the bedroom. Picking up the remote, he clicked on the TV and turned to ESPN. Glancing at the suitcase in the corner, he thought about the five days that he would be on the other side of the country. The five days he would be away from her.

Lying across the bed, he stared at the ceiling and exhaled a deep breath, asking himself for the hundredth time what his problem was. There was a woman who was beautiful, fascinating, exciting, and who he could be with right now. But no, he held on to his belief that it was time for him to settle down. To find that one special woman to share his life with. Now, as he laid in his bed alone, he began to think that he must be completely out of his mind. Was he being a fool to think that just because he wanted to take it slow that the results would be any different? Why shouldn't he move at whatever pace Alexis wanted?

She radiated confidence, beauty, style, grace, and class. Everything a man could want in a woman. Everything he wanted in a woman. Malcolm had never thought about accepting assignments that required travel. As he thought about his possible travel schedule over the next several months, it wasn't as appealing as it used to be. How long would he continue at this pace? How long would he want to?

Pursuing his career with a vengeance the past ten years, Malcolm accomplished what most writers only dream of. Investigative stories that have been published around the world and awards that recognized his work and contributions to his profession. His three years at *Image* had been magnificent, but he found himself wondering more and more how much was left for him to do. He thought about the novel he had started over five years ago. A sketchy outline and four chapters were all he had to show for it and he wondered when he would have the chance to finish. If he kept up his current work pace, it would be another five years. Pushing questions of his career to the back of his mind, he reached for the phone.

"Hello."

"I just want to let you know that I'll be thinking of you every day I'm in San Francisco."

Alexis snuggled under the covers and basked in the warmth of his voice. She had been tossing and turning every since she got into bed. Now she knew she would sleep like a baby.

"I'll see you five A.M. next Saturday," she answered.

"Good night, Alexis."

"Good night, Malcolm."

* * *

The next afternoon, Alexis could barely hide her anticipation and excitement as she headed to a studio north of Atlanta that the magazine was using for the cover photo shoot. She and the other two winners had talked briefly last night about the star treatment they were slated to receive. A stylist had contacted each of them two weeks ago for measurements because he was pulling several outfits to use from designers. Alexis had taken down her French roll and washed her hair in preparation for the famous hair dresser who was preparing her for the shoot.

Attending a variety of functions for her business, she had gotten to the point where she was able to style her hair and apply her makeup to fit any occasion, but today a famous makeup artist was being used, and she couldn't wait to pick up tips and see the final results.

As Catrena, Amanda and Alexis went through the preparations for the pictures, they all laughed and talked about being treated like a celebrity. Knowing how tough it could be starting and maintaining a business, they all shared their stories of triumph and failures.

Alexis relayed stories of some of her wildest events, such as parties based on movies and cartoons and she also shared some of her most memorable disasters. Alexis recalled having just hired Samantha and their schedule was hectic. They had several events on the calendar, meetings with vendors, and appointments with new clients, and she was trying desperately to hold it all together. In haste, she called Samantha on her cell phone because she forgot to order the gifts her corporate client wanted to give his foreign business associates at a special dinner they were hosting in an attempt to close a multimillion dollar deal. Instructing Samantha to order custom slippers for fifteen, her cell phone connection must have been horrible, because at the event three weeks later, instead of having fifteen pairs of custom slippers, the foreign business leaders were presented with fifteen buxom strippers. It was only her reputation for not making these kinds of mistakes, the fact that she waived her fee, and the fact that her client closed the deal with fifteen very happy businessmen that Alexis continued to get business from this particular company.

With everyone doubled over with laughter, the entire experience remained light and comfortable. Unfortunately, the makeup artist thought they were having too much fun. At one point, he begged them to stop sharing stories. Between the tears of joy and the tears of pain, all three kept ruining the eyeliner and mascara.

Sitting in a makeshift waiting area an hour later, Alexis and Amanda waited for Pierre to finish with Catrena's hair.

"Your job sounds fascinating, Alexis. I have to admit that the only types of planners I've heard of were meeting planners that put together conferences or weddings, but you don't do either. Why?"

Used to this question, Alexis said, "Conferences can be so impersonal. Thousands of people, coming and going over several days. I'd rather spend time with a client, giving them something special and unique. But I have worked with meeting planners to plan a particular event during the conference. And weddings . . . well . . . weddings are the biggest waste of money and creative energy there could possibly be. I've beared witness to the fiasco many times. 'In sickness and in health. For better or worse, richer or poorer.' Blah, blah, blah. What an absolute joke."

Older than Alexis by at least twenty years, Amanda was surprised at her answer. "You seem quite cynical about the institution of marriage for someone who hasn't experienced it."

"Institution?" Alexis said, eyes widening in disgust. "Did you just call marriage an institution? An institution represents something solid, a part of life, never to go away, always present. For most people, marriage is none of those things."

"I beg to differ," Amanda said. "I've been married for eighteen years, and have had the time of my life."

Alexis was unimpressed. "So that's two."

Confused, Amanda said, "Two?"

"Yes. That makes two couples I know who have experienced happy marriages," Alexis explained. "But I happen to know of many, many more married couples who are either divorced, getting divorced, or contemplating divorce."

"What about those dinner parties you have for married couples. Surely you don't think they are all headed for a separation?"

Thinking back over the last few years before her father left her mother, Alexis remembered the social and company events where her parents smiled, laughed, and held hands, hiding the fact that they had a screaming match just moments before they left the house.

"Things are not always what they seem," Alexis answered, sadness reflected in her eyes.

Turning to face her completely, Amanda said, "Are you telling me that you will never get married?"

"Marriage is a choice. And you know the old saying . . . just say no," she answered sarcastically.

"Aahhh, but that's just it, Alexis," she started, reaching for her hand in a motherly manner. "One day you'll meet someone who will set your entire world off balance. It will probably come at a time when you least expect it. And the result? Everything you think you know about relationships will be challenged. You'll find yourself caught up in not only a physical attraction, but a mental one as well. You'll try not to think about him and you will. You'll try to convince yourself that you don't need him, and you won't be able to. You'll go to bed thinking of him and wake up with him on your mind. His eyes will melt you, his touch will electrify you, and his words will seduce you. You may try to get away from him, but you can't—and you won't want to. He would have slipped under you skin and taken over your heart. And when he pops that magic question with those four little words, there will be no way on God's green earth that you will be able to 'just say no.'"

Alexis sat mesmerized as visions of Malcolm held her captive. Shaking his smile, his touch and his voice out of her head, she gave a nervous laugh and a half smile. "Don't be ridiculous. You're talking fairy tales. I live in the real world."

Watching Alexis shift in her chair uncomfortably, Amanda grinned with a look of understanding. Patting her gently on the leg, she said, "If you say so, my dear, if you say so."

Twenty minutes later, they were all escorted to the set of the shoot. Impressed with the lights, cameras, and the number of people needed to pull this off, all three women stepped into an arena set up like a boardroom with several props scattered all around. Laptops, briefcases, cell phones, two-way pagers, notepads, and palm pilots. Alexis unconsciously scanned the room for Malcolm and then remembered he was on a plane. *You'll try not to think about him and you will.*

"Okay, ladies. I think if we all cooperate, we can have fun, but get this done in a few hours."

Alexis turned to the voice and momentarily faltered. Rick Satchel! Rick was doing this photo shoot? All of a sudden, she felt a wave of nervousness and her mouth went dry. Spying a water cooler in the corner, she quickly made her way and filled up a paper cup. How someone like him became a well sought after photographer, she would never know.

"No, Alexis," the makeup artist frantically yelled from across the room. Everyone looked his way as his arms flailed and he sprinted, awkwardly avoiding wires, in her direction. "No water on my lips!"

Not professional models, the scene to the three woman appeared quite amusing and caused everyone to break out in laughter. That sound was just what Alexis needed. Realizing she was probably overreacting, she set the cup down and went back to join the others.

She had dealt with unwanted flirtations in the past and eventually the man got the message and left her alone. She was sure that if she gave no indication that she was interested, he would pick up the hint and leave her alone. Surely Rick wouldn't try anything in a room full of people.

"What we'll do first is take a few Polaroids to check the lighting and color. Then we'll do the real thing."

After the first half an hour, Alexis began to relax and get into the excitement of the moment. Rick had been on his best behavior, and even when he needed to adjust Alexis, his words were polite and his touch was aloof and professional. There were no sly comments, leery looks, or suggestive contact.

Two hours later, it was all over, and Alexis was exhausted. She wondered how supermodels did it. Someone always fussing with your hair, powdering your face, adjusting your clothes, and tilting your body. Glad to gather up her belongings, the free promotional makeup she received as a gift, she said good-bye to the crew and headed out.

As she walked out with the other two women, they spoke briefly for a few moments and exchanged busi-

ness cards, promising to keep in touch. Catrena and
Amanda were heading directly to the airport for the return flight home. Unlocking the door with her
automatic key, Alexis slid in and started the engine.
Pulling out of the parking lot as the sun began to set,
she never noticed the lone figure watching her from
the studio window.

Nine

Alexis arrived home from work on Monday to find a note from Melanie saying Celeste had taken her to rent a car and that she'd be back later. Hungry, Alexis went to kitchen to see what goodies Melanie left for dinner. It was great having someone around that could cook. Finding roasted chicken with sauteed vegetables, she put a plate in the microwave and headed to her bedroom to change clothes.

Stripping out of her suit, she tossed the skirt and jacket across her chair and kicked her shoes in the corner. Hoping her sister would be here, Alexis was anxious to talk to someone about Malcolm. Being so far apart in age, they didn't have the opportunity when they were growing up to experience the same things at the same time. But over the past few weeks, they managed to get along fairly well, excluding the conversations about their mother.

Standing at the entrance of her closet in her bra and panties, Alexis searched for her favorite T-shirt. Rummaging through a pile of clothes on her shelf, she came up empty and moved to a stack on another shelf. Still not finding it, she starting flipping through the shirts hanging on the top rail. Still not seeing it, Alexis realized how out of control her closet had become. Before she knew it, she found herself going through her clothes and shoes, organizing them and pulling out

those items that could go to charity. Two hours later, as
she looked at the four bags of clothes and shoes slated
for Goodwill, she realized her sister was right. Was all
the stuff she had accumulated over the years truly necessary?

Remembering her food was still in the microwave,
she headed back to the kitchen and reheated the plate
again, hoping it wouldn't dry her food completely out.
Grabbing some juice out the refrigerator she glanced
at the clock. Nine-thirty. Six-thirty California time. Immediately erasing that thought from her mind, she
grabbed her plate and went back to her room.

Turning on the TV, she flipped through one hundred and fifty channels before she realized she wasn't
in the mood. Remembering the new CDs she bought,
but had yet to listen to, she scanned through the titles
but quickly lost interest. Turning the lamp on her
nightstand, she saw three books she had bought. Not
one title caught her eye. Sighing heavily, Alexis considered working out, reviewing files, or returning
phone calls to friends. But none of those things appealed to her. She sat on her bed, hands folded in her
lap, and looked around her room. For the first time in
her adult life, Alexis was experiencing something completely new . . . restlessness. It couldn't have been
because she was home alone, she spent lots of evenings
by herself.

What was going on? Thinking she may be coming
down with something, she decided to go to bed. Tomorrow, when she woke up, she was sure she would feel
better.

Hours later, Alexis heard a ringing in the distance.
Slowly waking up, she reached aimlessly for the phone.

"Hello," she whispered, barely able to open her eyes.

"I would apologize for waking you, but that would be
a lie."

Sitting up, she was suddenly wide awake.

"Malcolm?"

"It's me."

Glancing at the clock, she said, "It's two o'clock in the morning."

"I know. I was the keynote speaker at the opening night dinner. Of course, everyone wanted to chat with me afterward. I got to a phone as soon as I could."

"I would say that you shouldn't have called so late, but I would be lying as well."

"I can't believe it," Malcolm said lightly. "I think we finally agreed on something."

"There's a first time for everything," she said, snuggling back under the covers.

"I'm counting on it," he said, growing serious.

"Excuse me?" Alexis said.

"I'm counting on this being the first time that you give a relationship a chance."

"Malcolm," she warned, "we have deal."

"But don't you think it's possible . . ."

"No, I don't," she said emphatically. Why was he trying to change the rules?

Hearing silence, Alexis said, "Look Malcolm, I'm not sure what you expect out of this, but let me tell you what I expect. Two people, having a good time, but not getting caught up in anything more."

"You can stay that emotionally unattached?"

"Yes," she answered, trying to convince herself more than him.

"Then how come I heard happiness and excitement when you got this call tonight?"

Ignoring the truth in his statement, she said, "What you heard was relief that you had made it safely. That's the same reaction that I would have given anyone who left for a trip."

Wanting to test her theory, he said, "So now that you

know I've made it safely, you wouldn't have a problem if you didn't hear from me the rest of the week."

"No problem whatsoever." she said, attempting to sound nonchalant. *Liar.*

"Fine, Ms. Shaw," he said, believing she was lying through her teeth. "I'll see you Saturday morning."

Hearing the click on the other end, it took several moments for Alexis's mind to register what just happened. After the dial tone buzzed in her ear, Alexis slammed the phone in the cradle.

No, he didn't just hang up on me! Too wound up to go immediately back to sleep, Alexis kicked the covers off and headed to the kitchen for a glass of water and the opportunity to calm down. Pacing the kitchen floor, she paused when she heard the front door open.

Stepping into the hall, she almost ran smack in to her sister. "Melanie?"

Caught off guard, Melanie stumbled backwards and asked, "What are you doing up at this hour?"

Staring at her sister dressed in a pink halter top and a black miniskirt, Alexis said, "I think the better question is, 'where are coming from at this hour'?"

Walking past her sister, Melanie headed for her bedroom. "I believe I left my mother in New York."

Following, Alexis said, "It looks like you left a lot of things in New York, including your clothes."

Twirling around, Melanie struck a pose like a model and said, "What are you talking about? I think I look fabulous in your clothes."

Taking a closer look, Alexis realized there was something very different about her sister. "Oh, my God! Did you cut your hair?"

Touching the short locks, a moment of panic crossed Melanie's face. "Do you like it?"

Alexis had to admit the Halle Berry style complimented her. and she said sincerely, "I think it looks great." Looking a little closer, Alexis rolled her eyes heavenward as she realized something else about her sister. "Are you drunk?"

Plopping unceremoniously on the bed and tossing shoes across the room, she said, "No, I'm not drunk. I only had one drink and that was four hours ago. Pausing a moment, she continued, "Maybe two, but definitely no more than three . . . and four at the absolute maximum."

Sitting beside her, Alexis said, "And where did you have this one, two, or three drinks . . . four hours ago?"

"After Celeste dropped me off to pick up the rental car, I stopped at this Jamaican restaurant. I was in the mood for some jerk chicken. Actually, it was the guy at the car rental place that recommended this restaurant. He said it wasn't much on ambience, but had the best Jamaican food around. It's located on . . ."

"Melanie," Alexis interrupted impatiently, "You're digressing."

Melanie giggled and Alexis shook her head in amazement.

"Sorry. Anyway, I went to order take out and I overheard the these two men talking about this Reggae club they were going to."

Alexis thought she needed her ears checked. "Are you telling me you went to a club by yourself?"

"No, silly," she said, slapping her sister's arm playfully.

Releasing a sigh of relief, Alexis relaxed. Celeste must have gone with her.

"I went with the two guys."

Jumping up, Alexis screamed, "Are you out of your freakin' mind? You're from New York! If anyone should know better than to get in a car with strange men, it would be you. What the hell were you thinking? I can't believe you. Anything could have happened to you. Have you totally gone crazy?"

Standing herself, Melanie stepped to her sister and said, "Who do you think you're talking to? I am a grown woman and I can do what I damn well please." Sticking her chin out defiantly, she continued, "I don't have to answer to anybody, and that includes you. Now I'll be happy to check into a hotel if I have to put up with an attitude about how I spend my vacation. Otherwise, I'll assume you'll respect my privacy."

Thinking of Malcolm's phone call and now her sister, Alexis had reached the boiling point and her patience reached the end of its rope. "If you want to act a fool, be my guest. I'm going to bed." Slamming the door, she stomped back to her room.

Yanking back the covers, she kicked off her slippers and cut off the light. Getting under the covers, she forced her eyes shut. No way was she going to let some man and a crazy acting sister keep her from getting a good night of sleep. But thirty minutes later, she was still awake.

As the week went by, Malcolm was true to his word. Not one phone call. And Alexis couldn't do one thing about it. She thought about calling Susan, but Susan would probably want to know why she needed to reach him. Besides, she wouldn't give him the satisfaction of proving him right. Determined not to miss him, she forced herself to take on an attitude of indifference. Still, it was the longest week of her life.

The following Saturday, Alexis moaned as she heard the alarm go off. For reasons she refused to acknowledge, she hadn't slept well all week and now she was forced to get up at this ungodly hour. What in the world was she thinking when she agreed to this date?

She thought of canceling, but realized the only number she had was an office number and she doubted very seriously that she would be able to catch him there.

Hitting the snooze button on her clock radio, she rationalized the added sleep time because he didn't contact her all week and since she had no idea where they were going, she wouldn't worry about dressing up. That meant she could cut out half of her morning routine. Turning over, she fluffed her pillow and closed her eyes, hoping for another thirty minutes of sleep.

At precisely 5:00 A.M., Alexis answered the door bell. With gray sweat pants, a matching top, her hair pulled back, and no makeup, Alexis greeted her date. However, her nonchalant attitude was immediately challenged when she drank in his broad shoulders, solid chest, and inviting smile.

Before Malcolm could say good morning, Alexis started, "First of all, don't say a word about how I look. You gave me no hint of what we were going to do, so I figured it didn't matter. Second, please tell me that's Starbucks in your hand."

Handing her a steaming cup, Malcolm leaned against the door jamb. "Is there ever a moment where you don't have to be the one in control?"

"It's rare. But you will probably be long gone when the occasion arises again," Alexis teased.

"Ouch!" Malcolm said, "You're crushing my ego."

"Yea, right," Alexis said, "You're the one who went the week without calling. If anyone's ego should be bruised, it's mine."

"Not hearing from me, did that bother you?" he asked, staring intently in her eyes.

"Not in the least." she said flippantly.

Malcolm secretly smiled at her forced air of indifference, but decided to let it slide. He would get her to admit soon enough that she missed him as much as he missed her. It must have been hard for her because it was damn near impossible for him. It took all his willpower for him to hold out, but he promised himself he would never go that long without hearing her voice again.

Taking in her casual dress, Malcolm realized this was the first time in his life he took a woman on a first date and she didn't look like it took her hours to prepare. Alexis stood before him completely natural and at ease. No pretense, no nervousness, no need to impress. Malcolm found the entire scene refreshing.

"Come in," she said, stepping inside. "Oh, no. I'm not coming in, you're coming out."

Groaning, Alexis tried one last time to get out of this early morning date. She offered to make breakfast, even cold, hard cash. But nothing worked.

Grabbing her keys, she contemplated peeking in her sister's room to let her know she was leaving, but quickly changed her mind. They had been polite to each other over the past week, but the closeness they had developed since she first arrived was no longer evident. Alexis figured she was going through some sort of identity crisis and decided to let her have her space. Hopefully, they'll work things out when she's ready to talk. Locking the front door, she followed Malcolm out to his truck.

As they headed out of the city, Alexis started a mental list of where they could be headed. There were very few things one could do when it was still dark outside. There was fishing, but Alexis prayed hard that that wasn't it. Hating the idea of putting little squirmy things on a hook, she took the fact that she didn't see any rods in the back of the truck as a good sign.

"So tell me about yourself."

Cutting her eyes at him, she smiled, "You just spent

two hours interviewing me last week. What more could you want to know?"

"That's not what I mean," Malcolm answered. "Those two hours revealed only one part of your life, your business. I want to know about the other parts of you."

"There is no other part," Alexis answered, taking a sip from her coffee cup. "The past five years of my life have been consumed with my business."

"What about that guy from the awards ceremony. You seemed to have had time for him."

She bit her lip to stifle a grin. "Jealous?"

"No," he lied. "Just curious."

"Yea, right," she said, her eyes brightening with laughter.

"Now who has the ego?" Malcolm said, turning off the main highway onto a two-lane road. Deciding to make it easier on her, he asked. "When is your birthday?"

"What is this? Twenty questions?"

"Humor me."

"March seventeenth."

"Favorite color?"

"Purple."

"Are you seeing anyone right now?"

Raising a brow at his backdoor tactic, she said, "No. I only do one temporary relationship at a time."

"Good."

Making the remainder of the drive in a comfortable silence, Malcolm turned onto a narrow dirt road and Alexis's eyes widened in surprise.

"I hope you're not afraid of heights, Alexis."

"What made you . . ."

"A colleague of mine did a story on this company a few years ago and told me I had to experience it first-hand one day. He said this is the best way to watch the sunrise."

Parking the truck and cutting the engine, Malcolm faced Alexis. "But I never had the urge to do it. Until I met you. For some strange reason, I wanted to witness that sunrise with you." Reaching out and covering his hand with hers, he continued, "From the moment I saw you at that restaurant, I have not been able to get you off my mind."

Reaching up, Alexis stroked his cheek with the back of her hand. "Oh, Malcolm. I hate to admit it, but I've felt the same way."

Pushing a few stray strands of hair from her face, Malcolm's eyes gazed downward at her lips. Believing that one kiss would not be enough, he raised his eyes to hers and said, "Let's do this."

Alexis didn't want to admit it, but Melanie was right. This was turning out to be the most romantic date she had ever had. Thinking about the "almost kiss" that just happened, Alexis was taken aback by the level of disappointment she felt in her heart. Physical attraction she could handle. But this this was something more. He was something more.

"Alexis, you coming?" Malcolm asked, when he realized she didn't follow him when he got out of the truck.

Pushing these new feelings aside, Alexis jumped out the truck and said, "I'm right behind you."

After the pilot briefed the couple on what would take place, they stepped into the basket and prepared for their first hot air balloon ride.

As they soared across the sky, words could not do justice to the beauty that was before them. Wrapped in Malcolm's arms, Alexis had never felt such comfort. Her previous relationships were always centered around her need to keep an emotional distance. But at this moment, all of her emotions were betraying her.

The ice around her heart was slowly beginning to melt, and Alexis wasn't sure if she wanted to refreeze it.

Two hours later, Alexis and Malcolm sat in a booth in the back of a local diner, enjoying fresh waffles and coffee. "I've never seen anything like that. It was beautiful. Thank you Malcolm. I enjoyed every minute of it."

"I'm glad to have shared it with you." Leaning back, Malcolm grew serious. "Alexis, I want to apologize for Rick's behavior last week, as well as at the restaurant."

Alexis felt her stomach turn at the mention of his name. There was something about that man that made her feel completely uncomfortable. "Are the two of you actually friends?"

Malcolm thought about their relationship and said, "I've known Rick since college. We both worked on the school paper. I was the writer, he took the pictures. We lost touch for a while, but ended up working together at *Image*. We don't hang out that often anymore, but I guess you could say he's a friend."

"I could say he's a lot of things, but a friend would not be it. How can you put up with him?" she asked, feeling the anger at his uncouth behavior rise in her.

"He was always a little rough around the edges, but deep down he's really a good guy."

Watching the waitress refill their coffee cups, Alexis thought about her run-ins with Rick. On the outside, he looked like any average guy, but that had nothing to do with what was on the inside. While his words were polite and there was a smile on his face, the friendliness didn't quite reach his eyes.

"Let's change the subject," Alexis offered. "When is your birthday, what's your favorite color and . . ."

He noticed her hesitation and released a slow grin as he knew her next words. "March tenth, black, and no, I'm not seeing anyone."

Alexis straightened her back and checked her watch, blocking out any physical sign that she was immensely pleased by that statement. "It's getting late. I need to get home and change for the picnic."

Signaling the waitress for the check, Malcolm read the look in her eyes. She was just as glad to get that little piece of information about him as he was to get it about her. "Before we go, I wanted to talk about that phone call last week." Reaching across the table, he held her hand in his. "I was serious about what I said."

Pulling out of his touch, she said, "So was I."

"I just think that if we take our time, we can get to know each other and see where it leads."

"And I think that people shouldn't make deals they can't keep," said pointedly.

Malcolm felt in his heart that her words didn't match her emotions, but he couldn't understand why she fought her feelings so hard. He knew she had hangups about relationships, but her refusal to even contemplate developing anything long-term revealed just how deep they were. Resigning himself to the fact that words were not the way to get Alexis to view their relationship differently, he decided to show her. Treating her with such tenderness and care, she would never want their relationship to end.

As they headed back into the city, Alexis took a call on her cell phone. Only hearing one side of the conversation, it wasn't difficult to figure out there was a problem.

"Don't worry about it, Olivia. I'll stop at the warehouse and pick them up."

Hanging up the phone, Alexis relayed to Malcolm that the centerpieces for her event this afternoon were mistakenly left at her storage warehouse. Noting that they were only about fifteen minutes from the facility, Malcolm agreed to swing by.

Pulling into the industrial park, Malcolm parked his truck and followed Alexis to warehouse twenty-three. Entering through a double garage-size door, Malcolm's eyes grew wide. He didn't know what to expect, but as he scanned the room, he began to understand the magnitude of Just For You.

In an amazingly organized manner, he saw life-size Santa Clauses, reindeers, and sleighs to the right. Beside that were harps, several cupids, candelabras in all shapes and sizes, and archways adorned with silk flowers. There were all types of electronics, including a Victrola, several jukeboxes, and instruments of every type. Continuing his walk into the warehouse, he saw the Egyptian pyramids, the Eiffel Tower, and horses with jousters sitting on top. There were palm trees, ski slopes, cactus plants, NBA-size basketball nets, bleachers, and several small boats. Amazed at all he saw, he followed Alexis to an office in the back of the room.

Malcolm looked around the small but functional office. The steel desk, file cabinets, and two chairs were nondescript and the two windows had industrial blinds letting in the sunlight. On the far wall was a huge six-month calendar with event times and delivery schedules. "This is incredible," he said, impressed.

Alexis pulled out a large cardboard box and began to put twenty-four musical minicarousels in it. The picnic had an amusement park theme and the centerpieces for the tables added the perfect touch.

Picking one up, Malcolm pushed the button. As the tiny horses rose up and down in a circle, he listened to the soft musical sounds. Setting the delicate piece in the box, the music continued to play.

"Beautiful, isn't it?" Alexis asked, placing the last one in the box.

Staring at her, Malcolm whispered, "It sure is."

"I just want to tape this shut, and then I'll be ready."

Malcolm watched her with appreciation. In the short time that she had been a part of his life, he was amazed at the many sides she portrayed. At the restaurant, she was full of fire and fight; when they settled into the interview, she was professional and poised. At the awards ceremony, she was sophisticated and elegant, yet when she gave her acceptance speech, she displayed an air of humbleness and gratefulness not often found in successful people. And now, in her sweatsuit, ponytail and a face devoid of makeup, he saw the essence of Alexis.

They always say, the bigger they are, the harder they fall. Malcolm knew he was about to hit the floor with a definite thud. He has spent his entire life placing his career before anything, but he felt a change taking place. And for the first time in his life, that didn't scare him. His life had become settled over the past few years. He found a home at *Image*, actually bought a condo instead of renting, and paid a car note instead of a lease payment. Atlanta had become his permanent home, and he wanted someone to share it with.

Reaching out his hand, he gently grabbed her arm. Alexis's eyes widened in surprise as he pulled her to him.

"What are you doing?" she asked.

Hugging her at the waist, he smiled and said, "Dance with me."

Alexis listened to the sounds of the carousel and almost allowed herself to get caught up in the moment. But she took a step back, separating herself from his touch.

The balloon ride, cozy breakfast, his alluring smile, and his sizzling touch were confusing her. If she wasn't careful, she could easily slip into something more than a temporary relationship.

Closing the space between them, he said quietly, "Just once, let's forget about our temporary agreement and enjoy this moment." Seeing the hesitation in her eyes, he opened his arms and encouragingly said, "Just take one step forward."

What harm could one dance do? Alexis started to take a step, and before it was complete, Malcolm stepped forward and clasped her body tightly with his.

Resting her head on his chest, Alexis allowed herself to lose herself in the moment. His nearness was overwhelming and everything about him turned her on. His masculine scent, his sensual touch, his melodic voice. Closing her eyes, she wanted to make this feeling last.

Malcolm fought for control of his body. His eyes loved to look at her, his hands couldn't resist touching her, his heart beat faster when she was around, and when she wasn't with him, she was always on his mind. Lifting her chin with his fingers, he slowly lowered his face to hers. The moment the connection was made, he couldn't hold back his desire as the touch of her lips sent a shockwave of complete awareness through his body.

Opening her mouth to receive all of him, his tongue explored her intimately while his hands went on an intimate exploration of their own. Gently rubbing her shoulders, he moved down her arms and around her waist. As the kiss deepened, Malcolm moaned in satisfaction.

Alexis was on fire. His hands were branding her with every touch and there was an intense physical awareness that she could not deny. Growing weak from the onslaught of desire, she bent her knees and leaned onto the desk, pulling him with her. Wildly reaching behind her, she haphazardly cleared the desk of papers, pens, and extraneous files, allowing him to gently lay her down.

As the carousel continued its serenade, Malcolm continued his assault of her body. His kisses seared her ears, neck, and shoulders. As his tongue left a trail of heat, the explosion of passion on the inside of him was larger than anything he had experienced and he was drowning in his uncontrollable desire to make her his. Physical attraction he was used to, but this was something beyond the physical. He had loved many, but never knew what it was to be in love. And while he didn't want to believe that he had fallen so quickly, he knew he would have to search far and wide to find another word to describe what was happening to him. This was it. This was the real thing.

It was that thought that snapped him back to reality. If this was the real thing, he knew he had to honor his promise to himself. He wanted to savor every moment of getting to know her, and if they moved too fast, deep inside, he knew it would only lead to heartache.

Pulling on every ounce of strength he could muster in his body, he slowed his touch and stood up, carrying her with him.

Breathless and confused, Alexis stammered, "Wha . . Wha . . . Why did you stop?"

"We're moving too fast," he said, fighting to return to his normal breathing level.

Straightening her clothes and catching her breath, Alexis felt the blood begin to pound in her temples.

"Too fast? What the hell is that supposed to mean?" she yelled, as raw, primitive anger began to overtake her.

"Alexis, let me . . ."

Screaming, she continued, "You take me through the whole seduction of gazing into my eyes, an intimate dance, and . . . ." Waving her arms around the scattered files and empty desk, "This." With a sarcastic laugh, she continued, "And I thought it was the woman who was supposed to be the tease."

Stretching his hand for her, Malcolm started, "Alexis, listen . . ."

Pointing her finger at him, she interrupted, "No, you listen. This little deal of ours is not working. You can't seem to make up your mind what you want. Last week it was 'take it slow' and today your lips are plastered all over my body. Well, I don't have time for games."

At that precise moment, the carousel song ended.

"How fitting," Alexis spat, as she replaced the files on the desk. Picking up the box of centerpieces, she walked to the door and turned to him. "I have work to do. Take me home."

The ride to Alexis's house was made in complete silence. She refused to talk and Malcolm didn't know what to say. Everything she said in the warehouse was right. If he was a woman, he would be called a "tease" and the last thing he wanted to do was appear to be playing games. This was the most serious thing he had ever done in his life. As he pulled up to her building, she opened the door before he came to a complete stop. Grabbing the box, she shut the door.

Rolling down the window, he said, "Alexis, can we talk later?"

She turned to him and simply said, "No."

He watched the doorman open the front door and she disappeared into the lobby. Malcolm sat there for several minutes. He wasn't sure if she would come back out or if he should go in. After contemplating the situation, he decided that neither would happen. Starting his engine, he headed home. Frustrated.

Ten

Alexis slammed the front door, set the box down, and pulled the clip out of her hair, allowing it to fall to her shoulders. Running her fingers through it, she hoped to relieve some of the pressure from her pounding head. Storming into the kitchen, she slammed cabinets and dishes as she fixed herself a cup of coffee. Glancing at the clock on the stove, she had a little over an hour before she had to leave for her event. That would give her just enough time to stop the steam from rising out of her ears.

"What in the world is going on in here?" Melanie asked, awakened by all the noise.

"What is going on is that I have seen the last of Malcolm Singleton."

Noticing her disheveled look, Melanie's face grew serious, "What did he do to you?"

Not getting an immediate response, Melanie said, "I'm calling the police."

Alexis sat down at the table and rested her head in her hands. Never in her life had she shed a tear over a man, and she didn't plan to start now. But she felt the drops welling in the corner of her eyes and she used every ounce of her willpower to keep them from falling.

Alarmed at the vulnerability she was seeing in her sister, Melanie replaced the receiver and sat across from her. "Alexis, what happened?"

Lifting her head, Alexis said, "What happened was a glorious hot air balloon ride where we watched the sunrise. What happened was a cozy breakfast in a quaint little diner where we talked and got to know each other. What happened was an unexpected stop at my props warehouse where we almost did the horizontal mumbo on top of my desk."

"Almost?"

Rising, Alexis poured herself a cup of coffee. "Almost."

"I hope he was a gentleman when you said no. If you weren't ready, he should understand."

Alexis glanced at her sister and shrugged, "Well . . ."

"Don't tell me he copped an attitude when you wanted to slow things down?"

"It wasn't me who pulled the plug."

Melanie's eyes widened in understanding, "You mean . . ."

"He said he wanted to slow things down."

Melanie watched her sister pout and attempted to hold her laugh, but she was unsuccessful, and as she let it out, her sister turned and glared.

"I'm glad I'm able to provide you a good laugh."

Melanie wiped the tears that gathered in the corner of her eyes and toned down to a giggle.

"Don't you see, Alexis? The route you laid out for your relationship with Malcolm is nothing like you planned. It sounds to me like he wants to make a stab at a meaningful relationship."

Everything you think you know about relationships will be challenged. Shaking Amanda's words out of her head, Alexis decided to change the subject. "I see you're speaking to me again."

Not responding, Melanie rose and went to the refrigerator and pulled out some eggs and cheese for omelettes.

"And I see you're cooking again. You know I've been really hungry this past week."

Cracking the eggs in a bowl, Melanie started, "I owe you an apology. I took my personal frustrations out on you and I had no right. And I didn't get in the car with those two guys. I followed them. I also stopped drinking hours before I left the club. But I did have one of the best nights of my life. Just dancing and hanging out."

Giving her sister a hug, Alexis said, "It's okay, but next time, let me know. I'll hang with you. Agreed?"

"Agreed."

"Good, I'm going to get ready."

Thirty minutes later, Alexis drove out of her parking lot, heading for her event. She never noticed the dark car following closely behind her.

Alexis pulled up to the valet and handed off her keys. It was Friday night and she was restless. Deciding to head to Buckhead, she knew she could always find pleasure in her favorite pastime: shopping. And Phipps Plaza was the place to do just that.

It had been a week since her blowup with Malcolm, and having not returned his numerous phone calls, she had no plans to ever see him again. The only problem was that she couldn't get him out of her mind. But she was determined. She was fine before Malcolm Singleton came into her life, and she'd be fine now that he was gone.

Having just left the estate of Harriet LeMeruix, Eric was shocked when Alexis announced he was in charge to complete the event. The reception, held for an exclusive's women's club, had just gotten underway when

Alexis made her departure. She usually never stayed until the end, but she had never left this early.

Melanie and Celeste were planning a movie, but Alexis wasn't in the mood. So she decided to do the one thing that always bought her pleasure. Shop.

Two hours into her outing, she entered Gucci, and headed straight for the shoe section. Having already visited three of her favorite stores, Alexis had yet to purchase one item. A fact that bewildered her. Normally, she would have made at least one trip to her car to drop off bags containing a new suit, a pair of pants or several blouses. But this time, she hadn't even felt like trying anything on, much less buying anything. Now, as she stood looking at the fall line of shoes, she mumbled under her breath in frustration. Her favorite pastime had never failed to bring her pleasure, always allowing her to relax from the stress of running a business. But she found none of that pleasure tonight. And she knew exactly who to blame. *You'll try to convince yourself that you don't need him, and you won't be able to.*

Amanda's words haunted her like a ghost and the more the phrase replayed in her mind, the more determined she was to prove her wrong. With deliberate movements, she picked up a pair of black and white pumps and searched for a salesperson.

"Alexis, is that you?"

Turning to the sound, she gave a genuine smile as she recognized Belinda Waters. Bride number three with the rainbow dress, she was also divorce number three.

Giving her a hug, they exchanged hellos.

"I thought that was you, but it's been over a year and your hair has really grown," Belinda said.

"Recognize me? I almost didn't recognize you." Alexis answered, taking a good look at her friend. And it was true. Belinda and Myron were married six years ago and divorced two years later when she found out

Myron had a six-month-old son. With her marketing career on the rise, and Myron's law degree, Belinda eagerly planned for the six-bedroom house, three-car garage, the minivan and the winter and summer vacations. But all her dreams of happily ever after were crushed when another woman showed up at her door on Christmas Eve with a bouncing baby boy in her arms.

The day she moved out, Belinda began to pull away from her friends, spending all her time at work or home alone. Over the next few years, repeated invitations were declined and Alexis only saw her occasionally. Last year, when several of their friends got together for dinner, Alexis tried to hide her surprise when Belinda walked into the room.

Having gained almost seventy pounds, Belinda's outer appearance reflected her inner depression. Throughout the entire evening Belinda whined about her failed marriage and the betrayal of someone who pledged to love and protect her. Concerned about where her life was headed, Alexis pulled her to the side and confronted Belinda about her state. Breaking down into tears, Belinda grudgingly admitted that Alexis was right, she just didn't know how to pull herself out of her misery.

A week later, Alexis got a message from Belinda that her company offered her a promotion if she was willing to move to Dallas. She left two days later. Aside from holiday cards and infrequent e-mails, Alexis hadn't seen nor heard from Belinda until today.

What a difference a year had made. The woman who stood before her was nothing like the woman who was crying and whining a year ago. This woman oozed radiance and life. Belinda had lost all the weight and had a sparkle in her eyes that hadn't been seen since that fateful Christmas Eve. Dressed to impress, everything about her screamed happiness.

"You look absolutely fabulous, Belinda."

"Thanks, Alexis," she answered, turning from side to side like a fashion model. "I just got back in town yesterday. I haven't been back home since I took that promotion and my parents were nagging me about coming back. I'm here on a short vacation."

Glad that she had run into her old friend, Alexis put down the shoes she was contemplating buying.

"Do you have time to grab a cup of coffee, to catch up?"

"You bet."

A few moments later, they were seated at a small coffee shop. Alexis couldn't get over the change in her friend. When she left a year ago, her clothes were sloppy, her auburn hair was unkept, and her pronounced features of hazel eyes, high cheekbones, and smooth almond skin were a permanent look of sadness.

"It looks like Dallas has been good to you."

Belinda laughed as she added cream to her coffee. "Is that your polite way of saying 'how the hell did you lose all that weight'?"

"Basically," Alexis said, breaking into a smile.

Leaning forward Belinda whispered happily, "I fell in love."

Alexis couldn't believe what she was hearing and her response reflected that. "Did you forget what happened to you the last time you fell in love? If I remember correctly, you put off graduate school because you were in love. You bought a house you hated because you were in love. You catered to Myron's every need because you were in love. And where did that get you, Belinda?"

Taken aback by the venom she heard in her voice, Belinda simply said, "It got me Jacob."

"And I suppose you lost the weight and cut your hair for Jacob."

Hearing her judgmental tone, she said, "You've always been so hard on me, Alexis. Why is that?"

"I can't believe you have to ask. You were a puppet for Myron, and look how he treated you. You're obviously doing the same for this Jacob guy. I just thought that at some point you would have realized that women were not put on this earth to please men, especially when they don't appreciate it." Wanting to drive her point home, Alexis reminded Belinda of the facts. "You know the numbers. Six weddings, five divorces. I just can't believe you're still setting yourself up for disappointment."

Belinda had heard all of Alexis's theories on the hypocrisy of love and marriage, and when her husband left her for another woman, she had to admit that Alexis had a faithful ally. But Jacob was not Myron, and that's exactly what she told Alexis.

"How can you say that?" Alexis asked, amazed at how quickly women forget the suffering they've done at the hands of men. "You swore off men, love, and everything it represented. And here you are, adjusting and changing yourself for a man. You lost weight for a man, you cut your hair for a man, and I'm sure there are plenty of other things you've done for this man that I don't know about."

Belinda stared at her friend with understanding eyes. Having met in college, Belinda knew Alexis came from a broken home and felt overshadowed by her mother. Alexis never had a boyfriend longer that a few months and her belief that all relationships were only for a season fueled her nonchalant attitude. Never letting a man get too close, Belinda believed that it wasn't because she didn't care, it was because she was afraid. Determined to help her see the light, Belinda decided to tell her the complete story. "For your information, I met Jacob the first week I arrived in Texas. Can you believe he lived in the apartment next door?"

Alexis seemed unimpressed. Belinda noticed and continued anyway, "I was overweight, depressed, and looked a complete mess. I managed to pull it together when I went to work, but around the house, I just let it all hang out, and it wasn't a pretty sight. But you know what? He didn't seem to mind. He would ask me out and I would say no. He would offer to fix things around my apartment and I would say no. Finally, after asking me over for dinner for the eighth time, I finally asked him, 'What do you see in me?' and do you know what his answer was?"

Alexis, trying not to show that her interest was piqued, simply shrugged.

"You."

"You?" Alexis said, perplexed.

"Yes," Belinda replied. "That's what he said. 'You.' What he saw in me, was me."

Seeing that Alexis was not quite getting the revelation, Belinda continued, "The weight, the hair, the sloppy clothes—that was the outer me. He told me the first time he looked in my eyes, he was drawn to the inner me. Kindness. Gentleness. A good heart."

Alexis sat forward. This was not what she expected to hear.

"We started dating, and not once did he try to change me. He just accepted me. Six months later, he asked me to marry him."

"Whoa. Wait a minute," Alexis said as her eyes opened in utter surprise, "You got married again?"

"No." Belinda replied, watching Alexis physically relax at that answer. "I told him I needed more time.

And while we continued to date, I began to take care of myself. I cut back on my work hours and started going back to the gym. I got active with our sorority again and started doing some volunteer work. Now, six months later, I'm healthy, happy, and content with me. I'm even thinking about going back to school. The important thing is now that I've gotten myself together, I can add someone else to the equation. When I get back to Dallas, I'm going to accept his proposal."

Reaching across the table, Alexis grabbed her friend's hand. "I know we haven't been in touch lately, but I still consider us good friends. So I have to ask you. How can you risk it all again? The heartache, the tears, the hurt. You have to remember the day we helped you pack your bags so Myron and Cassandra could raise their baby in your house. How do you know this time it will be different?"

Belinda sat quietly for several moments, hoping to find the right words.

"Because he met me exactly where I was in life and accepted me. Any man who is willing to do that, deserves the benefit of the doubt."

Alexis thought of Malcolm and their tumultuous relationship. He willingly accepted her demand of a temporary relationship and ignored her assumption that there could be nothing permanent between them. And that had not deterred him. Was he looking past her outward objections and into her inner self? If so, what did he see? In that instant, she knew exactly what he would see. A woman who was extremely attracted to a man, and who for the first time in her life, was seeking something permanent. Something permanent with him.

"Alexis?"

Jumping out of her thoughts, Alexis stared at her friend.

"Are you okay?"

Alexis squeezed her hands, and nodded in the positive with a growing smile. "Yes, Belinda. I'm just fine."

Malcolm sat in his living room listening to Jackson and Brent pluck his last nerve. After skipping the basketball game this week and bowing out on dinner last night, they came over to find out exactly what was going on with him. Dressed for a night on the town, they had spent the last twenty minutes trying to convince him to join them at The Mirage, the newest club in the city. Jackson, dressed in Tommy, and Brent, sporting Kenneth Cole, were ready for a night of hanging out and having fun.

In disbelief that Malcolm was turning them down again, Brent said, "This isn't like you Malcolm. You're moping around like you lost your best friend."

"And that can't be true," Jackson added, "because we're right here."

Malcolm glanced from one to the other and stood. "It's getting late, you guys better head out."

"Does this have anything to do Alexis?" Brent asked, believing full well it had to.

"Who's Alexis?" Jackson asked.

"The woman who screwed up our basketball game a couple of weeks ago and the woman who won Businesswoman of the Year from *Image Magazine*," Brent answered.

"I know you aren't still trippin' about this woman?" Jackson asked with a laugh. But as he watched Malcolm's nonresponse, he raised his brow and grew serious. "Tell me that's not the case."

Malcolm still took the fifth.

"She must have some good . . ."

Standing, Malcolm said, "Jackson, must you be so

crass? And not that it's any of your business, but I wouldn't know."

At this point, Brent and Jackson could have been knocked over with a feather.

"Let me get this straight," Brent started. "You blow off hanging out with your boys, you mope around your house all week, and now you don't want to go out. And all of this for a woman you haven't even slept with."

Jackson watched his brother's reaction closely.

Malcolm left them standing in the living room and went to the kitchen to get a drink, hoping to contemplate exactly what was happening with him. There were women that he dated for months that had never elicited this type of reaction. Women with whom he had spent time with, opened up his home and his bed to, but never his heart. But he realized the order was screwed up with Alexis. They had not spent that much time together, she had never been to his home, and she most definitely had not shared his bed. However, he felt he was slowly turning his heart over to her.

Heading back to the living room, his expression reflected the sadness of his reality. He was losing his heart to a woman who didn't want to have anything to do with him.

"Have fun tonight, guys. I'm staying in."

Before Jackson could protest Malcolm's decision, the phone rang.

Having given up hope that Alexis would call him, Malcolm made no move to answer it.

Brent grabbed the phone just before it would have gone to voicemail.

"Hello."

Malcolm watched the corners of his cousin's mouth turn into a smile.

"Yes, thank you."

Replacing the receiver, Brent looked at Jackson and said, "Let's go."

Confused, Jackson started to follow Brent to the front door.

"Wait a minute," Malcolm said. "Who was that?"

Putting his hand on the knob to open the door, Brent grinned. "That was the front gate. You have a visitor."

Malcolm, not in the mood for company, started to protest.

"I believe the name was Alexis Shaw."

Malcolm instantly smiled and Jackson moaned. He had seen that look on several of his fallen friends. Whether Malcolm was aware of it or not, he had it bad for this woman. And he had every intention of meeting the woman who'd managed to turn his brother's world upside down.

Facing Brent, Jackson said, "No way am I walking out this door until I meet this woman."

Fearing his two family members would be a total embarrassment to him, Malcolm quickly moved past them and opened the door. "Brent's already met her and you'll have your chance, but not tonight."

Jackson shut the door and patted Malcolm on the back, "Tonight is as good as any night to meet the woman who has taken over my brother's heart."

Malcolm started to protest his use of words, but decided to remain silent. Yes, he was attracted to her. Yes, he had missed her terribly this past week, and yes, he knew his feelings for her were growing, but was it possible to think that in a few short weeks he could have fallen in love?

Alexis followed the directions the guard gave her and pulled into a parking space in front of Malcolm's building. After talking with Belinda, Alexis had an overwhelming urge to see him. Turning on the inside car light, she checked her makeup. She knew it was a delay tactic, but now that she was here, she didn't know exactly what she was going to say. This was new territory for her. In all of her previous relationships, she was able to compartmentalize her emotions, but in this case, her emotions were running rampant.

Building a business required a large amount of her time, and when she focused on her events, she had no room to think about anything or anyone else. But in the past few weeks, all of that had changed. She had not been able to let one day go by without thinking of him. She would be in a meeting with a client and he was there. When she toured facilities and met with vendors, he was there. He irritated and annoyed her, but he also fascinated and warmed her by just being with him.

Cutting the engine, she took a deep breath. The security guard announced her arrival, so she couldn't sit in her car forever. Opening the car door, she slowly walked into the building. Stepping into the elevator, she prayed when he opened the door, her mouth would open and something coherent would come out.

Eleven

Malcolm resigned himself that Jackson and Brent weren't leaving and stood in the entranceway pacing the floor, wondering what he would say to her. She had every reason to be upset with him after that stunt he pulled at her warehouse, but he took her unexpected visit as a good sign.

Hearing the doorbell, he inhaled deeply and opened the door.

Alexis started to say hello and then abruptly closed her mouth. Standing tall in a tank top and a pair of shorts, his physique was breathtaking. His bronze skin, tanned from the summer sun, begged to be touched. Completely overwhelmed by the aura of virility that oozed from every inch of his body, Alexis was helpless to form one word. Her eyes perused his features from head to toe and she felt her body temperature elevate at least ten degrees. Forcing her eyes back to his face, Alexis opened her mouth, but still, not a sound came out.

Malcolm was not faring much better. A Friday night, he figured she must be coming from one of her events and she looked absolutely fabulous. Her hair was a sea of curls that hung loosely to her shoulders and the royal blue suit highlighted all the curves in her body. The short skirt showed off legs that he immediately envisioned wrapped around his naked body.

"Ah-hem."

Alexis looked past Malcolm and noticed two men. *Did I just make a complete fool of myself in front of these men?*

Stepping to the side, Malcolm motioned for her to come in.

"Alexis Shaw, I'd like you to meet my brother, Jackson. I'm sure you remember Brent. Both of whom were just leaving."

"Jackson Singleton," he said, reaching out to shake her hand. He now understood why his brother was so smitten.

"Nice to meet you, Jackson. Good to see you again Brent," Alexis answered, relieved for a break in the electric current that had sparked between her and Malcolm. The two men were a welcome diversion.

Malcolm hid his agitation as he watched Jackson and Brent follow her into the living room.

"Malcolm lied about you," Jackson said as they all took a seat.

"Oh?" she answered with a questioning gaze.

"He said you were beautiful, but that was obviously an understatement."

Seeing the playfulness in his eyes, Alexis decided to have some fun. "What else has Malcolm been saying about me?"

"It's not so much what he says," Brent said, "it's what he does."

Sitting forward, Malcolm cleared his throat and said, "I thought you guys had someplace to go."

Ignoring the rise in his annoyed brother's voice, Jackson continued, "First, there was the basketball game . . ."

"Thanks for stopping by," Malcolm said, standing. Grabbing Jackson by the arm, he forcibly lifted him out of his seat and pushed him out of the room.

Brent watched with amusement as the brothers left

the room before turning to Alexis. "I got your updates on the benefit dinner. Things really seem to be taking shape."

"Yes, they are," Alexis said, "I think you'll be pleased with the results."

After several seconds of silence, Brent hesitantly asked, "How is Melanie doing?"

"She's fine," Alexis said, curious about his tone.

"Brent, it's time for you to go," Malcolm yelled from the hallway.

"I guess that's my cue," Brent said, heading for the door. Pausing, he turned back to Alexis and said, "Let Melanie know I asked about her."

"Sure," Alexis said.

Brent and Jackson were still giving him a hard time when Malcolm slammed the door behind them.

"So what happened at the basketball game?" Alexis asked with a wicked grin.

"I believe it was you who came to see me," Malcolm said, attempting to turn the tables. "So why don't you tell me why you're here."

Her smile disappeared as she searched for the right words. "I wanted to see you."

"Why?"

Tilting her head to the side, Alexis stared into his eyes, and realized she didn't have an answer. Quietly, she said, "I don't know."

Malcolm moved to sit beside her and stretch his arm around her and gently stroked her neck.

"I missed every shot."

"Excuse me?" Alexis asked, confused at his words.

"The basketball game. I played the night of our interview. I missed every shot because I couldn't get you out of my head." Moving his hands from her neck to her cheek, he continued, "This week, I skipped the game altogether."

Alexis, embraced by the warmth of his touch, decided to make her confession as well, "I cleaned my closet."

Raising his brow, he said, "What?"

"I have never cleaned my closet. But I got so restless when you left for San Francisco, I started out looking for a T-shirt and ended with color coordinated separates and suits."

"Oh, baby." Without hesitation, his lips slowly descended upon hers. Forcing her mouth open with his thrusting tongue, he kissed her with the all the passion that had been stored in him since the moment he laid eyes on her. Moving his lips down her neck, he gently squeezed her shoulders. Between his words, he planted kisses on her ears, neck, and finally her lips. "I'm sorry about what happened at your warehouse last week. I was confused about what I wanted."

Breathlessly, Alexis answered, "And now?"

"Now, I know exactly what I want."

Pausing, his hazel eyes darkened with desire. "You."

As though his words released her from all of her doubts, she pressed herself further into him.

The simple word reminded Alexis of her earlier conversation with Belinda and she inwardly admitted to herself that Malcolm Singleton had managed to become what no other man had even come close to being. Permanent.

Leaning into his kiss, Alexis eagerly responded by locking her arms behind his neck. The pool of excitement swelling in the core of her being magnified to a level never before experienced.

At the reality of her growing feelings for Malcolm, she paused.

Malcolm immediately felt the change in her demeanor.

"Alexis, what is it?"

"I'm strong in the self-esteem and self-confidence area. But I don't know if I could take it if you stopped again."

Standing, Malcolm swept her up with him and held her hand as he led her out of the living room, down the hall and into his bedroom. Sitting her on the king-size bed, he picked up the remote, pushed a few buttons and the smooth jazz sounds of a saxophone filled the air. Disappearing into the bathroom, he came back with several candles and placed them strategically around the room. Without hurry, he lit each one, and a soft glow illuminated the room.

Alexis sat patiently as he left the room and returned a short time later with a bottle of wine and two glasses. Kicking off her pumps, she curled up on the bed and watched him open the bottle and fill the glasses.

"Leave a message for Melanie that you're okay, but you won't be coming home tonight."

With a sly smile, she answered, "I never stay the night, Mr. Singleton."

Grabbing the cordless phone off the dresser, he tossed it to her. "Call," he demanded as he turned to leave the room again.

A short while later, he returned with a small tray of cheese, fruit, and crackers. Without saying a word, he picked up the phone and pushed the redial button. As Alexis's voice came on the answering machine, Malcolm disconnected and said, "I think that's the first time you did what I asked without a fight. I could get used to this."

Pushing herself to her knees, she scooted to the edge of the bed and said, "Let's see how long your luck holds out." Unbuttoning her suit jacket, she dropped it the floor and said, "What would you like me to do now?"

Handing her a glass, he said "I'd like you to renegotiate our deal."

"Is that so?" she said with a playful sparkle in her eyes.

"Yes."

"And what would be the new terms of this deal?"

"I'm serious, Alexis."

After several seconds, Alexis erased all signs of a smile and said, "Me too. Let's negotiate."

"No more talk of a temporary relationship. I want to try and make this work between us, and we can't do that if we keep waiting for the end to come."

Alexis took a sip of the wine as a delay tactic. She had already admitted to herself that there was nothing temporary about what she wanted with the man. But to admit it to him would put her in a position she had never wanted to be with anyone: vulnerable. If she agreed, she would be releasing some control, and in doing so, setting herself up for the possibility of a broken heart.

"Alexis?"

"I don't know, Malcolm," she answered honestly.

Sliding the tips of his fingers lightly over her bare arms, he said, "Don't answer from your mind, answer from your heart."

Holding her breath, she decided to jump in with both feet. Clinking his glass, she whispered, "Okay, I accept the new terms of the deal."

Malcolm set his glass on the nightstand and kissed her sweetly on the slips, slowly moving to her ears, down her neckline. He slowly began to unbutton her blouse. Unhooking the last button, he gently removed the blouse from her shoulders and watched it fall from her body to the floor. Never once moving his eyes from hers, he knew that the passion and desire he saw in hers reflected the passion in his own.

Unhooking the clasp on her bra, he let the satin material follow her blouse.

"You are exquisite."

Laying her facedown, he gently rubbed her neck and shoulders before moving his hands to massage to her back.

Alexis moaned in pleasure and felt every muscle in her body unwind. Between the music, the wine, and the man, she was floating on a cloud. Never had a man taken such care with her body. She had been physically satisfied before, but she knew that this experience would touch the very core of her being. Mind, soul, and body.

Malcolm felt the tension leave her body as his hands kneaded, rubbed, and stroked her shoulders and back. They had the whole night ahead of them and he had no intention of rushing. Tracing a sensuous path down her spine, the warmth from her soft skin was intoxicating and he inhaled deeply as he headed for the high of his life. Moving lower, he slowly unzipped her skirt and removed her stockings and lace panties.

Continuing his sensuous massage, he listened to her moans of satisfaction as he moved down her legs, paying each one complete attention. As he rubbed each foot, every ounce of tension and stress evaporated from her body. Completing his rubdown from head to toe, Malcolm began to work his way back up. This time, it wasn't his hands that were his tool of choice. It was his tongue.

Alexis heart constricted in pleasure with every touch his tongue made to her body. Every spot sizzled from the scorching heat radiating throughout. As he worked her into a passionate frenzy, the internal battle in her mind had her stuck between riding out this assault, or putting an end to this torture by grabbing him and making their two bodies one. But as he reached the inside of her thigh, she sighed with contentment and decided to ride out the best foreplay she had ever experienced.

Malcolm turned Alexis over and his darkened eyes seared into hers. Removing his shirt and shorts, he reached in the nightstand drawer and removed a small foil packet. Removing his briefs, he quickly protected himself and laid on top of Alexis. He entered her and the uncontrolled passion caused both of them to moan in erotic pleasure.

Finding their rhythm, everything ceased to exist but the two of them. With each stroke, Alexis felt the stone walls in her heart that she fought her entire life to protect come tumbling down. Passion pounded through her and he matched her eager response, thrust for thrust. Amazed at the magnitude of her desire, Alexis allowed all of him to become a part of all of her. His body. His mind. His soul. As she called his name, her body exploded in a fiery sensation and he soon followed with his own release.

Malcolm gently pressed his lips to hers. Alexis Shaw captured his full attention the moment he laid eyes on her and he wanted to get to know her. But somewhere along the line, the want had turned to need. She was bright, spirited, and capable of giving of herself and her time and Malcolm believed that he had not only gotten to know her body, but he had indeed gotten to know her heart.

As Alexis moaned in pleasure and rested her head against his chest, Malcolm knew no words appropriate for this moment. He listened as her breathing became deep and she fell asleep in his arms. And, in an instant, he knew. This was love.

A few hours later Alexis awoke to the soft glow of candles and the scent of vanilla. Glancing at the clock beside the bed, she saw that it was just after three in the morning. Feeling Malcolm's arm wrapped around her waist, she gently extracted herself from his touch and headed to the bathroom. Quietly shutting the door, she flipped the switch and immediately squinted her eyes as they adjusted to the bright light. Facing the mirror, she turned her head from side to side, studying her reflection. Her makeup was gone and her spiral curls were more like big waves, but other than that, she found nothing out of the ordinary. Leaning closer, she stared at herself with eyes filled with questions. *How could I look the same when I feel so different?*

What she just experienced was the stuff that Hollywood movies were made of. Butterflies in the stomach, an aching need to be with him, total satisfaction in just laying in his arms, and the desire to have this relationship last forever. Could this be love? Was it possible that she spent her entire adult life criticizing those who gave their hearts away, making it her personal mission to spread the news of the hypocrisy of love, for it all to completely shatter when Malcolm Singleton walked into her life?

As these thoughts ran frantically through her head, Alexis turned to the door, suddenly afraid to go back out there. What if life was setting her up? Preparing her to prove her theory right? What better way to show the world that the Alexis Shaw love analysis was completely correct than to let her fall in love with the perfect man, and then have it fall apart, leaving her hurt, bitter and alone. Having no immediate answers, Alexis sat on the toilet. Resting her head in her hands, she contemplated her next move. If she left, could she bear to live without him? If she stayed, could she bear it if it didn't last?

The knock on the door startled her.

"Alexis, honey, are you okay?"

Feeling water fall down her cheek, she stood and rushed back to the mirror. *Oh my God, I'm crying.*

"Alexis, you have three seconds to answer me, or I'm breaking the door down."

Silence.

"One . . ."

Nothing.

"Two . . ."

He heard the lock turn and he took a step back when she opened the door. When he had turned over in the bed to an empty space, he sat up in fear. She had left without saying good-bye. But his body quickly relaxed when he saw her clothes. Seeing the light seep through the bottom of the bathroom door, he lay back down and waited for her to come out. But seconds turned into minutes and he became concerned. He didn't hear the toilet flush and there was no sound of running water. That prompted him to take action.

Now she stood before him, not with a look of power and control, but with vulnerability and fear. Alexis Shaw was scared. And when one was scared, there were only two choices. Fight or flee. Malcolm held his breath for her response. She could either fight to make this work, or run. As the seconds went by, he saw the struggle play across her face. He breathed a sigh of relief when she walked into his arms. Her decision made. She decided to fight.

"Come back to bed, Alexis. It'll be okay. I promise."

Pulling back the covers and blowing out the candles, he eased her down and followed. He understood her fear, not of him, but of what he represented. Wrapping her completely in his embrace, Malcolm provided a silent cocoon of protection, letting her know that whatever she was afraid of, he was here to help her overcome.

The next time Alexis awoke, it was she who was alone

in bed. It was just after ten and she was glad that this was a day off for her. Turning to the empty space beside her, she smiled when she noticed a single rose on the pillow with a note.

Just because . . . Malcolm.

Heading to the bathroom out of necessity, Alexis, glad to see that Malcolm had left a pair of sweats and one his T-shirts, turned on the shower.

Twenty minutes later, she found Malcolm in the kitchen by following the smell of fresh brewed coffee. On her way, she noticed another bedroom, his office, and a gym, complete with a treadmill, weights, and stair stepper. *That explains his rock solid body.* Immediate shivers raced down her spine at that thought.

"Good morning, beautiful." Malcolm said, placing two cups of steaming coffee on the kitchen table. As she stood in the entryway, Malcolm paused and swallowed deliberately to stifle the moan that threatened to escape his lips. In his baggy pants and oversized shirt, her sexiness was impossible to deny. Alexis stared at him with trusting eyes and he knew that she was where she belonged—with him. "I'm not much of a cook, but I did manage scrambled eggs and toast."

Taking a seat, Alexis tasted the eggs and quickly agreed with his assessment of his cooking skills.

"I'm not much of a cook either. That's why I love it when Melanie comes to visit."

"Can she burn?"

"Better than any chef I know."

"Is she a chef?"

Alexis sighed. "No, and that's been our biggest ongoing argument."

"I don't understand." Malcolm said.

Alexis wasn't sure if she was ready to open up her deep family wounds to Malcolm. But if they were going to make this relationship work, she knew she had to be willing to do something she had never done. Open her heart and her life to another man.

"Melanie followed the marching orders of our mother instead of the passion in her heart. With status, wealth, and social standing as the only important thing to her, our mother used everything in her power to manipulate any and all situations to the outcome she wanted." Alexis related some of her childhood experiences where she lived in the shadow of her mother.

"Some could say that she was just spoiling us, making sure we got what we wanted. But it never gave us a chance to see what we could accomplish on our own. The worst part was that she used her power and influence to get us into things that we had no interest in participating in. In her mind, she feared what her friends would think if her children weren't a part of the best this or the best that. The problem was, neither Melanie or myself were interested in serving out roles in bought positions. It was embarrassing to us because we feared that everyone understood how we got what we had."

Realizing she had revealed way more than she ever thought she would, she said, "Back to Melanie. Melanie loved to cook and wanted to go to culinary school, but that wasn't respectable enough for my mother. Her children would chose a more professional career. Lawyer, doctor, anything prestigious. And chef didn't count. A chef didn't have a bunch of letters behind your name, a corner office, and a huge expense account."

Malcolm heard the hurt and anger in her voice and thought about his interview a few weeks ago. He had asked about her family and she refused to provide any information. Now he knew why. They obviously didn't get along.

"In the end, she went to college, majored in business, got an MBA from Harvard, and took a job with Winston Marks. In a few short years, she had the big office, a long title, a secretary, two assistants, and a ton of money."

"I hear a 'but' coming," he said, rising to refill their cups.

"But she's miserable. Now she's been offered the promotion of a lifetime, and she doesn't know if she wants it. That's why she's here instead of New York—trying to get up the courage to do what she really wants to do."

Sipping his coffee, Malcolm asked, "But you're not a doctor or a lawyer. Why did your mother let you off the hook?"

With a sarcastic grin, she said, "She didn't. I let myself off. I left for college and never looked back."

"What about your dad?"

Pausing a moment, Alexis thought about her dad, It had been five years since he died, but the emotions could be as fresh as if it just happened.

"My parents divorced when I was twelve. I only saw him once a month, and he was no match for my mother's demanding ways. My mother came from nothing and my father represented everything she wanted in life. He was a prestigious doctor, had an extremely profitable practice, and was completely in love with my mother. But a strange thing happened on her road to high-class living. My father wanted out. He saw the changes that were happening to my mother and he believed he didn't know her anymore. Tired of the hectic schedules, their fake friends, and the city life, one day he announced that he had purchased a small farmhouse in Virginia and planned to close his practice and move us all there. Needless to say, my mother was livid. Coming from a small, hick town in Tennessee, she had no intentions of leaving New York. In the end, she selfishly chose her lifestyle over my father. She didn't even keep his name. Since the divorce, she's spent the majority of her time proving to the world that without my father, she still deserved the social standing she obtained when she married David Shaw.

Hearing her clear her throat, Malcolm knew that revealing such a personal part of her life was difficult. He doubted if she had ever done it before to another man. Beginning to understand the effects of watching her parent's marriage end, he renewed his commitment to show her the meaning of true love.

"That's what makes your magazine's award so special to me," she said. "It released the doubts that I've harbored over the years that I couldn't succeed on my own. I've committed the last five years to Just For You, and it's paid off."

"Yes, it has," he said, reaching for hand. "You've proven to yourself that you can accomplish your goals on your own."

"That's right," she said, rising and moving to stand in front of him. "I did it."

Wrapping his arms around her waist, he pulled her close and said, "Yes, you did."

Straddling herself across his lap, she reached under his shirt and traced his pleasure points lightly with with the tips of her fingers. Hearing him moan in pleasure she said seductively, "I can think of a few more things I'd like to do."

Reaching underneath her shirt, he cupped her breasts and responded, "Never let it be said that I keep my woman from getting what she wants."

Alexis stuck her key in the door just as the sun was going down. She had spent the entire day in bed with Malcolm and had a sore body to prove it. The only time he left the bedroom was to open the door for the pizza delivery guy. Neither wanted the day to end, but real life called. She had a brunch tomorrow and Malcolm hadn't worked on his latest story in a week. Turning the knob, the door suddenly swung open, pulling her with it.

"What the . . ."

"Get in here, you little skeezer."

She could barely get her key out the door before Celeste and Melanie attacked her with questions and snide remarks.

"Look who decided to come home."

"Is that a glow I see?"

"I've never known you spend the night with a man."

"Alexis has a boyfriend, Alexis has a boyfriend!"

"Oh, grow up," she snapped, heading straight for her bedroom.

Experiencing new feelings with Malcolm, she needed time to herself to sort them out. Slamming the door, she walked into her closet to hang up her suit. Wearing his clothes home, she couldn't fathom the thought of taking them off. She would never admit it to anyone, but she felt comfort and peace inside his clothes. With the faint smell of his scent, she figured that if she couldn't cuddle up with the real thing, the sweat pants and T-shirt would have to do.

Walking back into her bedroom, she sighed in disgust as two pairs of eyes stared at her from her bed. Resigning herself to the fact that she was not going to get a moment of peace until she satisfied their curiosity, Alexis playfully shoved them out of her way. "Move over, at least let me get comfortable."

Propping her pillows up, she leaned back and looked into the expectant faces of her friends. "I ran into Belinda at the mall yesterday."

Melanie and Celeste exchanged confused looks and

Celeste said, "That's nice, but you can tell us about that reunion another time. Right now, we want to hear about the cause of that glow on your skin and that sparkle in your eyes."

"Do you want to hear this or not?" Alexis said.

"Okay, okay," Celeste said, "we're listening."

Alexis rehashed the night, leaving out some of the most intimate details, but nonetheless giving her sister and friend the understanding that something very special had happened between herself and Malcolm.

"From what I can see, Malcolm has been good for you. He may be the one," Celeste said.

"I don't know, it's still new," Alexis said thoughtfully. "I've had milk longer than this relationship."

Ignoring her snide remark, Melanie said, "But you're giving him a chance, and that's more than you've given to any other relationship. And that's good news to me."

"Well, since Alexis shared her good news, I'd like to share some of my own," Celeste said excitedly. "I'm pregnant!"

Alexis and Melanie screamed in delight as the tears began to form in the corners of their eyes. Alexis knew that Kenneth and Celeste had been trying for almost two years. It was truly a miracle.

Rising, Melanie walked to the dresser and fiddled with the various perfume bottles.

"What is it, sis?"

Hesitantly, she said, "If this is a night of confessions, I have some confessions to make of my own." Looking from one to the other, she thought it best to quickly spit it out before she changed her mind. "I slept with Brent the night of the award dinner, quit my job last Friday, sent my engagement ring back to Darius, and enrolled in culinary school."

At that moment the entire world stopped. There was a full two minutes of total silence. Finally, Alexis found

JUST FOR YOU   183

her voice. "Let me get this straight. Did you just say you slept with a man you just met?"

Melanie shook her head slowly in agreement.

"And you quit your job and your fiancé?"

Boldly, she said "Yes . . . and don't forget about culinary school."

"What in the world has gotten into you?" Alexis said.

Staring at her sister, Melanie answered, "You."

"Now this I have got to hear," Celeste said, finally recovering from the announcements. She had only hung around Melanie on her infrequent visits to Atlanta, but she could tell that this type of behavior was way out of the ordinary. It was unheard of for anyone to turn down a job that paid well into the six figures with amazing perks and bonuses. She was not only saying no to a coveted position, she was leaving the firm. And her man. And she said it was all because of Alexis?

"As I watched you pick up that award a few weeks ago, I realized what a pathetic life I live."

"No one would call your life pathetic," Alexis said with quiet assurance.

"Pathetic or not, I was living for everyone but me. I hated it. The funny thing about it is that I always thought you were the dumb one. I just knew you were going to be a failure because you went your own way. But that wasn't the case. You followed your heart, and you succeeded. I decided that night to do the same thing."

"Help me out here, sis," Alexis said, confused. "What does that have to do with you sleeping with Brent?"

"He was cute and I wanted to. So I did."

"And you got that from Alexis?" Celeste asked, finding that concept amusing.

"What I've gotten from Alexis is that you need to live the life you want to live. Do the things you want to do to make yourself happy. And that's what I'm starting to do."

Alexis, not quite ready to let her off the hook, said, "All that time you were telling me to take it slow with Malcolm, let our relationship develop, you went out and slept with someone you just met?"

"I didn't plan it, but after all of you left the hotel, we sat and talked until the hotel staff asked us to leave. The night was so beautiful, that we took a stroll around the grounds of the hotel. Brent was so easy to talk to that I found myself unleashing all the things I've kept bottled inside for the last thirty years. I talked about my career choices, my love choices, and my complete dissatisfaction with the road I was on. And you know what he said?"

Completely captivated by her words, Alexis and Celeste just stared at her.

"Nothing," Melanie said with a sincere smile. "He said absolutely nothing. For the first time in my life, I felt like someone was truly listening to me. Not to tell me what to do. Not to judge me. Not to offer advice. He just listened. And when I was finished, he responded by saying the only thing I was guilty of was trying to make others happy, and if I made myself miserable in the process, then I owed it to myself to finally do what made me happy."

As Melanie grabbed a tissue from the nightstand, she quickly dabbed her watery eyes and continued, "So when he hailed a cab for me and asked to see me again, I realized I didn't want the night to end."

Even though she heard every word her sister said, Alexis still couldn't believe it. Never in a million years would she have thought her sister capable of this. Suddenly, she wondered about Brent and felt a sliver of anger rise in her.

"What kind of man would take advantage of a woman who was obviously in a vulnerable state?"

Thinking back on that amazing night, Melanie said, "Actually, it was just the opposite. Believe it or not, he asked me several times if I was sure. He wanted to continue seeing each other, but I thought it best not to. I knew what I wanted. Just one night."

Alexis thought about Brent's strange tone when he asked about Melanie and said, "I think he really would like to see you again."

Melanie didn't respond.

"All this time you've been telling me to give Malcolm a chance. Take things slow. Let our relationship grow into something more. And here you are, cutting off the chance of developing a relationship with Brent, whom you obviously like."

"You're different. You need to love and be loved. And I think you can find that with Malcolm . . . if you haven't already."

Alexis gave her sister a hug. "I'll support you, regardless of what decisions you make. And you're going to need it when mother hears about this."

Melanie cringed at the confrontation she knew would come. "I know, I'm planning on going back to New York soon to clean out my desk and pack up my stuff."

Celeste, realizing that they were all facing major changes in their lives, wanted to lighten the mood. "I have the goofiest idea."

"Oh, Lord," Alexis said.

"Let's have a pajama party."

"You're right, Celeste," Alexis said sarcastically. "That is goofy."

"It'll be fun," she said, jumping to her feet and picking up the phone. "I'll call Kenneth and let him know

I'm not coming home. Melanie, you pop the popcorn. Alexis, you find me some PJs. It's girl's night out."

Getting into the spirit, they all got into Alexis's bed, and talked, laughed, and planned their future all through the night, just like giddy teenagers. A month ago, Alexis didn't think she would allow herself to engage in something as silly as this, but a month ago she didn't know Malcolm Singleton.

As Celeste and Melanie finally fell off to sleep, Alexis lay awake deep in thought. This was the first time she talked about her future and it included a man. Closing her eyes, she tried to fall asleep. But one thought kept running through her mind. She had opened her heart and her future to Malcolm. And she only hoped she wouldn't live to regret it.

Twelve

Alexis sat in her office humming one of her favorite tunes. It had been several weeks since the first time she spent the night with Malcolm and things could not have been going better. Even her staff had noticed a significant change in their boss. Less controlling, Alexis cut back on some of her input into her other planners' events to spend more time with Malcolm. Knowing she had hired competent, capable associates, it was okay to let them run their own show. They showed their appreciation by booking more events the past two weeks than they had the entire previous month.

Malcolm and Alexis ate leisurely dinners, took strolls through museums, and even took another balloon ride. Celebrating with their country, they shared fireworks on the Fourth of July—and sparks were flying, both in the park and in the bedroom. Malcolm had done what Alexis thought impossible. He had actually gotten her thinking about sharing her life with another person, forever—and to top it all off, the Businesswomen of the Year issue of *Image* was scheduled to hit the newsstand next month.

Checking her watch, she realized she had just a few minutes before Brent was scheduled to meet with her. Putting the finishing touches on their fund-raising plans, the invitations and announcements were slated to go out at the end of this month.

"Alexis, a Mr. Portman is on line three."

"Thanks, Sherry," she said, hitting the line for speaker. "Alexis Shaw . . . hello . . . hello."

Alexis hung up the phone and tapped her pen on her desk. That was the fourth time this week she had taken a call and no one was there. When she questioned Sherry about it, she said she thought all the voices sounded different, but she couldn't be sure. She would now instruct Sherry to get the purpose of the call before she transferred it to her.

Reviewing the invitation choices for the fund-raiser, she wondered if she would be able to refrain from asking Brent about the night he spent with her sister. Knowing Melanie was a grown woman and could take care of her own affairs didn't negate that fact that she was meeting with the man who slept with her the same night he met her.

"Alexis?"

Waving her in, Alexis said, "What is it, Sherry?"

Stepping into the office, Sherry carried a huge floral arrangement filled with exotic flowers whose amazing scents quickly filled the room.

"How beautiful," Alexis said, as Sherry placed the vase on the desk.

"Now this just beats all," Sherry said with a grin.

"What are you talking about?"

"First of all"—she started, playfully putting her hands on her hips and pretending to pout—"I gracefully bow out of my pursuit of Malcolm since he only had eyes for you. Next, I've watched the two of you leave for fancy restaurants that I can't afford on the money I make. Which reminds me, I would like to discuss a raise. Finally, I have to be the one to bring in the biggest flower arrangement I have ever seen in my life. I should have never passed Malcolm off to you."

By the time Sherry finished, Alexis couldn't help but

smile. Her receptionist was the most dramatic person she knew and since she had come onboard, the fun and laughter in this office had elevated several notches.

Picking up the card inside, she opened it and replied, "I do thank you for bowing out gracefully. Your sacrifice is greatly appreciated."

Peering over her shoulder, Sherry asked, "What does it say?"

Putting the card close to her chest, Alexis smiled. "Do you mind?"

Stepping back, Sherry smiled and said, "Okay, okay, I guess I can let you have one private moment."

Reading the card, Alexis smiled weakly and said, "It's personal."

"I bet it is," Melanie joked. "You better thank that man for sending you something so beautiful."

Setting the card aside, she said, "I'll be sure to give him a proper 'thank you' next time we get together."

"Girlfriend, with a man that fine, there should nothing 'proper' about how you thank him."

Alexis faked a laugh and said, "Get back to work. I think I hear a phone ringing."

Alone, Alexis picked up the card and reread it. "Enjoy the good life while you can—very soon you will lose it all."

"I don't want this assignment."

"Excuse me?" Jeremy said, wondering if he needed to get his hearing checked. He had never heard these words uttered from this man in the three years that he'd worked for him.

Malcolm sat in his editor's office doing something he had never done his entire career: turn down a lucrative story. He had built his career, first by taking on any assignment given to him, and then by only taking on stories that were the cream of the crop. And the story that his editor was offering had meat. Had this been two months ago, Malcolm would have accepted without a second thought. But a lot can change in sixty days, and in his life, change came in the form of Alexis Shaw.

"Let me get this straight," Jeremy said. "I'm offering you what could be the story of the year, and you're turning me down? Well, guess what. You work for me, so you don't have the luxury of saying no."

"But this assignment will put me out of town for at least two months."

"And your point?" Jeremy asked. "If you want your ego stroked, then fine. Here I go."

Dramatically clearing his throat, Jeremy said, "Malcolm, you're the best I have and I would never consider putting this story in the hands of anyone but you." Pausing to let the words sink in, he followed sarcastically with, "Is that better?"

Malcolm ignored his attempt at humor and thought about his predicament. He was being offered to cover the race discrimination trial of Endonite Industries. It was the largest class action suit against a manufacturing company in the history of the country. The trial, in Los Angeles, could take up to two months. Searching his memory, Malcolm could not recall a time that he had let the length or location of an assignment determine whether he would take the job or not. But this time it was different. He was different. And he knew why. His time with Alexis had been electrifying. When she wasn't in his arms, she was in his thoughts. Never had he met someone who seemed to be such a perfect fit for him. They enjoyed the same things and seemed to be compatible in just about every area. Whether they were engaged in a heated debate about a current news topic or enjoying the roller coaster at Six Flags, it didn't matter. He just liked being with her. And he couldn't fathom the thought of being apart from her right now. Even for one of the biggest news stories of the year.

Jeremy removed his glasses and said, "I don't recall *asking* you. I make the assignments around here. Endonite's lawyers agreed give you an exclusive interview with the CEO, not just cover the trial. The only reason they did that was because they know you to be a fair reporter."

Standing, Malcolm walked to the window that faced the open area where people worked at a steady pace to produce the number one African American magazine in the country. For so many years, his career had been his life. And when he came to *Image* three years ago, he put that same passion and commitment into the magazine. He worked all hours, traveled the world without complaint, and wrote some of the best stories ever published in the history of the thirty-year-old publication. And if he wanted to turn down one assignment, he should have the right to do so.

"I've never let you down, Jeremy. I've never said no. Of the three years I've been with *Image*, I've been on the road at least half the time. This time I'm saying no."

Jeremy stared at Malcolm with curious eyes. Having been in the publishing business for thirty-five years, he had worked with a lot of writers, and Malcolm was one of the best. Confident, but not egotistical, fair, but not one to mince words, and hardworking, without being obsessive. That's why he was not prepared to hear his superstar tell him no.

Malcolm had always been the one to jump on a hot story, push the envelope, work his stories from every angle, regardless of what he had to do or where he had to go. Jeremy had watched Malcolm's career before he came to *Image*, and was thrilled when Malcolm came onboard to make this his home. He saw a lot of himself in Malcolm, and took it upon himself to nurture Malcolm into becoming the best writer he could be, and then to help him make whatever career moves he wanted to make.

As he looked at Malcolm, he remembered the time he was at the same place in his career as Malcolm was today. He had written award-winning stories, traveled the world many times over, and had earned the respect of peers and the public. But he also remembered when he tired of chasing the story and looked for a more slower, steady pace. It happened when he met Patricia. The woman who became the love of his life, the mother of his three children, and the one who would share that condo in Florida with him in five years after he retired. Taking a closer look at Malcolm, he wondered if they were more alike that he could have ever thought.

"What's her name?"

Turning away from the window, Malcolm attempted to pretend he had no idea what he was talking about.

"If that's supposed to be a look of confusion at my question, it's not working," Jeremy said.

Malcolm remained silent. Thinking of someone else when considering an assignment was new to him. He wasn't sure if he was ready to share that with anyone, especially his boss.

"Susan has narrowed it down. One, Alexis Shaw, the winner of our award. Two, Denise Edwards from Advertising, and three, Arlene Perez. No one's quite sure who she is. We're leaning toward eliminating Denise, knowing that it didn't work out the first time."

Seeing Malcolm's irritation grow by the grimace forming on his face, he knew he had hit a nerve. "Something about voicemail being down and a goofy grin on your face."

Malcolm tried to keep his expression unchanged,

even though on the inside, he was planning to have a little talk with his efficient assistant.

"Now, for my money, I'd go with Ms. Shaw. Business owner, beautiful, and from my brief encounter with her at the awards ceremony, I think she is someone any man would love to get to know. Not to mention that moment the two of you had on stage. Now Arlene, I'll have to get my research department on that one."

"Susan needs to learn how to keep her thoughts to herself," Malcolm mumbled.

"Are you kidding? That's how I keep up with what's going on around here."

Malcolm erased all signs of humor and said, "I've never said no, and I think you should cut me some slack on this one."

Realizing he wasn't going to get any more information out of him, he said, "You're scheduled to leave in three weeks."

"But," Malcolm started.

Raising his hand to cut him off, Jeremy continued, "If in two weeks you still want to pass, I'll give it Morgan. He's been itching for a cover assignment."

Malcolm smiled at the tactic. Peter Morgan had been a thorn in Malcolm's side from the first day he came through *Image*'s door. Always working to grab the coveted cover story, he usually fell short. A good, solid writer, he had been biding his time at *Image* for five years, waiting for his chance to become the top person at the magazine. But that plan was put on hold when Malcolm came on the scene. There was no love lost between the two and Jeremy knew that offering this story to him if Malcolm turned him down would ensure that Malcolm would think long and hard before passing on his assignment. The stakes just got higher.

Malcolm opened the door without saying a word.

"Talk to you in two weeks."

Malcolm slammed the door and failed to hear the laughter coming from his editor.

"Everything you've planned is fantastic. We usually do a dinner and dance. But the casino night and silent auction will add another dimension to the event."

"Another dimension?" Alexis said with a sly grin. "You know as well as I do that 'another dimension' is not what we're adding. What we're adding is another way to get people to donate to this worthy cause. With the venue being comped, the caterer charging us cost for the food, and Just For You owning the casino equipment, Men of Standard should walk away with enough money to add that computer lab you so desperately need, and send two more students to college."

Brent leaned back in his chair and said, "Sounds like you've done your homework."

"You sound surprised."

"To be honest, when I heard you were going to plan this fund-raiser for us, I thought you would find a cheap place, order some dry chicken, and charge outrageous ticket prices so that you could justify finding some way to take payment for your services. I have to say I owe you an apology."

"I like what your organization does. I'm impressed with the services and programs you provide for young men. I know how important fundraising can be to sustain and grow your programs. And to be honest with you, Mr. Fund-raising Chairperson, your work in that area has been shoddy."

Brent smiled. "Malcolm said you pulled no punches."

Leaning forward, Alexis raised a brow, "What's the most you've ever pulled in from one of your dinner dances?"

"We've had about two hundred people attend, and after expenses, we've cleared about ten thousand dollars."

Pulling the samples for the invitations and tickets, Alexis slid them across the desk and said, "That's pocket change."

"I know. I'm a stockbrocker. The investment company I work for makes that every millisecond. It's just that Atlanta is full of worthy causes, so the donation dollars are spread thin."

"That was before me."

"And what makes you so special?"

"Sylvia's mansion can hold up to three hundred people in the main ballroom. Five hundred, if we utilize other rooms and the grounds. With the reduced expenses and a sold out event, that will more than double your funds. Add in the money from the silent auction and casino play, and that should cover the computer lab and the scholarship fund."

Not wanting to burst her bubble, Brent looked at the invitations, picked his favorite, and said, "Our organization is only a few years old and our mailing list has about one thousand names on it. Most of those people, although supportive of the cause, have yet to dig into their bank accounts to make a significant monetary contribution. We'll be lucky, and I'll be satisfied, if we fill half of that mansion."

Glancing at the selection, Alexis nodded in approval and said, "Luck has nothing to do with it. It's all about hard work. Celeste works in PR and she's comping some services to help us get as much coverage as possible.

Brent said, "Now I know why Malcolm is so taken with you."

"Tell me more," she said playfully.

Just then, the intercom on Alexis's desk buzzed.

Rising, Brent smiled, "Saved by the bell."

"Yes, Sherry?"

"Your next appointment is here."

"Thanks, I'm finishing up."

As their meeting came to a close, Alexis thought about Melanie. Forcing herself to mind her own business, Alexis said, "The invitations will be ready next week. You said you have volunteers to stuff envelopes?"

"Yes, we have a group of men who want to help out with the event as much as possible. Let me know what day you want to mail them out."

Gathering up her notes, she closed the file and said, "I'll touch base with you next week."

Brent didn't move and Alexis said hopefully, "Was there something else?'

When Brent and Melanie spent the night together, she said she was looking to have some fun and he said he could handle it. But that one night stand had haunted him. With each passing day, it became much more difficult not to contact her. She made it painfully clear that night what she was wanted and it wouldn't be fair of him to try to make it any more than that. But he was having second thoughts about that decision.

"Did Melanie tell you what happened between us?"

Relieved that Brent had opened the door, Alexis marched right in.

"Yes, and the only thing I want to say is that my sister is not that easy. You caught her in a rare moment."

"I never thought your sister was easy. We spent quality time getting to know each other before we decided to . . ."

Holding up her hand, she interrupted, "No need to give details."

"All I'm saying is that I enjoyed the time I spent with her." Pausing, he said, "I should have never agreed to her stupid deal."

Alexis looked intrigued, "You made a deal with her?"

"Yes, the deal was one night. No more, no less." Thinking back to that night, he cynically laughed, "Can you believe she actually made us shake on it?"

Alexis cleared her throat, thinking she knew where Melanie got that idea from. "Why are you telling me this, Brent?"

"Because she told me that night that she might stay in Atlanta, and well, I'd like to see her again."

Hearing the sincerity in his voice, she said, "I'll see what I can do."

As Alexis walked Brent out, the woman sitting in the lobby raised the magazine over her face to cover her identity. Just her luck to schedule an appointment the same day Brent Harrison was here. But she quickly breathed a sigh of relief when the elevator doors closed and he was out of sight.

"Good afternoon, I'm Alexis Shaw."

Standing, the woman outstretched her hand, "Denise Edwards." About the same height, that's where the similarities ended. With her short haircut, and slightly heavier frame, Denise studied Alexis and wondered what Malcolm saw in her. Hiding her discontent, Denise smiled politely.

"I understand you're interested in planning a surprise party?" Alexis asked.

"Yes, I am."

"Let's go to my office and we can discuss if my services fit your needs."

As Alexis shut the door, Denise saw the flowers and gave a sly smile. "Must be nice to have someone love you that much."

Alexis just smiled and pulled out her notepad. "Let's talk about your party."

* * *

After her meeting with Denise, Alexis picked up the flowers and headed out. Stopping at Sherry's desk, she said, "I'm going out for the afternoon. I'll see you tomorrow."

In the lobby, she dropped the flowers in the trash. Pulling out of the parking lot, she pulled out her cell phone and called Melanie, making plans to meet at her favorite restaurant. Enjoying a late, leisurely lunch, they decided to treated themselves to a pampering session at Filani's Day Spa. An exfoliating facial, a hot rocks massage, and a manicure and pedicure had left them in total laziness. Not ready to call it a day, they decided to go to Saks and picked out new clothes for Melanie. As they moved through the various departments, Alexis was surprised to see the vibrant pinks, oranges, and yellows her sister chose.

As they browsed through the latest sportswear fashions, Alexis thought this would be a good time to bring up Brent. Being sure to watch her sister's reaction, she said, "Brent came to the office today."

Refusing to make eye contact, Melanie said, "And . . ."

"And he asked me to talk to you."

Flipping through a rack of summer dresses, Melanie said, "About?"

"Seeing you again."

"Why?"

Stepping between her sister and the rack of clothes, Alexis said, "Will you cut it out with the one word answers?"

"No." Stepping around her, Melanie moved to a rack of blouses.

"Melanie, I'll butt out if you want me to."

Staring her sister directly in the eye, Melanie answered, "I want you to butt out."

"Okay, so I just lied. What could be the harm in seeing him again?"

Selecting three blouses for the dressing room, Melanie said, "I'm just starting to find myself, I don't need to get involved with another man right now."

Looking at her three selections, Alexis shook her head in the negative at two of them and put them back on the rack.

"He's talking dinner, maybe a play . . . not marriage."

Melanie would never admit it to Alexis, but she had been unable to get Brent Harrison off her mind since that fateful night. Feeling a sense of freedom she had never felt before, she was uninhibited that night as their physical attraction to each other was completely satisfied. When she awoke early the next morning, she thought she would feel embarrassed or humiliated, but instead she felt completely liberated. Quietly, she got dressed and let herself out of the suite. That was the last time she saw him. But she wouldn't deny that despite their agreement, she had thought of calling him on several occasions. "I'll think about it."

Her statement garnered a smile from her sister as they made their way to the dressing room.

A couple of hours later, they entered the condo building, laughing and talking about their day. This outing, on top of the past couple of weeks, had done wonderful things for their relationship. They had spent their adult lives not only separated geographically, but professionally. Alexis always felt Melanie had sold out to their mother and Melanie thought Alexis was too frivolous and carefree, never giving much thought to the future. But the past few weeks that they'd spent together had allowed them to have a better understanding of each other.

Melanie was suffocating with her life in New York, and Alexis was finally turning her attention from her business and making room for other things. And other people. Namely Malcolm Singleton.

"Isn't this a sight. Both my daughters goofing off on a Monday afternoon."

Both women froze and stared at the approaching figure. Alexis blinked twice, hoping that this was a cruel joke. There was no way on this beautiful southern afternoon, after enjoying lunch at one of the best restaurants in the city and relaxing at the spa, that Melanie and Alexis Shaw would come face to face with their mother.

"I called your office, Alexis, and they said that you had taken the afternoon off. I've been waiting since two thirty. I thought about going back to the hotel, but I didn't want to miss you."

Dressed in white linen pants and matching top with her hair pulled into a tight bun, her flawless makeup and petite body portrayed a look that was regal and majestic.

Melanie spoke first, "Mother, what are you doing here?"

Beverly Jefferson glanced from one to the other and folded her arms across her chest. "You say that as if I'm not welcome. I would expect that from Alexis, but not from you."

Waiting for Melanie to defend her, Alexis was not surprised when she didn't. Believing they had made some headway in their relationship over the past weeks, Alexis hid her disappointment and said, "I'm going to get my mail."

As she headed off, Melanie glared at her mother. "Was that really necessary? You treat her as if she's beneath you. No wonder she doesn't want to have anything to do with you."

Beverly stood stoic before her daughter with the only indication her mother even heard her words being the slight roll of her eyes.

"I'm not here to discuss Alexis. I came to Atlanta to take you back to New York."

Melanie laughed, "Take me back to New York? What do I look like? A twelve year old? If I decide to go back to New York, I'll go when I'm good and ready."

Appalled at the tone her daughter was taking with her, Beverly gasped. "Melanie Angelique Shaw. I have no idea what has gotten into you, but it better get out . . . and fast. I've heard about this nonsense of you quitting your job, but you'll be glad to know that Constance Lanier, your CEO's wife, is in my Pilates class. It's been explained that you were just going through a little phase and that you'll be back at work the first of the month."

Appalled at her unwelcome interference in her life, Melanie said, "I'll do no such thing. And you had no right to involve yourself in my business affairs."

"Involve myself," Beverly cryptically laughed. "Melanie, darling, I have always been involved in your affairs. In elementary school, how do you think you were chosen to be the captain of the hall monitors? When you were in junior high, you were smart, but do you think you would have gotten into those advanced classes without my help? And senior class president in high school? Why do you think the principal worked so hard to steer votes to you? And your job? You really think you got a management position right out of college on your own? Lawrence and Constance Lanier have been tennis buddies of mine for years."

Melanie stared at her mother as the tears welled up in the corners of her eyes.

Alexis returned, and at look of raw pain and anger on her sister's face, said, "Melanie? Is everything alright?"

Without saying a word, Melanie walked to the elevators and stepped in when the doors opened.

"What did you say to her?" Alexis demanded. Used to her mother's antics, she was strong enough not to let anything her mother said get to her. But Melanie was different. While Alexis believed she had become stronger since coming to Atlanta, she wasn't completely immune to the power of her mother to emotionally affect her.

Calmly taking her sun shades out of her purse, Beverly put them on and said, "I've done so much for both of you and this is the thanks I get."

"When are you going to realize that we are adults and we don't need you?" Alexis asked.

Giving a slight smirk, Beverly said, "How wrong you both are. Both of you need me more than you know." Turning to leave, she glanced over her shoulder and said flippantly, "Tell Melanie I'm staying at the Ritz, room 843. When she's ready to end this nonsense, she can call me."

Alexis entered the condo and called out for her sister. If that women weren't her mother, she would have cussed her butt out in three different languages.

Finding Melanie in the kitchen, she stopped short when she noticed the bottle of vodka.

Surpressing a laugh, Alexis said, "And what are you going to do with that? You don't even know what to mix with it."

Getting a shot glass out of the cabinet, she said, "I'm drinking it straight."

"Yea, right," Alexis said, taking the bottle out of her hand. "That woman can drive you out of New York, she can drive you out of your job, but she will not drive you to drink."

Grabbing the bottle back, Melanie sat down at the table and poured herself a shot. Just staring at it, she said, "Last month when you picked up that award, that was proof that you were good enough. That you did something on your own. Something that didn't require our family's money or name. I thought I had done the same thing. But it was all a lie. My education, my job, my ex-fiancé. It was all carefully crafted by mommie dearest. Well if I ever had any doubt about my decision to quit my job, my fiancé, and my life in New York, it's gone now." Raising her glass as a toast to herself, she said "Atlanta Culinary Institute, here I come." She threw her head back as she downed the shot and Alexis watched as her eyes watered and her faced turned a deep red. Jumping out of her chair Melanie frantically paced the kitchen, arms flailing.

Alexis couldn't hold her laughter.

"Www . . . www . . . w-h-h-y-y did you let me do that?" Melanie said.

Grabbing the bottle off the table, she screwed on the top and put it back in the cabinet.

"Some things you just have to learn for yourself."

Finally regaining some sense of normalcy, Melanie grimaced and said, "Don't ever let me do that again."

"Don't worry." Growing serious, Alexis said, "Don't let her get to you. She's old, mean, and spiteful. And she'll be back in New York soon enough."

Resting her head in her hands, Melanie contemplated her sister's words. "That's easy for you to say. You severed the ties years ago. But me? I worked hard to make her proud. Getting good grades, going to the college she chose, and moving up the corporate ladder. But now I realize that it all came with a price . . . my happiness."

"She's not going to let you go without a fight," Alexis said sadly. "You're all she has left."

"She'll have no choice."

For a moment, they just looked at each other, both

wondering if Melanie had the guts to go through with her plan.

"I'm meeting Malcolm later, but if you want me to stay, I can. We can talk."

"No, no, I'll be all right. You go ahead and have a good time."

"Okay, but call me on my cell if you need me."

Giving her sister a hug, she said, "You really look happy, Alexis."

"It's only been a few weeks."

"Actually it's been over a month."

"A week, a month, it's still no time."

"But hasn't it been the best month of your life? I know it's been mine."

Reflecting on how important Malcolm had become to her, Alexis had to admit that she had never been happier in her life.

An hour later, she pulled out of her parking lot, oblivious to the sedan two cars back.

Thirteen

As they waited for their food to arrive, Alexis reached in her purse. "I got a flower delivery today."

Arching his brow, Malcolm playfully asked, "Should I be jealous?

"Read the card."

"Is this some kind of sick joke?" he asked as he scanned the words, annoyance evident in his voice.

Alexis told Malcolm about the hang-ups at work and that Melanie said she had answered the phone a few times at home, but no one was there.

"I'll hold on to the card. I'll check with the florist, see if they remember anything about the order."

Feeling slightly better, Alexis said, "Thanks, Malcolm."

"Now isn't this a cozy scene?"

Alexis and Malcolm turned to the voice and neither could believe it.

"Denise Edwards?" Alexis asked.

Hearing her speak her name, Malcolm turned to Alexis. "You know her?"

Confused at the fact that he seemed to know her as well, Alexis answered, "She was thinking of planning a surprise party for her boyfriend and came to see me today."

Enraged that it appeared that Denise was up to her

old tricks again, Malcolm said, "What game are you playing now?"

Alexis glanced from one to the other and realized there was something between Malcolm and Denise. Something bad.

The sweet smile that Denise wore when she stepped to their table disappeared and her expression became unreadable. "No games, Malcolm. I was just having dinner, saw the two of you, and thought I would come over and say hello."

"Well, you've said it. Now you can leave."

Turning her attention to Alexis, she said, "He can be so demanding, can't he? That's one of the things I like about him. Makes for great sex between us."

Alexis was speechless as this woman stood before her admitting that she had slept with Malcolm after sitting in her office for an hour today.

"It felt good to be in your arms a few weeks ago, Malcolm. Maybe we can get together again soon."

"That's enough, Denise," Malcolm warned.

Staring at Malcolm for several seconds, she suddenly broke into a sugary smile and said, "I've taken up enough of your time. Enjoy the rest of your evening."

Malcolm watched her walk out of the restaurant alone and wondered if she was really here having dinner as she claimed.

"You want to fill in the gaps of what she was talking about? I got the part about you sleeping together, but I'm a little fuzzy on the 'in your arms a few weeks ago' thing."

Malcolm knew her stab at humor was a cover for the anger that was bubbling right beneath the surface.

"She's someone I used to know."

"I got that much."

"She was a long time ago, and she was referring to a dance. We had one dance at the awards dinner."

Alexis remembered seeing Malcolm on the dance floor with another woman, but hadn't recognized her.

Malcolm gave her the abbreviated version of their relationship and ended by telling her that their dance was the first and last contact he'd had with her in years and he had no idea why she came to see Alexis or stopped at their table tonight. Then he thought about Denise showing up at Alexis's office on the same day she got the flower delivery. Was it just a coincidence?

They managed to salvage their dinner, and by the time they were served dessert, the mood had almost returned to normal.

Not wanting to delay having this conversation any longer, he said, "I might have to leave town on assignment for a couple of months." He had wrestled with this decision for the past few weeks and was torn. The woman sitting in front of him had become an important part of his life and he couldn't imagine being away from her for any extended period of time. But Endonite's CEO would only talk to him, and he owed it to the magazine. Coming back on weekends wouldn't help because of her limited time due to her events.

Watching her take a sip of coffee, Malcolm wondered if she heard him.

"Alexis?"

Wanting to mask her feeling of disappointment that he would be leaving, she said, "Give me a call when you get back. Maybe we can hook up."

"Is that all you have to say?" he asked.

"Let's face it, Malcolm, it was fun while it lasted, but life calls. You have your career and I have my business. Those things will always come first."

"No wonder your relationships never last."

"Excuse me?"

"You are always looking for a way out," he said, not

fooled by her nonchalant attitude. "I said I had an assignment, I didn't say I wanted us to end."

"But there will be more assignments. It will be a month here, three months there, you'll spend more time out of town than you will in town. And don't say it's not true. Before my interview, you were gone for three weeks. So don't tell me it won't happen again."

"It won't happen again," he said.

"I'm not in the mood for games, Malcolm."

"I said it won't happen again," he repeated.

"The only way you can make a statement like that would be to quit the magazine and we know that's not happening anytime soon."

"I quit today."

Alexis stared at him, waiting for him to crack a smile and say it is was all a joke. Not that she wanted him to give up his career, but if that was the case, it was the most unselfish act he could have committed. Not sure what to say, she asked. "Why did you do that?"

Understanding Alexis's fear of commitment, he wasn't sure if she was ready to hear that he loved her and wanted to change the focus of his life from career to family. He had come to Atlanta searching. Searching for a home, a sense of stability, a sense of peace. And he found that—not in his work, but in her.

When he talked to Jeremy today, his editor didn't seem surprised. Of course he tried to talk him out of it, but knew that Malcolm's mind was made up. Malcolm would still freelance, but he would finally be able to devote some serious time to writing the novel that sat unfinished on his computer. He had already contacted an agent and had some serious interest from publishers.

"I want to take a stab at writing a novel."

"Oh," Alexis said, somewhat disappointed in his answer. She didn't realize until that moment how much she wanted him to say it was because he loved her and couldn't stand the thought of being apart from her.

Watching the emotions play across her face, he added, "And to spend more time with the one who has come to be the most important person in my life."

Her mouth widened into a smile, and she said, "That's better, Mr. Singleton. Much better."

Melanie sat in the living room making a list of the things she wanted to bring back to Atlanta and the items she would put in storage or sell. Just after nine, she was surprised when the doorbell rang. Looking through the peephole, she sighed and leaned her head against the door. Was she up to this tonight? She knew it would happen sooner or later, just not this soon. Deciding that she was through running, she decided to deal with this situation right now.

Opening the door, she said, "What are you doing here?"

"Hello to you too, Melanie."

"Hello, Darius."

Standing, just staring at each other, he said, "Can I at least come in?"

Stepping aside, she shut the door and led him into the living room.

"You cut your hair," he said, taking a seat on the sofa.

Melanie remained silent and he shifted uncomfortably.

"What's going on with you, Melanie?

"Didn't you get my message?"

"What I got was a voicemail from my fiancé breaking off our engagement and a FedEx package with a ring in it. Regardless of what's going on with us, I think I deserve better than that."

Melanie realized he was right. Her life crisis didn't

give her the right to treat people badly, even if it was deserved. "I'm sorry, Darius. I'm trying to handle this the best way I know how."

"That's what I don't get. What are you trying to handle? You get the job offer of a lifetime, a man who wants to marry you, and friends and family who miss you."

"I wasn't happy, Darius."

Reaching in his pocket, he pulled out the flawless three-carat square cut diamond in the platinum setting and held it out to her. "Come back where you belong, Melanie. Back to your life in New York."

Melanie stared at the man who had meant everything to her, yet he had no idea who she was. "Did you not hear what I just said? I said I wasn't happy."

Dropping the ring on the coffee table, Darius clasped his hands in frustration. "I don't get it, Melanie. Most women would kill for the life that you have. Your job, your money . . ."

"My man," she finished for him.

Losing all patience at her sarcastic tone, he said, "Yes, Melanie, your man. There is a city full of women who would think twice—probably three times—before they tossed me aside. And to be quite honest with you, I have some open invitations I'd be happy to accept if you don't come to your senses."

Melanie knew there was no exaggeration in his statement. He was considered one of the most eligible bachelors in New York. Rich, powerful, and sinfully handsome, she had no doubt that some women would think long and hard before they let him go. But not once since he had entered this house did he say he loved her. And that spoke volumes about their relationship. "Is that why you're here Darius? To get the green light to go on with your life . . . with someone else?"

"Not if you end this nonsense. Your mother said the job offer was still on the table and if you come back to New York, we can pick up where we left off."

At the mention of her mother, Melanie felt her blood pressure rise. "And where did we leave off? The latest company event, the next charity ball, the next country club social? Our relationship was one big business deal. Not once have you asked me what I needed or what I wanted. The woman you were suppose to marry just told you she wasn't happy, and you didn't even bother to ask why." Pausing to catch her breath, she continued, "I want out."

Standing, he said, "I've tried to be patient with you while you go through this juvenile phase of 'finding yourself,' but enough is enough. If you want out, you better understand that I don't believe in second chances, Melanie. If I walk out this door, that's it."

Standing, Melanie said, "Good-bye, Darius."

Giving a cynical laugh, he said, "I'm staying at the Ritz tonight, but I'm leaving in the morning. If you change your mind, you can reach me on my cell. But if you don't, keep the ring. I wouldn't want to give my wife a used one."

After he left, Melanie sat staring at the ring. Seconds turned into minutes, and minutes into an hour. Did she really know what she was doing? Moving to Atlanta, becoming a chef. Was that really what she wanted? Or was she just going through a rebellion period late in life, living to regret it once it passed? Contemplating the impact of her decision, she picked up the phone and dialed.

Malcolm dropped his keys on the living room table and offered Alexis something to drink. She had been quiet most of the evening and he wondered if Denise's surprise visit unsettled her. He thought the Denise situation was over years ago, but suddenly she was back, showing up in his life at the most unexpected times. He considered going to her office tomorrow and confronting her. The last thing he needed, as his relationship with Alexis developed, was a pain in the butt ex-girlfriend upsetting her.

"I'm sorry about Denise. She was a long time ago and I don't know what possessed her to come over to our table tonight."

Not getting a reaction, Malcolm said, "Alexis, did you hear me?"

Looking up, Alexis focused her attention on Malcolm and realized she hadn't heard a word he said. "I'm sorry. What did you say?"

Moving to sit beside her, Malcolm rubbed her shoulders and said, "You seem to be preoccupied. At first I thought it may have been because of Denise, but now that I think about it, you've been this way all night. Are you thinking about the flowers and the hang-ups?"

This man had penetrated her heart, her soul, and her spirit, and she knew she had found someone that she wanted to fully commit to without fear. He had proven to her that she could trust him and she knew that he was the one for her.

"It's been a very trying day."

"What else happened?" he asked, concern etched across his face.

"My mother showed up announced at my condo."

"Did she say or do something to upset you?"

"Did she?" Alexis said sarcastically. Thinking back over her teenage years, she said thoughtfully, "I wish I knew why she hates me so much."

Hearing the pain in her voice, Malcolm reassured her. "I'm sure she doesn't hate you."

"You don't know my mother. She hates anything or anyone who doesn't bow to her every command."

"Why is she here?"

"Can you believe she declared that she had arrived to take Melanie back to New York? Talking to her like she was a child."

Pulling her into his arms, he said, "If your mother doesn't want to be a part of her daughter's life, then that's her loss. You can't take responsibility for that."

"It was because of her so-called friends. All their children were Ivy League, Rhodes scholars, doctors, lawyers—anything that had prestige and honor written all over it. To her, I was one big disappointment."

Kissing her tenderly on the forehead, he said with confidence, "That's just to her. To the rest of the world, you're just fine. You've got a thriving business and a wonderful man who loves you." The words came out before he could stop them. And he was glad.

He felt her body go stiff and he waited for her reaction.

"What did you say?"

Malcolm looked in her eyes and knew it was time to speak what was in his heart. "You are the best thing that has ever happened to me and I can't imagine how I survived thirty-four years without you. You have touched me in a place no other person has even come close to. I love you, Alexis."

Kissing her with unbridled passion, Malcolm felt lighter now that he had set free the love that had been harbored in his heart. As they stood, he bent down and picked her up in his arms. At the romantic gesture Alexis smiled. But a few moment later, as he led her to the bedroom, her smile turned into a soft giggle.

"What is it?" he asked.

Not answering, Alexis tried to control herself. "I'm

sorry, Malcolm," she said trying to contain her amusement.

"Now you're really hurting my ego."

"I'm really sorry. It's nothing."

As they made their way down the hallway, Alexis suddenly broke into a laugh.

"Okay, that's it Ms. Shaw," he said, opening the bedroom door with his feet. "You're throwing a monkey wrench in my seduction thing I have going here. What is so funny?"

"I was just thinking what an idiot I've been."

Plopping her unceremoniously on the bed, Malcolm smiled. "Now, this I've got to hear."

"I've spent my entire adult life declaring the complete absurdity of falling in love. Do you know how many times I've gotten a call at work from women asking me to plan their weddings? After hanging up, I would think about the waste of creative energy, valuable time, and hard-earned money this poor woman was about to experience. I've preached to my friends, irritated my sister, and been an all around pain in the butt to anyone who declared themselves in love. Even when I dressed up for those six weddings, I tried to be supportive, but underneath, I was calculating how long I thought each relationship would last. And here I am, with a man I couldn't stand the moment I met him, in his house, in his bed, and in his heart. My friends will make me eat a huge helping of crow."

Joining her on the bed, he tipped her chin up to look him directly in the eyes. "What are you saying, Alexis?"

With all traces of amusement gone, she said, "I'm saying I love you."

"Come here, beautiful," he said, reaching behind her shirt and unzipping it. "You've just made me the happiest man on earth. And if anyone gives you a hard

...me about being in love, you tell them to see me. Even know a woman has a right to change her mind."

Later that evening, totally spent from the heights of passion they had reached, Alexis lay in Malcolm's arms contentment raining through her. Gently running her fingers up and down his arm, she finally understood love. It was about acceptance. Alexis grew up believing her parents loved each other, but when it was all said and done, they couldn't accept each other, and her father left. Alexis's mother claimed she did everything for her children because she loved them, but the moment Alexis stepped outside of the boundaries her mother set, she snatched that love away. She refused to accept Alexis for the person she was.

But Malcolm was different. With her bossy ways, demanding job, and opinionated manners, he accepted her. He never asked her to change and he never forced his opinions or his expectations on her. He simply loved her. Snuggling closer, Alexis moaned in contentment.

"Malcolm?"

"Uu-umm-m," he answered, not opening his eyes as he dozed off to sleep.

"You're right. My life is perfect. And it doesn't matter whether Beverly Jefferson approves of it or not. If she doesn't want to be a part of my life, that's my mother's problem, not mine."

Malcolm opened his eyes when he heard that name. Did she just say that Beverly Jefferson was her mother? Swallowing deliberately, he grimaced at the revelation just handed to him. For a moment, he hoped that he could be wrong. But he quickly realized that was impossible.

Just in case his memory wasn't what it used to be, he would check with Susan first thing in the morning. Hoping against all odds that he was wrong, he won-

dered what he would do if it was true. How would the
woman lying beside him feel if she knew that Beverly
Jefferson pushed for Alexis to win that award and made
a fifty-thousand-dollar contribution to the McKnight
Foundation in the process?

Fourteen

Melanie heard the doorbell for the second time that evening. Checking the peephole, she closed her eyes and sighed. *What am I doing?*

After the scene with her mother earlier and with Darius tonight, she wanted to talk to someone, get these feelings off her chest, and he was the first person to come to her mind. And before she could change her mind, she whipped out the business card he gave her with his home number on the back and called. He said he would come right over, and here he was.

Unlocking the door, she stepped aside and watched him enter. Amazingly handsome in black jeans and a button-down shirt, she drank him in, quenching a thirst she didn't know she had. "Thanks for coming."

Giving her a sexy grin, he pulled his left hand from behind his back and said, "These are for you."

Seeing the bouquet of flowers, Melanie smiled. "Thanks, Brent."

Never having a one night stand in her life, she worried what she should say or how she should act, but now that he was here, she was surprised that calmness prevailed.

"I was surprised to get your call, Melanie. Glad. But surprised." Taking a seat on the sofa, he watched as she sat in the chair opposite him. Dressed for a night at home in sweat shorts and a tank top, Brent remembered their night together and realized he knew every part of the body beneath her clothes.

"The night of the award's ceremony . . . before we . . . u-u-m-m . . . you know."

Seeing that she was a little embarrassed and nervous, Brent gave her a reassuring smile and said, "I know."

"Anyway, you really listened to me and I know this may sound weird, but I really needed someone to talk to tonight and I thought of you."

"I'm glad. Because to be honest, Melanie, I've been thinking of you. I don't know why I agreed to that stupid deal, but I'd like to renege."

Knowing she was just beginning to get to know herself, Melanie had no intentions of jumping into another relationship, no matter how much she liked the guy. And she really liked Brent Harrison. "I just got out of a relationship. I don't think I'm ready to get involved with anyone right now."

"You said you wanted someone to talk to and here I am. Why don't we just start with that, and see what develops."

"Now that's a deal I can live with."

Malcolm stepped into his office the next morning with a fierce determination to find out the situation with Beverly Jefferson and the selection process. He knew it would crush Alexis if she realized that her mother's contribution to the McKnight Foundation influenced the selection committee's final decision. Searching through his files, he needed to figure out when the contribution came through in relation to the selection process—and who knew about it.

"What's going on in here?" Susan asked, standing in the door, watching Malcolm flip through files like a madman. "What are you looking for?"

"I can't find my file on the Businesswoman of the Year selection process." Throwing papers to the side, he slammed his file cabinet shut and cursed in frustration.

Noticing a few people pausing in the hall at all the commotion, Susan stepped inside and shut the door.

"Do you want to tell me what's going on?"

Malcolm sat down and ran his hand over his face. "You coordinated the selection process for the awards. I need to have a look at your files."

"No problem, but is anything wrong?"

"Let's hope not."

An hour later, Malcolm sat at his desk trying to piece together the information before him. The magazine ran full-page ads three consecutive months before the selections were made to solicit nominations for the awards. The nomination letter for Alexis came from Celeste Daniels. The selection committee compiled statistical information on the company and narrowed the candidates down to ten finalists in each category. At this point, the committee contacted clients, customers, and business associates to solicit information and feedback on the finalist. In addition, a statement from each nominee was also considered.

The selection committee was made up of a cross section of people in the McKnight Publishing family, which included representatives from the McKnight Foundation, the recipient of the fifty-thousand-dollar contribution. Could it be possible that their votes were skewed by the fact that the same woman who made the contribution also had a daughter as a finalist for Businesswoman of the Year? Malcolm prayed that it was all a coincidence. But he knew there was only one way to find out. If anyone could shed light this situation, it would be the three people who were on the Board of the Foundation and also on the selection committee. Picking up the phone, he called their New York office.

Malcolm slammed the receiver into the phone and wondered what he was going to do next. Bob Foster, James Billingsly, and Constance Wright would only say that they got strong support from Alice Milestone and Beverly Jefferson for Just For You, and days before the vote, a letter came pledging the contribution to the foundation. There was no solid proof that Alexis only got that award because of her mother's influence, but there was also strong circumstantial evidence to show that the results may have been skewed. Not knowing much more than he knew when he arrived this morning, the million dollar question remained whether he should tell Alexis.

Alexis arrived at Just For You looking radiant in burgundy and black. She was just in time to meet with Hannah Witherspoon. Throwing a birthday bash for her husband who was from New Orleans, she wanted a Mardi Gras theme, even though it was the middle of summer. The event would be spectacular, complete with a miniparade and funeral marching bands.

Entering her office, her eyes zoomed in on a small gold box in the center of her desk. Eyeing it suspiciously, she buzzed Melanie.

"It was delivered to the lobby desk this morning. It had your name on it, so I just set it on your desk. Probably a fabulous gift from Malcolm."

Disconnecting the call, Alexis stared at it for several seconds. Turning it around, she saw no return address and no delivery receipt. Feeling a little apprehensive, she called Malcolm.

Confirming that he wasn't the sender, he could hear

fear and concern in her voice. "Don't open it, sweetie. Bring it with you tonight and we'll open it together."

Realizing how silly she was acting, she said, "It's probably a thank you gift from a client or a sample from one of my vendors."

"Then we'll laugh about it together," he said lovingly.

Alexis left the office a little early and headed for the grocery store. Melanie was leaving for New York tomorrow to take care of some business before moving to Atlanta and Alexis thought it would be nice to cook for her sister for a change. Finding a simple recipe on-line, she could only hoped her dish would look half as good as the picture. Working her way up and down the aisles, she ticked off the ingredients as she added them to her basket.

"Fancy meeting you here."

Alexis turned to the voice and had to force herself to smile. How many time could they "accidently" run into each other?

"Hello, Denise," she said, careful to keep moving so not to encourage a lengthy conversation.

Walking briskly to catch up with her, Denise said, "Since we've run into each other, I was hoping we could take this opportunity to talk."

Pausing, Alexis said, "And what could we possibly have to talk about?"

"It's not a what, but a whom. Malcolm."

"I have absolutely no intention of discussing anything or anyone with you, especially Malcolm," she answered, turning to walk away.

"Now just a minute," Denise started, grabbing her arm.

Alexis paused and looked from Denise's face to the hand on her arm and said in a calm, but lethal tone,

"You don't know me very well, so I'll let you in a little secret. If you don't get your greasy paws off of me, every person in this store will bear witness to you getting your annoying butt kicked."

Releasing her arm, Denise put on a fake smile and occupied herself by removing an invisible piece of lint from her linen dress. Standing tall, she said, "I'll let you get back to your shopping. We'll talk another time."

"Malcolm?"

"Yes, Susan?"

"Alexis Shaw is here to see you."

"Thanks, Susan. Send her back."

Lowering her voice, she whispered into the intercom. "She's the one, isn't she."

Knowing exactly what she was asking, Malcolm ignored the question and said, "Send her in."

"I'm happy for you, Malcolm. You're shifting your career for the right reasons."

Susan had been with him for three years and she would be missed when he was no longer working out of this office. Sometimes overly protective, sometimes a little too nosy, she was always there when he needed her. Resigning himself that it wouldn't be a secret for long, he said, "Thanks, Susan. And yes, she is the one."

As soon as Malcolm saw her face, he knew something was wrong. Was it possible that she found out about the award?

"What's wrong, baby?"

"I'll tell you what's wrong," she answered, taking a seat. "It's your little ex-friend."

"What are you talking about?"

"Denise."

Thinking about her impromptu visit at the restaurant, he said, "Did something else happen?"

"She keeps managing to show up."

"What do you mean?"

Alexis relayed what happened at the grocery store and watched Malcolm's expression grow dark with concern. As he listened to her tell the story, flashbacks to the end of their courtship surfaced to the forefront of his mind. He remembered that she would show up at the oddest time, or stop by his office for unknown reasons. But that was two years ago. Why would she start with these games again?

Cursing under his breath, Malcolm picked up the phone. "I'll talk her and put an end to her harassment this instant."

Seeing how worked up he was getting, Alexis stroked his cheek trying to calm him down, "I don't think that will be necessary. I made it quite clear to her that if she stepped to my face again, her health insurance better be up to date."

Replacing the receiver, he wrapped his arms around her waist and smiled. "Listen to my tough lady."

"That's right. I can take care of myself, and Miss Denise learned that firsthand today."

Still, as he listened to her, something didn't sit right with him. "Did you bring the gift box you received today?"

"It's in the car." Watching his thoughtful expression, she continued, "Do you really think Denise has something to do with this?"

"I don't know, but I don't like it," he said.

Wrapping her arms around his neck, she leaned in to kiss him, "Let me help you take your mind off your ex-girlfriend."

Hearing the door open without a knock, they didn't have time break their embrace.

"Malcolm, I have those photos for your review."

Both turned to the door as it swung open.

Caught off guard by seeing the two of them in an intimate embrace, Rick put his annoyance in check and said, "Excuse me, I didn't meant to interrupt."

Taking a small step behind Malcolm, Alexis said nothing.

Malcolm felt her body grow tense. "You can just leave them on the desk. I'll take a look at them later."

"Sure, no problem," he answered. Turning his attention to Alexis, he said, "It's hard to believe you look better every time I see you. Let me know when you're ready to move to a real man."

"Rick," Malcolm warned.

Cracking the corners of his mouth upward, Rick said, "Just kidding. Can't you two take a joke?"

Malcolm watched as Rick stared at Alexis a little too long. "Was that all?"

Quickly averting his gaze back to Malcolm, Rick smiled and said, "I'll talk to you later."

As soon as he left, Malcolm said, "Something's not right."

"What are you talking about Malcolm?"

"First you get strange gifts, and now he comes in here and looks at you like you're a prize in a big contest."

"Don't you think you're overreacting? A few minutes ago, you pegged Denise as some over the top ex-girlfriend and now you say it's Rick."

"I think we should call the police."

"Do you honestly think they can do anything?" she asked, eyes widening.

"I'll call my friend on the force and see what he thinks."

Rick sat in an empty cubicle outside of Malcolm's office and stared at the closed door. This was the story of his life with Malcolm. In college, they were the players of the campus, however, Malcolm's girlfriends always seemed to be one step above his. They were a little prettier, a little smarter, and had a little more class. And every time they came head to head over a girl, Malcolm prevailed. Now he sat watching him prevail again. With Alexis. And he was tired of playing second fiddle. Just plain tired.

"What are you doing here?"

Trying to cover up the fact that he was caught daydreaming, he decided to turn the tables.

"I could ask you the same thing, Denise. Advertising representatives don't have business on this floor. Don't tell me you're still pining away for Malcolm," he asked with a sneer.

"If I was, that would explain why I'm here. But I believe the original question was what are you doing here."

Just as Rick opened his mouth to respond, the office door opened and Malcolm and Alexis stopped short when they saw the two topics of their conversation standing in front of them.

An uncomfortable silence ensued as all four stared at each other. Alexis was the first to speak up.

"Nice seeing you both. Again." Turning to Malcolm, she said, "Ready?"

Locking arms with her, he said, "Right behind you."

Denise and Rick watched them walk out, both reeling on the inside at how happy the two of them looked together.

Alexis and Malcolm stood beside her car as she nervously bit down on her bottom lip. "I'll feel so silly when I open this up and find chocolates or a party favor. Taking a deep breath, she removed the gold ribbon and pulled the lid off.

Malcolm heard her gasp as the color drained from her face and he grabbed the box and looked inside. Replacing the lid, he threw out a string of expletives and pulled out his cell phone.

Not saying a word, Alexis listened as he left a message for Detective Anthony Summers. Ending the call, he spat, "Someone's idea of a joke is not very funny."

The black doll was dressed in what appeared to be a replica of the dress Alexis wore to the award ceremony. Only the head was snapped off and the note around the neck repeated the same words as the note that came with the flowers.

"I'll hold onto this until I hear from Anthony," Malcolm said.

Alexis nodded her agreement. Never one to frighten easily, she did have to admit that this was a little too much to be a coincidence.

Embracing her at the waist and pulling her to him, he said, "In the meantime, I want you to stay at my place."

"Don't you think you're overreacting?"

"When is Melanie leaving for New York?"

"Tomorrow morning."

"I don't want you staying at your condo by yourself."

Patting him on the back, she said, "That's so sweet. My big, bold man wants to protect little ole me."

Not getting a return smile at her comment, she said, "You're serious?"

"You're damn right I'm serious. My community is secure. No one can get in unless I let them. I know you're planning on having dinner with Melanie tonight, so you can pack and come tomorrow."

"I don't know Malcolm. That's too much like . . ."

"Like what?"

"Like living together. I don't think that's a good idea. I'm already giving more than I've ever given. I like things the way they are."

Malcolm listened and realized that while they had come along way in their relationship, they still had a ways to go. They had fallen in love with each other, and

Malcolm actually liked the idea of waking up to her every morning and kissing her good night every evening. He understood that she wasn't ready for that. But that didn't change the fact that he was worried about her. That someone was trying to spook her. And he needed to keep her safe. To protect her.

"Alexis, I understand how you feel, but I don't want you staying by yourself. Melanie's going to be gone at least a week. Why don't you come and stay the week with me. By that time, I would have had a chance to talk to my suspects."

"Suspects?" she asked. "Don't you think you're carrying this thing too far?"

"If I am, humor me."

"Okay. I'll stay."

Kissing her squarely on the lips, he said, "Thank you. I feel better already."

Fifteen

Alexis balanced the two bags of groceries in her arms as she opened her front door. She thought it ridiculous that Malcolm insisted on seeing her home. But if it made him feel better, then so be it. Promising to call him later, he waited until she was safely in her building before he pulled off.

Stepping into the foyer, she called out to her sister.

Meeting her at the door, Melanie smiled sweetly, "Alexis, I'm so glad you're here."

Giving her a strange look, Alexis said, "I live here."

With a nervous laugh, she relieved her of one of her bags and said, "Of course you do."

Eyeing her sister suspiciously, Alexis headed for the kitchen.

"Mother's here."

Alexis froze at those words and slowly turned around. "What did you say?"

Moving toward her sister, Melanie started, "I called her and told her to come over."

"You did what?" she said through gritted teeth.

Melanie knew that if she was ever to fully move on with her new life, she had to deal with the one factor that had always held such a tight hold on her. Beverly Jefferson.

Asking her to come over, she wanted her mother to know that in no uncertain terms would she have any input on her life. Changing the clothes she wore, cutting her hair, leaving her job, fiancé, and New York—those were all cosmetic changes. Melanie knew that she had to experience an internal change as well. A change of heart. She no longer lived for the satisfaction of others; she was finally living for personal satisfaction, and no one was going to take that away.

"I didn't know you would be home so early, but now that you are, maybe we could all talk."

"I'm not interested in talking to her."

"As usual, it's always about what you want."

Both turned to the sound of the voice and Alexis stared at the woman who had given her nothing but grief since she divorced from her father. "No, mother. The problem is that it's always about what you want." Alexis set her bag on the floor and headed for her room.

"Alexis, wait," Melanie said.

"Let her go," Beverly said. "She's at her best when she's running away from me."

"Excuse me?" Alexis said.

"You know exactly what I'm talking about."

"I have no idea what you're talking about. The only thing I've run away from in my life is an overbearing mother."

"If you hate me because I wanted my children to have the best things in life, then so be it. I won't apologize for that." With her chin high and her voice steady, Beverly meant every word of it.

"What you need to apologize for is trying to use my father's money and power to buy us the life you never had."

"How dare you talk to me like that?" Beverly said with an air of superiority.

"You're in my house, I can talk any way I damn well please." With her heart racing, Alexis worked to control her breathing. She could not recall a time when she had been angrier. "Without our father you would have been nothing. It was his name, his money, and his practice that gave you the fancy clothes and a position in society. Everybody knew it. That's why when daddy left, you had to prove that you were worthy of maintaining the status you had come to enjoy by being Mrs. David Shaw. The only way you could do that was to push us to accomplish all those things you couldn't. The social clubs, the elite schools, the ivy league colleges, and the professional careers. You didn't have our best interest at heart. It was for your own selfish reasons. Your selfishness had already led to a failed marriage. You couldn't fail at being a mother too."

"You ungrateful little . . ." Beverly started.

"Little what?" Alexis challenged. "You couldn't stand the fact that I didn't follow the plan you laid out for me. How embarrassed were you when your friends found out I wasn't going to that fancy college you bought my admission into? Or better yet, how did you explain the fact that I wasn't going to law school? But you know what, I fooled you. I didn't need you. I made it on my own. I was chosen Businesswoman of the Year. I built my own company and made a success without you.

"The day you found out I started Just For You, you stuck your nose up in the air and proclaimed that I was wasting my life. Well, look at me now, Mother. I have a thriving business, friends, and a man who loves me. And what do you have? NOTHING! And I want you out of my house. I don't need you."

Storming past them, she headed for her bedroom.

Before opening the door, her mother said, "You are so foolish. Money and influence always makes a difference. That was the problem with your father," she said sarcastically. "Always thinking those two things didn't matter. But in the real world, that's all that matter."

Turning to face her, Alexis said, "Maybe in your world, but not in mine."

Pausing, she stepped inches from Alexis and said, "How do you think you got that business award?"

The room began to spin as her words registered. "What do you know about that award?"

With a cynical smirk, Beverly said, "When Alice Milestone told me that you were one of the finalists, I made a few phone calls—and a charitable donation."

"Wh . . . wh . . . what are you saying?"

"I'm not saying anything," she said with a satisfied grin. "You can figure it out."

"Why?" Alexis cried, feeling as if the rug was being pulled from under her feet.

"Because I plan to shove that issue of *Image Magazine* in the face of every person who made snide remarks about me and what I could accomplish."

Anger flared in Alexis with lightning speed as she glared at Melanie. "Get this selfish woman out of my house before I do something I may or may not come to regret."

Melanie said, "Mother, maybe you better go."

"Alexis, what is the problem?" Beverly asked. "Don't you see? We both got what we wanted."

Alexis slammed her bedroom door and paced the floor, trying to calm down. A million thoughts were running through her head. How could this be happening to her? Falling on her bed, she curled up like a child and felt the hot teardrops falling from her cheek to her pillow. The faint knock on the door didn't move her.

"Alexis? Are you okay?"

"I'm fine Melanie. I just want to be left alone."

"Alexis, I . . ."

"I said leave me alone."

"I can change my travel plans. I don't have to leave tomorrow."

"I'll be fine, Melanie. Go. Take care of your business."

Alexis reached for another tissue off her nightstand and blew her nose. All of her hard work meant nothing. The only thing that mattered when it was all said and done was her mother's name and her mother's money. Consumed with hurt and anger, Alexis started to call Malcolm, but remembered he had a basketball game. Planning to call him later, she fell into a fitful sleep.

The sunlight beamed through the window and Alexis turned over and looked at the clock. Just after eight in the morning, she realized she hadn't even bothered to change out of her clothes. Knowing her sister had already left for New York, she called Malcolm. She had meetings today, but she had to see him before she went to the office.

The minute he answered the phone, he heard the emotion in her voice. She wouldn't say what was wrong, only that she needed to see him.

Twenty minutes later, he stood at her door, not sure of what to expect. Dressed in black slacks and a white blouse, her hair was in a simple pony tail and the makeup did little to hide the puffy red eyes, a result of dried tears and a night filled with too little sleep. Her cell phone rang and she didn't even look at her hip.

"What is it, baby?"

"I can't believe it," Alexis cried. "I left New York to get away from her, and she still won't stay out of my life."

"What's going on, honey?"

"My mother. I can't believe that self-serving woman."
She found out!

"Everything I've accomplished was one big lie. I won that award because of her interference, not on of my own ability. She used her position and money to influence *Image* and . . ."

She stopped abruptly and stared at Malcolm.

"Did you know about this?" she asked pointedly.

Malcolm frantically searched his mind for the right words. "There is no evidence that your mother's actions had any influence on the selection process."

"What do you know about my mother's actions?" she said, eyeing him with raw suspicion.

"Alexis, let me explain . . ."

"Oh my God . . ." she yelled. "You knew!"

"I only found out a couple of days ago."

"And you never said a word! I bared my soul to you about my mother. I never opened myself up to anyone the way I've opened up to you," she screamed. "I violated my own life rule and became vulnerable to you and this is how you treat me?"

"Calm down. Let's talk this out."

"There's nothing to talk about. I never want to see you again."

"You're not being rational."

Opening the front door, she yelled, "GET OUT!"

Malcolm refused to leave.

"Fine," she said, grabbing her purse and keys. "I'll leave."

Alexis stormed out of her condo without looking back.

Hearing his cell phone ring, Malcolm said, "Anthony, thanks for calling back."

Spending the next few minutes telling him about the phone calls, flowers, and the doll, Malcolm agreed to stop by the station and drop off the card and doll later that afternoon.

Alexis hit the remote on her keychain and the automatic locks on her car were released. Swinging the door open, she felt her fury reach the point of explosion.

"Give me your keys, get in, and don't make a sound."

"What the . . ."

Feeling a cold, steel object in her side, she froze and dropped her purse.

"You have three seconds to get in or I blow you away right now."

Sliding into the driver seat, she stepped over the gears to get to the passenger side. As the other person got in, she reached for the handle to jump out the other side. Before she could open it, she heard the locks click.

"Try something like that again and I'll snap your neck, just like the doll." Starting the car, she turned to her attacker and gasped as reality set in.

"It was you. The flowers, the doll, the phone calls. What were you trying to do?"

"Shut up! I don't want to hear one word from you."

"Why are you doing this? What do you want from me? You won't get away with this. I won't let you."

"I said shut up. If you don't, I'll keep you alive and kill your little boyfriend."

"Is this was this is about? Malcolm? Are you that jealous?"

Not getting a response, she continued, "It's broad daylight and you're driving my car. How far do you think you'll get?"

The blow came without warning. Alexis screamed as the fist connected with her jaw.

"One more word and the next hit will do permanent

damage." Watching her grow quiet, her captor laughed. "Not so tough now, are you?"

As silence engulfed the car, the driver nervously checked the rearview mirror. Little did Alexis know, her comment about it being daylight made the driver nervous. But the anger had gotten so strong that something had to be done. Alexis had it all. A successful business, respect, and Malcolm. It was enough to spread the cancer of jealously quickly.

But now that she was captured, the next step was not completely clear. Glancing at the highway sign, the driver broke into a smile. A plan was beginning to develop.

Malcolm walked out to his truck and saw the empty parking space beside it. On the ground, he noticed a Fendi bag with a few items strewn about. Moving closer, he realized it was Alexis's purse. Picking up the purse and the items, he wondered how she could leave her purse and not know it. Dropping it in the passenger seat, he got in his truck and dialed her cell phone.

Getting no answer, he called her office.

"Malcolm?"

"Yes, Sherry. I'm trying to reach Alexis."

Sighing, Sherry said, "I was hoping you could tell me where she was."

"What are you talking about?"

"She had an appointment with a caterer this morning at eight and never showed."

Trying to sound normal, he said, "I know she got off to a late start. I'm sure she'll be there shortly."

Malcolm began to feel a churning at the pit of his stomach. He knew Alexis was upset, but was she mad enough to blow off her business meetings without telling anyone?

"Have you checked with everyone on the staff?" Malcolm asked.

"Yes, and no one has heard from her."

"Are there any events today?"

"There's nothing until Saturday night."

Where was she? "Melanie, I'm going to try her again on her cell phone."

Hearing the slight tremor in his voice, Sherry asked, "You don't think something has happened to her?"

Not wanting to cause unnecessary worry, Malcolm said confidently, "I'm sure everything's just fine. I'll call you later."

Calling Anthony back, he got voicemail. Leaving a message didn't make him feel any better. He could almost hear what the detective would say, friend or no friend. *She found out some disturbing news and had a fight with her boyfriend. She was probably somewhere letting off steam. It has only been a couple of hours, call us back when she's been gone two days.*

Cursing under his breath, he threw his cell phone on the seat. Still no answer on her cell. *I hope you're just ignoring my call, Alexis.* Remembering that Melanie was going to New York to clean out her office, he dialed information. A few minutes later, he was listening to her voicemail at Winston Marks. Trying to sound calm, he left a message for her to call him as soon as she got the message.

Thinking about the mysterious gifts, his mind began to work overtime. The flowers, the doll, the phone calls. Obviously they were all tactics to scare her. But who would want to do that to her? Reaching for the card that came with the flowers, the answer hit him with brute force and he made a left at the next light and headed across town, determined to get some answers.

Fifteen minutes later he was banging on the door.

"Malcolm? What are you doing here?"

Pushing past him, he headed to the living room. "Where is she?"

Following him as he opened and slammed doors shut, Rick said, "What is your problem man? Where is who?"

Storming past him, he headed up the stairs and checked all the bedrooms.

"Have you lost your mind? You come in here like a vigilante, poking around my house. What the hell is your problem?"

"You are my problem. Now where is she?"

"Who?"

"Don't play dumb with me," he said, his lethal stare bearing into Rick. "I know you sent those flowers and now she's gone."

"You must be on crack. I have no idea what you're talking about."

"Peachtree Florist? I saw the card. Isn't that the only shop you use? I know it was you."

"Like I said, I have no idea what you're talking about."

"And I suppose you don't know anything about a doll or crank phone calls."

"I don't know anything about any dolls or calls," he said, making no attempt to hide his anger.

Grabbing him by the collar, Malcolm slammed him against the wall. "I'm not playing games with you, Rick. If you know anything about her disappearance, you better come clean. If not, and I found out you knew something, I'll . . ."

Slapping his hands away, Rick said, "Or you'll do what? You think you scare me? What you do is make me sick. I'm tired of playing second to you."

Startled at his confession, Malcolm said, "What are you talking about?"

"You always win. In sports, in school, and with the

women. Especially the women. I tried to get with Denise for two years. But she wasn't interested in me. You're at *Image* for one week and you've got her in your bed. And now Alexis. Once again, a classy woman was choosing you over me."

"Rick, I had no idea," Malcolm confessed

With a knowing, cryptic laugh, Rick said, "Why am I not surprised. You were too busy becoming the great writer, Malcolm Singleton. But don't worry. I've had enough. I'm leaving in two weeks."

"What?" Malcolm asked.

"I took a job at a paper in Seattle. I gave my notice and I'm leaving town."

Realizing he had nothing to do with Alexis's disappearance, Malcolm said, "I'm sorry you felt that way, man. But it wasn't like that."

"Whatever. Just shut the door on your way out."

"Rick . . ."

"Just go."

Malcolm got back in his truck and decided to head for Just For You. Frustrated, he checked his messages at home. Nothing. *I tried to get with Denise for two years. But she wasn't interested. You're at* Image *for one week and you've got her in your bed.*

Malcolm dialed and pressed the extension for the Director of Advertising.

"Lenore James."

"Hi, Lenore. This is Malcolm. I was trying to reach Denise but got her voicemail. Have you seen her today?"

"Actually, she left me a message this morning. She's not feeling well. She called in sick."

Malcolm made an illegal U-turn and headed straight for Denise's apartment.

* * *

Alexis sat in the chair beside the desk trying to block out the painful swelling in her left cheek. Her hands were tied behind her back and her feet to the legs of the chair. She watched her captor pace nervously back and forth. Thinking about the last couple of days of her life, Alexis seethed with agitation. Between her mother, Malcolm, and the award, she felt like she was losing complete control over everything in her life. And now she had a gun being waved at her. Feeling her temper rise, she only had one person available to take it out on.

"Is this your grand plan?" Alexis asked sarcastically. "To hold me here?"

"That smart mouth of yours in going to get you in trouble. For your information, looking at that big calendar on the wall, no one should be coming through these doors for at least three days. That will give me just enough time to decide exactly how I will ruin your life. Just like you've ruined mine."

Alexis felt a moment of panic when she realized the truth of that statement. This place would be empty for three days.

"Why are you doing this? What do you want? You know you won't get away with this," she said, trying to sound bold and confident.

"What I want you to do is shut up so I can think." When her captor walked out of the small office, Alexis took her time alone to figure out a way to get help. Her hands and feet were tied, but there had to be something she could do to get her out of here. Then she heard her cell phone ring again. It rang several times in the car ride here, but her captor couldn't reach it across the seat. This was the first call in hours and her heart told her it was Malcolm.

The thought of him gave her a burst of energy and confidence. She had to find a way out for him. Looking at the other end of the desk, she had an idea. She only hoped she had enough time.

Denise opened the door and smiled. "Malcolm, how nice to see you, come in."

Malcolm strode past her and took a good look at her. Her hair was disheveled and she held several tissues in her hand. "You're sick," he said, obviously surprised.

Smoothing her hair down, she said, "Yes, but that doesn't mean you have to leave. Would you like some coffee?"

Remembering his mission, he said, "Listen Denise. This isn't a social call. Alexis is missing and I thought . . ."

"You thought what, Malcolm?"

"I thought you might have some information about that."

Realizing what he was thinking, she yelled, "Get out!"

"You have to admit that you have been less than amicable to her since we got together."

"I might have done a lot of stupid things to try to win your love, Malcolm, but I resent what you are implying. If your girlfriend is missing, believe me when I say I am not broken up over it, but I definitely didn't have anything to do with it. Now get out."

Holding open the door, Malcolm paused and turned to face her. He spoke in a voice cold and even, "Leave us alone, Denise. I mean it."

She slammed the door, causing the paintings on the wall to shake. Holding her emotions in check, she refused to shed one more tear for him. It was over. Whatever hope that she held on to that she and Malcolm would someday get back together was just crushed by his final words. He loved Alexis. She could hear it in his voice and see it in his eyes. Malcolm Singleton was lost to her forever.

Alexis worked at scooting her chair to the other side of the desk so she could reach the phone. She was halfway there and prayed that the door would not swing open before she got to the other side. Just a few more feet. With each inch, she felt the ropes cut into her wrists and ankles, but she had to keep trying. Her inspiration came from thinking of Malcolm. Being with him again would make all the pain worthwhile.

When she reached the phone, she hoped to bend over far enough to hit the speaker button and using her tongue, chin, whatever. She would need to only hit three numbers: 911. *That's it, Alexis. You can do it. Just a little more.*

"What do you think you're doing."

Alexis froze at being caught in the act.

This time the slap was open handed and the sting caused tears to well up in her eyes.

"I should kill you right now." She watched as the phone was snatched off the desk and ripped out of the wall. Throwing it across the room, it hit the floor with a crashing thud. "You think you're smarter than me? Huh?"

Walking to the file cabinet, the doors were yanked open and files started flying out.

"What did I ever do to you, Gary?" Alexis screamed, refusing to let the tears fall.

"You have to ask?" he said, staring at her, his eyes ablaze with fury. "You ruined my business."

"What are you talking about?" she asked, trying to make sense of what was happening to her.

"I'm talking about you being a stuck-up, selfish little

witch. All I needed was a few leads, a few contacts to get my business going, and you turned your back on me."

She watched in horror as he turned over the file cabinet, and all the files came tumbling out. Panic like she'd never known before welled in her throat. Was it possible that this was it? That she would never see Malcolm again? Hoping to calm down, Alexis ignored her ferociously beating heart and said "Gary, I did help you. I offered to give your information to clients who were interested in your services."

"I didn't need you to hand out packages," he hollered. "I needed you to tell people to use my services. With all your contacts, I could have been a success. Instead, I'm out of a job, out of business, and very soon will be out of my home."

"Gary, be reasonable. What is holding me here going to accomplish? You have to let me go. If you let me go, I promise I'll call every person in my Rolodex and set them up to meet you."

A shadow of anger swept across his face.

"I must look like a fool. The only reason you want out is so that you can be with that writer."

"What does Malcolm have to do with this?" she asked, confused.

"I've watched you two together," he said with a demonic sneer.

"W-w-what do you mean you watched us?"

"I've followed you. To restaurants, to the movies. To his house. I've seen you hug, kiss, and act as if you hadn't a care in the world. Tell me, Alexis, how come you wouldn't let me get to first base with you, but he hit a home run the first time you went to his house."

"You bastard," she said through gritted teeth as she struggled to get loose.

With a sinister laugh, he said, "But I'm the bastard with the gun and that means I'm the one in control.

That's right, Alexis. You're finally not the one in charge. I am."

Watching him carelessly wave the gun around, she decided on another tactic. "You're sick, Gary. You need help. Let me call someone."

"There you go again, trying to take control. But you're not in control, I am. Want me to prove it?" he asked, his eyes darting around the office. "Watch this."

Picking up a box of glass vases used for centerpieces, he started dropping them on the floor, one by one, the shattering glass echoing throughout the room. "I can do whatever I want to anything in this office, including you."

Alexis choked back a frightened cry as she realized she was dealing with a madman. "Gary, calm down."

"Shut your mouth right now," he said, pointing the gun directly at her. "Do not speak unless I give you permission. I have to think and I can't do that with you blabbering in my ear."

Alexis stopped talking. As long as he wanted to think, that meant she still had a chance. She hoped that if he really wanted to kill her, he would have done it by now. She prayed that she was right.

Sixteen

Malcolm sat in his living room, his head buried in his hands. It was almost dark and he was no closer to finding Alexis than he was when he picked her purse up off the ground early this morning. Celeste and Kenneth waited impatiently by their phone, while Jackson, Brent, and Sherry were all there to offer what little comfort they could. Unfortunately, all of them understood that no words could be said, and no action could be taken, to help the situation. They could only do what the police had told them when they left hours ago. Sit tight and be patient.

Malcolm was not able to do either. He alternated between pacing the floor and sitting with his head buried in his hands as the tears flowed. He tried not to blame himself, but he knew she never would have stormed out of her condo if she had not been so angry—at him.

Courtesy of his media connections, her picture ran on the evening news. But it didn't seem like it was enough. With an APB out on her car, and her picture flashing across the television screen, no one had reported seeing her. It was like she simply vanished. Standing, he began to pace the floor again. With his cell phone in one hand and his cordless in the other, he silently willed one of them to ring.

Jackson watched his brother suffer and wished he could do something to ease the pain and fear. Seeing the change in his brother the past few months, he knew that Malcolm had found his soulmate in Alexis Shaw. She was the woman he would spend the rest of his life with. It was obvious that he loved this woman deeply, and Jackson only hoped that they would be reunited soon. If not, he wasn't sure if he would be able to pull Malcolm out of the abyss he knew he would fall into.

Sherry sat restlessly in a chair in the corner of the room, twisting a well-used tissue. When she realized that her boss was missing, she spent the first few minutes in uncontrollable tears, overcome by emotions.

Alexis had been wonderful to her. With no formal education beyond high school, she was glad to be working for such a fun company and for such a phenomenal woman. For all of Alexis's trappings of success, she never acted as if she was better than her. They may not have been best friends, but they had definitely moved beyond the employee-employer relationship. She wasn't sure how much of a help she would be, but she was just glad to be here, to offer and get support.

"Malcolm," Brent said, "you haven't eaten all day."

"Let me fix us something," Sherry volunteered, glad to be able to keep busy.

"I'm not hungry," Malcolm said without turning around.

"Come on, Sherry," Jackson said. "Let's see what's in the kitchen."

At that moment, Malcolm's cell phone rang and everyone froze. Malcolm looked at the number and shook his head in the negative. Jackson and Sherry, visibly disappointed, made their way to the kitchen.

Taking a deep breath, Malcolm knew that he would have to be strong if he was going to have this conversation. "Hi, Melanie."

Not wanting Malcolm to have to relive the entire day

again, Brent took the phone and told Melanie the situation. Melanie tried to remain calm, but found that she couldn't hold back a cry of fear. She would be on the next flight to Atlanta and Brent agreed to pick her up from the airport.

Disconnecting the call, he set the phone on the table, only to have Malcolm immediately pick it back up and stare at it. Brent cleared his throat and left the room. He wouldn't be any help to Malcolm if he fell apart in front of him.

Just wanting to hear her voice, Malcolm dialed her cell phone.

"It's getting dark outside, this will be a good time to head out," Gary said.

Alexis, tired and a little weak from struggling with the ropes, tried once again to reason with him. "Gary, you don't want to do this. If you let me go, I promise, I won't tell anyone what happened."

With a laugh, he repeated, "Let you go? What kind of idiot do you take me for?"

"No, Gary. You're not an idiot. You're a smart man, and the smart thing to do would be to end this right now."

"Don't tell me what to do," he yelled. Picking up the box of minicarousels, he threw it at her, and groaned in disappointment when it narrowly missed her head. Landing behind her, she heard the music start to play from several of them, and it immediately reminded her of the time she and Malcolm spent in this room. This time, she couldn't stop the tears from falling. She loved him so much, and now that she may never see him again, she realized that it didn't matter how she won that award. The only thing that mattered was that she get out of here alive to spend the rest of her life with him.

Just then, her cell phone rang again. "It's been ringing all day, Gary. They probably already know something is wrong. If you let me answer it, I can say everything is okay. That I just need some time to myself. That will buy you some more time."

Walking to her, he snatched the phone off her hip, prepared to slam it against the wall. Glancing at the caller ID, he paused. "On second thought, I think I will take this call."

Pushing the green button, Gary said gaily, "Malcolm, have you called to join the party?"

"Who is this? Do you have Alexis? Let me talk to her."

"I guess it's only fitting to let you say good-bye. Enjoy the moment," he said with a sinister sneer. "It will be the last time you'll ever hear her voice."

Holding the phone to her ear, Gary warned, "One word about where you are and I'll shoot you and let loverboy hear you scream."

Swallowing deliberately, she said quietly, "Malcolm, listen . . ."

"Alexis, honey, are you okay? Where are you?"

"Malcolm," Alexis said, in a controlled, level tone. "Listen."

Not knowing exactly what was going on, he knew from the purse, flowers, the doll, and the hang-ups that she had been taken against her will. She was probably scared out of her mind, yet he wondered how she could remain so cool and calm. As precious seconds ticked by, he said nothing. Then he heard it. Exactly what she wanted him to hear. The music of the carousels.

"Time's up, lovers," Gary said.

Disconnecting the call, he threw her phone across the room.

"Don't worry, Alexis," Gary said, running his fingers across her breasts, "I can make you forget all about Malcolm Singleton."

"There is no way you could ever make me forget him," she spat. "You're not half the man he is."

This time, the numbness from her previous bruises kept the sting out of the next blow.

Malcolm grabbed his keys and headed out of the condo with Jackson, Sherry and Brent hot on his heels. Malcolm called the police as he sped down I-20. He had no idea who was holding her or why, but he did know where they were. There was only one place where he had heard that music before. Her warehouse.

Ten minutes later Malcolm pulled into the industrial park and cut his lights. Jumping out of the truck, he turned to see two police cars arriving. No sirens. No flashing lights. They knew they had a hostage situation and weren't sure if they wanted to tip their hand yet.

He ran to the officers and pointed out the building.

"Stay here. We'll take it from here."

"I don't think so," Malcolm said. "Whoever's inside has my woman and there's no way I'm staying out here."

"Malcolm, be reasonable," Brent pleaded.

"Let the authorities handle it," Jackson said, "Your emotions are running so high right now, you can do more damage than good."

"Listen to them," Sherry pleaded.

Relenting, Malcolm stood and watched as his life was put in the hands of strangers. Even though it was Alexis in that building, she was so much apart of him, that if she didn't make it, he knew his life would be over.

Backup officers arrived on the scene, and they quickly checked the perimeter of the building to assess the situation. Two officers returned from the back area and conferred with the other officers. Quietly peering through a back office window, they saw one man and one woman. Not giving any indication of the state of the woman, they went on to say that they could hear him yelling and that he appeared to be working alone.

Sherry provided the officers with a key to the front entrance. Taking their position around the building, they planned to storm the building through the front entrance and both back windows. Using surprise as their tactic, they believed that by the time the man inside figured out what was happening, it would be too late.

Malcolm held his breath as he watched the scene unfold. The emotions swirled inside of him at a ferocious pace. Anger. Fear. Frustration. Pity. He felt pity for the man that had tried to take away the love of his life. He had never been a violent man, but he knew that if he got a hold on whoever was inside, he would kill him with his bare hands.

The signal was given and, in an instant, all hell broke loose. Men were running, glass was shattering, and orders were being yelled through a bullhorn. Then he heard gunfire, and Malcolm's heart skipped a beat. Having no concern for himself, he took off running toward the building. Not getting more than ten feet, he was tackled from behind.

"Get off me," Malcolm yelled.

"Are you out of your mind?" Jackson said, pinning his brother to the ground. "Do you want to get yourself killed?"

"I can't lose her," he cried.

As the headlights from the cars were turned on, Jackson released his brother and helped him up. A few seconds later, they saw a small figure being helped out of the building by one of the policeman.

Malcolm ran to her, relief flooding his body. Wrapping her in his arms, he inhaled everything about her, as the officer stepped aside to give them a private moment. Pushing her hair out of her face, he notice the swollen jaw, dried blood, and the bruised cheek. Reaching for her hands, he saw her face contort in pain and he looked down. The rope burns and cuts were fresh and painful. "What the . . ."

"Get your hands off me!" Gary yelled at the officers dragging him to the squad car.

Turning to the voice, Malcolm took another look at Alexis's battered face and said, "Wait right here."

With deliberate steps, he raced toward Gary and before anyone knew what was happening, Malcolm punched him in the nose, followed by a blow to his gut. Not letting up, Malcolm connected blow after blow, all of his rage and fury flowing from him to the man who held Alexis captive.

Gary screamed, "Help me!"

After several minutes, one of the cops finally pulled Malcolm off. "That's enough. He's not worth it."

"I want to file assault charges," Gary screamed as blood oozed down his lip and he doubled over in pain. Turning to the officer on his right. "Arrest him. You saw what he did to me."

"I didn't see a thing," the officer said. "The only one who's going to jail is you."

Alexis slowly made her way over to Malcolm. "Are you crazy. What were you thinking?"

Catching his breath, Malcolm worked hard to put his anger under control. He knew if they hadn't pulled him off, they would have taken Gary out of here on a stretcher, maybe even in a body bag. As his breathing returned to normal, Malcolm realized the officer was right. He wasn't worth it.

"Come on, sweetheart, it's over. Let's get you to a hospital."

Six weeks later, Alexis danced in the arms of her man as the music blared through the speakers. The nightmares had subsided and Gary was secure behind bars, unable to hurt her anymore. Her face was almost completely healed and the only reminders she would have of her horrific ordeal were the slight scars from the rope cuts.

For the first few weeks, Malcolm refused to leave her side for any length of time. Every time she woke in a cold sweat, he was there, calming her back to sleep. Her opinion about love had completely changed and she couldn't imagine living life without him. Refusing to go to L.A. for the Endonite trial, Morgan got his cover story after all, and Malcolm could not have cared less.

The fund-raiser for Men of Standard was the perfect event to ease Alexis back to work. Checking with the volunteer coordinators an hour ago, she knew the evening turned out to be a huge success. Men of Standard was on track to reach their target amount, getting the computer lab, and adding to their scholarship fund. Alexis, once again, had pulled off a memorable event.

Looking around the room, she was glad to see all her closest friends. Celeste and Kenneth both glowed as Celeste's pregnancy was beginning to show. Melanie and Brent were dancing alongside them, smiling and talking. Even Jackson was falling prey to the spirit of love that floated in the air as he and Sherry sat talking at a corner table.

The issue of *Image Magazine* hit the newsstand and, as expected, her business experienced extraordinary growth. But even with all her friends and her success, she still had one unresolved question. Initially, she had feared asking, but now she just wanted closure.

"Did I win that award fair and square?"

Malcolm knew she would ask sooner or later. Having survived the nightmare, he understood that to put that time in her life completely behind her, she had to know the truth. "I have no idea what impact Beverly Jefferson had on you winning the award. All I know is that you were a finalist and your mother made a few phone calls and a large donation to the McKnight Foundation."

"So the answer is no."

"The answer is I don't know. I talked to the selection committee and they will only confirm the facts of what happened during the process. No more, no less."

She stopped swaying to the music and looked to him with a sense of needing to know. "What do you think?"

"I think everything that made Just For You a finalist is true. I think everything that was said about your accomplishments were true. I believe you built a company in five years that demonstrates your knowledge, skills, and abilities as a savvy businesswoman. I believe that you represent everything *Image Magazine* was looking for in a Businesswoman of the Year."

Hearing the sincerity in his voice, she knew he was right. No matter what impact her mother had on the award, nothing could change the fact that Just For You met all the criteria for a successful business worthy of *Image*'s award.

"She called again."

Knowing exactly who she was talking about, Malcolm said, "And?"

"And I refused to talk to her."

Alexis may have been physically healed from her ordeal, but she wasn't ready to take on the mental challenge of dealing with her mother. The last message from her mother said that when she heard what happened, she knew she wanted to work out their problems. Understanding there was a lifetime of issues to be worked out, she would be there when Alexis was ready. Hearing the sincerity in her voice, Alexis believed she was telling the truth. But Alexis needed time to sort out her feelings. She would call her mother when she was ready.

"Let's take a walk on the grounds," Malcolm said.

As the fall breeze wisped through the trees, Alexis gloried in the peace and joy she felt in just being with him.

"Alexis, when I walked out in that parking lot and saw your purse on the ground, I swear my heart stopped beating. I knew at that moment that loving you wasn't enough. I needed you to be more than that. Alexis, I know how you feel about marriage, but . . ."

"Yes," she said.

"I want you to know that I think we could . . ."

"Yes."

"There's no one else I'd rather be with . . ." Finally registering her responses, Malcolm looked expectantly at her and asked, "What did you just say?"

"Yes."

Realizing what word she was saying, he asked, "Yes, what?"

"If you're asking me to marry you, the answer is yes."

Wrapping her in his arms, he said, "If I'd have know, it was going to be that easy, I wouldn't have spent the past hour coming up with a list a reasons of why you should marry me."

Softly brushing her fingers against his cheek, she said, "Malcolm, when I was tied up in that warehouse, the only thing I could think about was you. My business, the arguments with my mother, the award? They were so minimized compared to the thought of never seeing your face, never feeling your touch, and never letting you know that 'us' is the most important thing in my life. If you didn't ask me, I was going to ask you."

"Will Just For You make an exception to its 'no wedding' policy?"

"Exception?" she asked, a sparkle in her eyes. "I guess I forgot to mention that we've started a wedding planning department."

As Malcolm threw his head back in laughter, Alexis gloried in the sound of his voice. It was that sound that had first captured her attention and it was that voice that now possessed her heart. It was deep. It was smooth. It was sexy. And it belonged to her.

Dear Readers:

Greetings! I hope you enjoyed the story of Alexis and Malcolm. They were two people that I truly enjoyed bringing to life. Although they got off to a shaky start, they managed to move through their challenges and find true love.

I want to thank all of you for making my debut novel, *Foundation for Love*, such a huge success. I look forward to continuing to bring you stories that touch your heart and soothe your soul. After all, isn't that what romance is all about!

As always, I would love to hear from you. I can be reached at www.doreenrainey.com or by mail at P.O. Box 1263, Alexandria, VA 22313.

Until Next Time . . .
Doreen

ABOUT THE AUTHOR

Doreen Rainey graduated from Spelman College and resides in the suburbs of Washington, DC with her husband, Reginald. Currently, she works as a Human Resources Manager at a CPA firm. Her first novel, *Foundation for Love*, received excellent reviews and was named a Top Pick from *Romantic Times*. Doreen enjoys reading and traveling to new places.